Alive at Sunset

Rituals of the Night Series

Book Two

Kayla Frederick

This is a work of fiction. All the characters and events portrayed in this novel are either products of the author's imagination or are used fictitiously.

Alive at Sunset

Cover by Betibup33

Edited by Danielle Yeager, Hack & Slash Editing

ISBN: 978-1-950530-41-0

Library of Congress Control Number: 2025919837

First Edition May 2026

https://authorkaylafrederick.com/

Other Books by the Author

Voices
Flirting with Death
After the Devil
What I Did
Runners (The Core #1)
The Residency
Memento Mori
The Council (The Witch's Ambitions Trilogy #1)
Dead by Morning (Rituals of the Night #1)

Rituals of the Night Series

Book One: Dead by Morning

Book Two: Alive at Sunset

Prologue

BLACKNESS SMOTHERED HIM. It wasn't only an absence of light. It was a complete, suffocating void that pressed against his skin and seeped into his thoughts. He couldn't remember where he was. Or who he was. His own name felt like a foreign concept, buried beneath the murk of his consciousness.

Something inside him begged to slip back into that blank silence. It would be easy. *So* easy. But another part warned him that if he did, he might not return.

With effort, he opened his eyes.

Gray light bled into his vision. A featureless field stretched out in every direction, shrouded in a dense, pale fog that clung to him like cobwebs. The air buzzed with a low, electric hum, almost too faint to hear. He tried to stand. His legs trembled under his exhaustion, breath fogging in front of him.

Where am I? he wondered, turning in a slow circle. The white haze wrapped around him like a wall, the air impossibly still. Was he alone or were people watching him from the fog?

"Hello!"

Tiny lights drifted through the mist. They bobbed and hovered like insects, but they didn't blink like fireflies. They circled him, and when he took a step forward, they retreated.

He followed.

With each footfall, something tugged at the edges of his thoughts. A silent force. Something ahead wanted him to come closer.

The fog thickened. Tendrils slithered into his mouth and eyes. He gagged, waving his arms to push it away, but it clung, sticky and cold. His foot caught on something, and he toppled forward, the frost-kissed grass scraping his skin.

"Ugh!" The wind was knocked from him. Cold blades of grass brushed his nose, and damp earth soaked through his sleeves as he pushed himself up.

He crouched low, hoping the fog might be thinner near the ground, but it wasn't. The same cold nothing. He stood again. Walked. The silence made his own footsteps sound like gunshots.

A piercing wail came from somewhere deep in the fog. Distant, but not far enough. High-pitched and raw, it tore through the mist like a knife. He wasn't frightened in the way he should've been. There was something . . . familiar about it. Like a memory. The scream cut off as suddenly as it began.

"Hello?" he called to it. "Where the hell are you?"

Had the scream been in his head? Five minutes in this strange place, and he was already going crazy. *This is hopeless.* For all he knew, he was walking in a circle back to where he started.

Ting. The lights appeared again, brighter now and pulsing red at their core. He followed them. What else was there to do? Trying not to get disheartened, he focused on the things he *could* control, such as his breathing and footsteps.

The grass beneath him faded to dry, cracked dirt. Then, something coiled across his path. A thick vine, slick and dark like wet rope. He tried to step over it, but it moved. Fast. It wrapped around his ankle and squeezed.

"Hey!" He kicked, but it coiled tighter, slithering up his leg. He clawed at it, fingernails sinking into its bark. It oozed thick sap, green chunks caked under his nails. The vine tugged, and he hit the ground hard, then was dragged backward.

A red glow flared ahead, cutting through the fog like a blade. The scream returned, so loud it rattled his skull. He covered his ears, heart jackhammering. The vine kept climbing. Alarms rang in his head. If it squeezed his stomach or his ribs, breathing would become impossible. Panicked, he fumbled in his pocket and yanked free the object hidden there. A dagger.

He slashed wildly. The vine shrieked as it was severed, flopping onto the ground like a dead limb. He scrambled away on hands and knees, wary of it rearing up to grab him again.

The red glow intensified, a presence, hidden and watching. The scream grew louder, the ground vibrating as if the earth itself was letting out its rage. He reached toward it, compelled beyond reason, and his fingers brushed against something smooth.

A searing bolt shot up his arm. He screamed, trying to wrench himself free, but the object clung to him, digging in. A paralyzing sensation worked its way up his wrist. Struggling between life and death, he fought to stay conscious but wasn't sure how long he could keep going. Pain was everywhere, alerting him to places he hadn't known existed. It rioted in every vein, bone, tendon, muscle, and even his blood.

The haze began to thin, but he failed to notice. The pain had consumed him, hollowed him. His vision blurred. He was slipping again. Fading back to that black place of unconsciousness.

When he was about to give in and let this place take him away, the hurt and the fog vanished at the same time. He lay alone in a wide circle of scorched earth. In his trembling hand, where the red light had been, he now held a long, yellow bone. A red rose entwined around it, the stem coiled in perfect spirals. The petals shimmered with moisture, but they weren't wet. They were *alive*.

A single thorn pierced the meat of his palm, absorbing the blood that leaked free, bringing the flower to life. It pulsed once, then twice, the petals stretching out larger.

Faces and moments lost in shadow stirred in his chest. He clenched the bone tighter, holding fast to that flicker of himself.

A ghost of a smile graced his face, haunted and knowing.

Chapter One

LUNA KETZ SCRIBBLED on the Scantron sheet until the little bubble darkened. It was the last question on the test, and she let out a huge sigh of relief to be done. Then she scanned her classmates. Everyone else was still working. Certain she'd done something wrong, Luna reread her answers, patiently waiting for someone else to finish. Her anxiety would never allow her to be first.

Twenty minutes later, a girl at the front of the room rose and turned in her test. Luna gathered her things and followed suit. In the hallway, it felt as if a literal weight was lifted off her shoulders. Today wrapped up another semester of college. Her fourth one, in fact.

As she crossed campus, long glimpses of evening light cut across the concrete, leaving gaps of shadows between them. Footsteps echoed against the stone paths as students moved around her, some heading to the library with bags slung low and others clustered together, making dinner plans with their friends after class. The buildings, the trees, the sounds. It was all familiar now, though very unlike the town she'd grown up in. The town she no longer wanted to think about because doing so, even fleetingly, would take her on a trip from hell down memory lane. Once upon a time, she'd adored her life there. Back then she'd been a firsthand witness to a serial killer, nearly becoming a victim herself. Her classmate, Chance Welfrey, was behind the string of murders, and he had an . . . *odd* infatuation with her.

Unconsciously, she grabbed her stomach where a lasting scar reminded her daily that yes, she *had* been kidnapped, and yes, she *had* been stabbed. Quickly, she moved her hand to her backpack strap, worried someone might have noticed the gesture and would ask about it.

Luna walked a bit faster, trying to escape the memories as she sought out her roommate. Near the parking lot, several benches lined the path. A blonde woman sat alone on one of them. When she spotted Luna, she rose to her feet, waving excitedly. She was pretty and wiry, her long hair reaching all the way down her back. She reminded Luna a lot of Rapunzel in both appearance and energy.

Amanda Grey. Being the youngest of her siblings, she'd decided to try her hand at college to prove a point to her parents, though her dream was to one day open her own boutique. They'd met freshman year and clicked in a way that Luna hadn't with anyone except her old friend, Violet.

In the early days of college, Luna had still been living at home and either took the bus to Bowling Green or borrowed her father's car to make the hour drive. Amanda, having recently rented her own apartment, had invited Luna to move in with her. They'd been glued at the hip ever since.

"How'd it go?" Amanda asked, shouldering her big gaudy purse.

"I think it went well," Luna said as they descended the

slope to the parking lot.

"Ugh, I envy your confidence. I'm pretty sure I *flunked* all my finals."

"You think that every semester, and it hasn't been true yet."

"Never say never," Amanda said.

Luna giggled and rolled her eyes as they searched for Amanda's vehicle. Her shiny purple sedan was nearly on the other side of the lot, which felt abandoned with only a scattered handful of cars still remaining at this hour. They climbed inside and Amanda started to drive. Luna melted into the seat, ready to get home and relax.

As Amanda eased out of the parking lot, the joy started to leave Luna. She loved how her life had turned out but none of it had been her first choice. She'd dreamed of an Ivy League university and a posh future.

But life had different plans for her.

From the day of her high school graduation, Luna had slowly, *painstakingly*, done the work of piecing her life back together. Six days out of the week, she could pretend to be normal. To be the girl she might've been had Chance not intervened in her world.

On day seven, however, she needed to find peace.

Amanda peeked at her, her face tightening at whatever expression Luna wore. "That time of the week?"

Luna nodded, her bobbed black locks bouncing around her jawbone. Amanda put her blinker on, ready to exit the highway. She didn't know about Luna's past, nor the truth behind the visits. Luna explained them away by lying about a sick aunt, and Amanda believed her. The only people who knew the truth were Max, Amy, and her. Though Luna had always wondered how much of the puzzle Amy was aware of. Amanda was a fresh piece of Luna's life, not stained by tragedy, and she planned to keep it that way.

When Amanda pulled into the hospital parking lot, Luna was so lost in her thoughts that it took a gentle prod to bring her back to reality.

"Are you okay?" Amanda asked, light but searching.

Luna blinked, forcing herself up from the dark place she'd sunk into. "Yeah. Yeah, I'm fine," she said, the words hollow and brittle. She ran a shaky hand down her face, trying to wipe away the shadows clinging beneath her eyes. "I won't be long, I promise."

The door popped open, and she slid out of the car, steadying herself.

Amanda waved her off with a casual flick of her hand, unfazed. "Take your time."

"Okay." Luna wouldn't mention that the last thing she wanted to do was *stay* here.

She turned away and hurried across the lot. The sliding doors of the lobby whooshed open and closed behind her like a gate sealing her inside. Check-in was mechanical. After a brisk elevator ride to the third floor, she walked the length of the hallway toward the last door, each step heavier than the one before. Nurses passed by, careful to avoid her gaze, their sideways glances full of whispered questions and silent judgments. Most of them watched her coming and going from the room with misguided pity. The relationship they thought she shared with the patient was the same one *he* had wanted. The one he had gone to great lengths to try to cultivate.

Luna stopped outside the door, taking a deep breath to settle her nerves. It didn't matter how many times she did this, it never got any easier. The door opened with a soft *squeak*. Inside sat a single hospital bed.

She pressed her back against the wall, forcing herself to study the man lying on it. Wired with a multitude of cords running from his arms and chest, a beeping monitor signaled he was alive, though his closed eyes and unmoving head on the pillow might've suggested otherwise.

He was unconscious, deep in the recesses of a coma that had been his fate since the end of their senior year of high school. Luna knew this, but it didn't stop the fear that came from being in his presence. The blankets had been changed since the last time she'd visited. Other than that, everything was the same. She let her eyes rest on his face. The oddly angelic face that was uncommonly beautiful until the demon that lay beneath it made an appearance.

She felt a sense of justice every time she remembered that she'd been the one to put him in his coma. It was the only way to contain his evil short of killing him. Seeing him in the same condition week after week, month after month, brought her fragile peace that held the terror at bay—the deep-seated fear that one day, she might open this door and find him awake.

That won't happen.

Her old friend, Max, had told her years ago that if Chance

woke from the coma, his memory would be gone. Luna wasn't convinced. Evil wasn't so easily erased. He'd been in this coma state for three years now. Odds were, he would never wake from it.

At least, Luna hoped not.

Chapter Two

MAX CAZMEA GROANED, dragging himself up from the depths of a sleep so heavy it felt like drowning. His limbs ached, his head throbbed, and for a moment, he wasn't sure if he was still dreaming or awake. It was hard to tell the difference sometimes.

He opened his eyes to darkness.

The room around him was quiet, shrouded in heavy shadow. Faint moonlight bled through the edges of the blackout curtains, casting a thin, silvery haze across the floor. His desk sat cluttered in the corner. A hoodie was draped over the back of his chair like a slumped ghost. The air was cool and still.

The shadows beside his bed were thick. Too . . . *solid*. It took a second for his brain to register what his eyes saw.

A figure hovering over him.

Max jolted sideways, and his pillow exploded in a burst of feathers. With a *thump*, he landed on the floor as the figure raised the knife again. Timing the trajectory, he dodged the attack and landed unsteadily on his feet. The man jabbed the knife toward him again and again. Max dodged most of the flurry, holding up his arm to block the blows he couldn't evade. Two fresh lines opened across his forearm. He roared with pain, but the man didn't stop and neither could Max.

The knife came at him again, and this time, he grabbed the man's wrist. With a squeeze and jerk, the assailant dropped the weapon. He tried to lunge, but Max grabbed the knife and slashed once, twice. Blood bloomed, then cascaded down the side of the man's face and his arm. He took a step backward with Max pursuing him. When he tried to flee, Max grabbed the back of his robe and plunged the blade into the side of his neck with a wet ripping sound.

The man coughed and gurgled. Max dropped him. Blood poured from the attacker's wounds and oozed across the floorboards, splattering up the wall when the weapon landed in it. Max closed his eyes, trying to wrench himself out of the dream and back to the Real World. A trick he'd taught himself to get out of any particularly sticky situations on the Other Side.

Max gasped awake, and after ensuring he was alone in his room, relaxed against the mattress and let himself breathe. The blood from his new wounds squished into the mattress, and he groaned. Running into unsavory people as a Keeper wasn't anything new. What *was* new was the frequency with which the encounters were happening. There were similar elements to the attacks. The men wore some sort of cloak, either red or black, and they always came at night.

Someone else he knew had worn a red cloak too. But that had been years ago, and it was part of the reason he'd landed himself on the radar of those strange men.

Was his partner in danger, too, or was it only him they were interested in? Max had so many questions and no one to answer them.

The alarm clock beside his bed blinked *3:00 a.m.*

Perfect time for the supernatural.

A heavy wave of unease surged through his stomach. It wasn't uncommon for Max to feel these pulses of energy from the Other Side, but this one was different—darker. Familiar, but not in a way that brought comfort. It reminded him too much of the first time Chance's twisted games in DreamWorld had begun.

It's someone else, he tried to tell himself, but he couldn't be convinced. Chance's presence left a mark. An undeniable imprint. Maybe it was his power or the madness in his decisions, but Max *knew* when he was up to no good on the Other Side. If he was right, this was bad. He couldn't take this on alone.

But who would help him?

He hadn't been able to contact his partner in some time. Occasionally, he'd pick up a hint of her essence, but nothing more solid than that. He concluded that she was intentionally avoiding him, always just a step out of his reach. So Max continued on, the best he could, alone.

I can't do this forever.

The constant stress and minimal sleep were starting to wear him down. He needed help. No harm in trying to reach out again, he supposed. Bracing himself, he opened the channel of communication between himself and his partner.

Partner, are you there?

As predicted, he received no response.

I need your help, he tried to tell her anyway.

The channel shut with a violent *clang* that made the inside of his head ache. Squeezing his eyes closed, he pressed his pillow over his face, waiting for the sensation to pass.

How can she do this to me?

Max flopped onto his side, letting the weight of his situation crash down. Through a gap in his curtains, pale moonlight shone into the room, illuminating a picture on the nightstand. It was an old photo from freshman year of high school. He and his friend, Luna, both of them smiling, both so young and unaware of the darkness that would later haunt them. Max could barely remember the boy in the photo. The one who smiled without fear, without regret. That boy had disappeared long ago.

He picked up the photo, his fingers tracing the edge of the glass. Luna's smile stared back at him, full of life. It was the smile of someone who thought things could only get better, not worse.

He clenched the frame tighter. He wasn't alone in this fight after all.

Chapter Three

L UNA'S FOOTSTEPS ECHOED in the suffocating darkness, each step booming in the void. Her ears strained to catch any sound beyond her own, but there was nothing. Only silence. Her eyes were useless. The blackness swallowed every hint of light.

She took two steps forward and crashed into a wall. Alarmed, she reached out, pressing her palm to it. She felt her way along, using it as a guide. Maybe if she followed it long enough, she'd find the way out of this place . . . wherever she was.

Crash!

She hit another wall. *That's impossible*, she thought, then spun around, following the new wall. That dead-ended as well.

She was in a box.

Luna whipped her head back and forth, trying to find a way out. Her lungs refused to expand, restricted by an oncoming panic attack. A light flicked on so bright that she was blinded after spending so long in the dark. Transparent walls came into view and so did the pair of sapphire eyes on the other side of them.

Luna screamed and the scene blurred, slipping away to Amanda's concerned face hovering above her. "Luna! Wake up! You're having night terrors again."

Luna licked her dry lips, trying to process the events of the last thirty seconds. Holding a hand to her chest, she sat up. The inside of her room brought little relief as her heart continued to pound. "Yeah, sorry."

"Are you okay?" Next to Amanda, Luna's border collie, Lucky, watched with the same level of concern. Dogs used to terrify Luna, but when that fear had been used against her, she decided it was time to face it. It didn't help that her mother, Rose, had insisted on giving her a puppy for protection when she moved to Bowling Green.

"I'm fine," Luna said quickly, probably *too* quickly. There was more she could say, but she didn't know how to explain herself to Amanda. There was too much trauma packed into the dream for her to casually talk about it.

"If you say so," Amanda said, unsure. "But, hey. Get dressed. I wanna take you to lunch."

Luna racked her brain for an excuse, but Amanda's expression halted her mid-sentence. "Okay."

With an approving nod, Amanda left the room.

Lucky tilted her head, watching Luna expectantly.

It was just a night terror, she told herself as she climbed out of bed. They were annoying but also expected after all she'd been through. That was why she limited the amount of sleep she let herself get daily. Less chance of danger.

Luna rummaged through her closet, throwing on a baggy dark blue T-shirt and black capris. "Comfy and cute," as Amanda called the outfit. By the time Luna slid her shoes on, Amanda was already in the car waiting for her. The silence of the apartment was unnerving, plunging Luna back into the box and the hauntingly familiar eyes watching her from the darkness.

Stop it, she chided herself. *He can't hurt me again.*

Saying so didn't make her feel better. Her trauma had started with a simple nightmare, and that ended in murder.

AFTER DRIVING AROUND for a while, debating where to eat, Amanda settled on a café in the middle of town. She picked out a table on the patio, then went inside to order. Luna watched as she came back with a black tray full of food. Setting it down, Amanda tucked her miniskirt beneath her thighs and sat.

"See? This place is pretty fly, isn't it?" Amanda prompted as she picked up a white plastic fork.

The sun warming Luna's skin eased away some of her anxiety. Not all of it, of course, but enough for her to pretend to be normal . . . for a little while at least. "Not bad at all."

"It feels like forever since we've been able to hang out," Amanda said.

It was the truth, though Luna wouldn't point out that she didn't really hang out with anyone. Amanda was the only person she saw daily, and that felt like more than enough social interaction on some days. "So, you got any big plans for the summer?"

Amanda shrugged. "Not really. Cassie wants me to help her with the wedding stuff."

"That's what a maid of honor is for, right?"

Amanda smirked. "Okay, smart-ass. Yeah, but there's a lot more to a wedding than I thought. If I ever get married, I'm going to elope. None of this planning nonsense."

Luna raised her eyebrows in silent agreement, not that she ever planned on getting married. Dating in general was an activity she didn't care for. Her last romantic encounter had ended in disaster, and she had no desire to repeat the experience.

Amanda pulled a tube of lipstick from her bag and glided the red substance on her lips. It was such a natural gesture for her that she didn't have to think about it, she just did it. Luna tried to imagine doing the same without looking in a mirror and thought clown makeup would look similar to any attempts she'd make. "There are some really cute guys here today."

Luna used her drink to hide her face and the lack of interest Amanda would see there. Cute men had no appeal to her.

Amanda focused on something behind Luna as she dropped the lipstick back into her bag. "Ooh, I wonder if he comes here often." Luna couldn't care less, but Amanda gestured with her eyes and said, "Take a look."

Luna forced herself to do it, knowing Amanda wouldn't drop the subject until she did. Light glinted off the window, making it impossible to see inside, but she wouldn't mention that. Shifting her gaze back to Amanda, she said, "Yeah," and picked at her salad, hoping to end the conversation with her blunt disinterest.

"You should ask him out," Amanda practically dared her.

Luna chuckled darkly, imagining such a venture ending in failure. "No, that's okay, Mandy. I'd rather not. If you think he's so cute, why don't you ask him out?"

"Maybe I will," Amanda said, but made no move to leave her seat.

Luna offered nothing else as she stared out at the road. Behind Amanda, the sun glinted off a new surface, and Luna narrowed her eyes to focus on the image. A man with shockingly blond hair, cloaked in all black. Blue eyes flashed from pale ivory skin. The world around her vanished. She couldn't breathe. Couldn't think. He was all she could see.

"Uh, Luna?" Amanda broke through the haze with a sharp snap of her fingers. "Hello? Earth to Luna!"

Luna tore her eyes from the road, struggling to focus.

"You okay? You totally zoned out," Amanda said, chuckling softly. "Where did you go?"

Luna didn't answer, her mind still miles away. Her gaze shifted back to the street, to the place where she'd seen the figure. Whoever it was, they were gone, but who she *thought* she'd seen made her stomach twist. She pushed her half-eaten salad to the middle of the table, no longer hungry.

When would the hauntings stop?

Chapter Four

FOR THE REST of the outing, Luna tried to shake off that clinging unease, but it stayed, eating away at the back of her mind. She went nonverbal in the car, but she doubted Amanda was aware. She was chatting away with her sister on the car phone about wedding plans.

Luna normally didn't eavesdrop on her friend's private life, but Amanda also didn't put forth any effort to hide it. So she sat in silence, ready to fling herself out of the car by the time the black gate surrounding their apartment complex came into view. Amanda parked in their assigned spot, and Luna slipped out of the car and walked up the path.

The apartment complex consisted of a series of two-unit structures, each standing side by side like neatly arranged bookends. Each building resembled a house divided into two, with front doors placed next to one another. A field in the center of the complex had a few trees and flowers, a bit of nature to offset the rest of the concrete jungle. Luna and Amanda lived in a building toward the back of the lot.

Amanda caught up to her as Luna reached the door and unlocked it. She hummed as they went inside, immediately making a beeline for her room. Luna set their lone key on the kitchen counter in a place visible from the living room. When Luna had first moved in, Amanda promised to make her a copy but hadn't followed through. Luna didn't mind. She felt more secure knowing there was only one thing able to unlock her little piece of the world.

On her way through the kitchen, Luna pressed a button on the answering machine. There was one message. She hit another button to load it.

"Luna . . ." it began.

She couldn't turn it off fast enough. *Max.* Arguably her closest friend now that Violet was dead. She hadn't heard from him since the day everything had gone down. For a time afterward, she'd waited for him to make contact.

But he hadn't.

And she hadn't either. It was easier to distance herself from everything that tied her to it. Growing apart was the best thing for them both.

Why would he call now? she couldn't help but wonder. Then she thought, *He's your friend. Maybe he's just checking in.*

When she tried to restart the message, she accidentally deleted it. "Divine intervention," her mom would say. *If it's urgent enough, he'll call back*, she decided, then went to her room, flinging herself onto the bed. Lucky's claws clicked against the wooden floor as she bayed in the hallway outside. "Hey, girl," she cooed to her.

Lucky let out a happy yip and trotted into the room, bright eyes shining. She tilted her head, allowing Luna to scratch the white space beside her left eye. "Want to go for a walk?"

An excited bark tore through Lucky's chest, and the dog bolted into the living room. Luna snagged the leash off the dresser and followed her down the hall. She stopped by the door, hand hovering over her shoes, then reconsidered and strapped her rollerblades on. Amanda lay lazily on her stomach on the couch, pillow propping up her chest.

"Where are you off to?" she asked.

"Taking Lucky for a walk," Luna answered, clipping the end of the leash to her dog's collar for added effect.

"You feel like going out when you get back?"

"We'll see," Luna said, already knowing she'd come up with an excuse by then. Taking Lucky for a walk would take every ounce of energy she had.

Amanda yawned, oblivious to the storm in Luna's mind as she flicked through channels on the TV. "Okay. Have fun."

Luna silently pushed the door open. When the fresh air touched Lucky's face, she was off, bolting like a rocket. Luna's hair streamed behind her in a cascade of dark strands as the dog towed her through the complex, out of the gate, and into the world beyond. Luna let her, offering little guidance aside from leading her across streets and through crowds.

Ten minutes later, Lucky's energy began to fade. Her eager strides slowed to a sluggish trot, and then to a tired, half-hearted walk. Luna gave a soft tug on the leash, and the dog came to a stop. She flopped down on the pavement, tongue hanging out, eyes heavy as she rested her head on her paws.

Luna scratched her behind the ears, surprised at how far they'd come. This wasn't a part of town she visited often, usually passing through on her way to school or back to the apartment. Aging brick buildings and small shops lined the street.

In a place like this, she could almost make herself believe she belonged here. That she was as normal as the people around her. And why not? She'd put in the work to make Bowling Green feel like home, and yet, something still felt off.

A tingling sensation ran up her spine, the feeling of being watched. Whipping on her heels, she glanced around, but nothing appeared out of the norm. People lived their lives, driving, walking, and moving past her without a second glance. Luna glanced down at Lucky, but her dog's gaze was focused on the road ahead. Out of the corner of her eye, she spotted a bright blond head of hair and turned to better see it. It disappeared.

I didn't even talk to Max, but he's still in my head, she scolded herself.

Except that wasn't it. Not really.

From the moment she'd escaped Chance's clutches, she became paranoid. The world didn't look the same after trauma. She'd never felt particularly close to other humans, but now she had a deep-seated fear of them. How could she know if she was being watched? If she was being stalked? Chance had been at the periphery of her life for years, and she'd never thought twice about him until he'd given her no other choice.

"Let's go home, girl," Luna murmured, gently tugging on Lucky's leash. The dog rose to her feet, whining when she sensed Luna's shifting mood. Luna imagined it as Lucky's way of asking why she continued to torture herself.

I don't know.

She'd let her past trap her rather than conquering it and moving on. Problem was, she had no idea how to free herself.

24

Chapter Five

LUNA EXPECTED TO be ambushed by Amanda as soon as she got home, but found her to be, thankfully, asleep. She stripped off her skates and unhooked Lucky from the leash. As she went to put everything away, the phone in the kitchen rang.

The caller ID said it was her mother. Luna eagerly took the call. It had been a good month or so since they'd last spoken and she missed her. "Mom! Hi!"

"Luna, sweetheart. Have you got plans for today?" Rose asked.

Luna thought of Amanda's request before she left the house. She glanced at the couch just as Amanda let out a loud snore. "Nothing definite. Why?"

"I was hoping you and Amanda would come by for dinner tonight."

Distance had always made Luna's relationship with her mother tough, but over the course of the past year, Rose seemed to make more of an effort to spend time with her family rather than traveling for work. Of course, most of that decision had to do with her father's declining health, but she would take it.

"Yeah, of course, Mom."

"I'll see you soon."

Elated, Luna hung up and took a step toward the living room to wake Amanda, when the phone rang again. Thinking it was her mother calling back, she scooped it up. "Hello?"

"Hey, Luna," a husky voice replied.

Chills ran down Luna's spine. "Max."

"I think we're past due for a conversation."

A rock settled in her stomach. Whatever conversation they owed one another had long since passed them by. "I've been meaning to get in touch, but you know . . . life." She hoped he wouldn't ask for specifics.

"Yeah, I know you've been busy." She couldn't tell if Max was being sarcastic or not. "Last I heard, you were settled in the apartment."

"It's been great actually. I finished another semester of college," Luna said, barely hearing herself speak. She was waiting for him to drop the bomb, the real reason for his call. He was a harbinger of doom, appearing prior to disaster. "How've *you* been?"

"I've been all right . . ." Max said, trailing off.

"But?"

"I'm not happy to be the one to tell you this, but I think, and you need to hear me out on this one, something is wrong in DreamWorld." His words came rapidly as if he wanted to say his piece before Luna could interrupt him. The joke was on him because she didn't have the words anyway. "I woke up with the worst feeling this morning. It's familiar, Luna, too familiar."

Luna tried not to think of her nightmare: the shining sapphire eyes and the box. "Chance is *gone,* Max," she found herself saying, because entertaining any other idea would destroy her. "He can't hurt us because he's not him anymore. We beat him. We won. You said so yourself." A cold rock of dread settled in the pit of her stomach. *What if he was wrong?* asked the little voice in the back of her mind, and she couldn't argue with it. It was too loud.

"There are . . . others. I've been seeing them more often," Max explained. "I don't know how much longer I can keep them away. I need your help."

The word "help" caused her to bristle, and so did the thought of other shadowy figures lurking in her dreams. "I can't help with any of your Keeper stuff. I've done everything I can to forget about all that."

"I know," Max said, and it sounded like he was disappointed in her. Maybe he'd expected the experience in high school to bring them closer together rather than apart.

He didn't contact me either, she reminded herself.

Max continued. "But you're the only one who can help me."

There was that word again. As if she were in any position to help others when she was barely holding on herself. "No," she blurted out.

Max let out a bitter chuckle. "You think we have a choice? If we don't stop them, who will?"

"*You* don't have a choice," she pointed out. "But *I* do. I don't want to be involved."

"You already are," he reminded her.

"If it involves Chance, that's a given. But it's not him, so it's not my problem to solve."

"We can't rule out that they're not connected."

Luna took in a deep breath and held it until her lungs burned. Slowly, she let it out and said, "Okay, I'll humor you. Who are these people? Other Keepers?"

"No. I don't *know* for sure who they are, or what they want, but I think they're connected to what Chance was trying to do," Max explained.

A memory played at the front of her mind. Chance's devastated face in the temple when he realized he was losing his control over the situation. *I need you to see the big picture. This is the only way, or I'll never be free from that place. From them. They'll kill me*, he had said.

She had no idea who they were then or now.

Max dragged her back to the conversation. "What if Chance knew all the risks that would come with fusion, and he exploited a way to recover? What happens then?"

"He'd be pissed," Luna mumbled. It was as easy as it ever had been to imagine his eyes smoldering with rage. For as long as she lived, she would never forget that sight.

"He knew how to plan and manipulate. Maybe he had something planned to get others to take over for him if he failed."

Luna didn't have a chance to process the awful implications of Max's words before a searing pain shot through her stomach. It was so sudden, so intense, that it froze her in place. It twisted into a chilling cold that crawled down to her bones, spreading like ice through her muscles, her blood.

What's happening to me? she wondered, eyes darting around the room as if she'd find the solution nearby.

Her hand curled around the phone, finger hitting the end call button as it dropped to the floor with a *thump*. The pain moved across her abdomen, sharp and direct, as though she were being gutted one organ at a time. When it became too much, she bent forward, toppling to the floor beside the phone. Curling into a ball, she wrapped her arms around herself and cried until a puddle formed beneath her face.

Worried, Lucky circled her, nudging her face with her nose. When Luna didn't respond, she licked the tears, smearing them across Luna's cheek. The pain moved up to her brain, serving as the world's worst migraine. She opened her mouth, ready to scream, when it vanished. Lucky nudged her again, concerned.

"I'm okay, girl," Luna said, dragging herself to a sitting position. Lucky scrambled a few steps back but stared at her anyway.

Tentatively, Luna placed a hand on her stomach, wary of igniting the pain, but it didn't hurt anymore. She knew how to handle intense aches; Chance had made sure of that.

Max said something about feeling familiar things, hadn't he?

Oh no, she thought when her eyes landed on the phone. How much had Max heard?

She picked it up, listening to the dial tone buzz. Two very different instincts came. The first was to hang up the phone and pretend the past few minutes hadn't happened. The second urged her to call back and find out exactly when the call disconnected and how much he'd heard.

She chose the latter.

"What the hell happened?" Max demanded as soon as he picked up. "Why were you screaming?"

That answered Luna's question. "There was . . . a pain in my stomach."

Max fell quiet, and Luna started to think he had hung up. A whirlwind of emotions hit her—disbelief, anger, sadness, but the majority was relief. If he ended the phone call now, she'd be just fine with that.

"Max? Are you still there?"

"I'm gonna ask you one more question, and I need your honest answer," he said in a stern monotone voice.

Luna didn't want to do this, didn't want to play this game, but Max wouldn't let it go until she did. "Okay. Just one."

"Do you think your pain could've been from your gift?" he asked. By his tone, Luna would never guess the thoughts running through his head. He sounded so calm, cool, and collected, yet she knew him well enough to know he felt none of those things.

She wished she could do that too. Her life had never been normal, but it would be nice to pretend.

"No, Max, I don't," she answered stiffly.

"I feel like you're saying that to avoid this conversation," he said, his irritation starting to bleed through.

"You'd be right in that assumption."

Max huffed. "I get that you don't want to do this, but you have to man up here. We all have our demons, Luna! I lost a goddamned leg, remember? Like it or not, we need to do something. Or would you rather wait until Chance's cronies show up on your doorstep?"

"Goodbye, Max," Luna said unceremoniously, then hung up.

The ordeal with Chance had been the most frightening experience of her life. To think of the curtain rising on Act II made her want to board a plane and flee as far as she could. She'd barely made it out alive last time and Chance had gotten away with everything.

Police didn't suspect him of a thing.

Luna never asked Max how he'd explained himself to the cops three years ago, but she had heard the story on the news. They thought Violet's death had been the result of an unfortunate hunting accident and that the serial killer of Lima was responsible for whatever it was that happened to Chance and Susan. With Max unwilling to say the truth, and Chance unable to offer anything, they'd had no choice but to accept Chance as another victim.

Luna couldn't be mad at Max for that. Had he told the truth, he'd have to talk about the nightmares and the magical world that made them exist. They would've sent him to Brentwood Psychiatric Hospital and thrown away the key.

She shook her head, desperately trying to dislodge the clinging thoughts. What happened in the past was over and done with. Chance wouldn't come back, and if he did, his mind would be a blank slate, a wiped hard drive. He wouldn't have memories of whatever life had led him to commit such evil. He'd start anew.

Other people might come after them, but they weren't *him*. Max and his people could handle it.

I'm safe, she told herself, staring down at the puddle of her tears. But her doubts only dug in deeper.

Chapter Six

AMANDA WOKE TO a series of loud gasping sounds. At first, she assumed she was in a dream, reliving the time her father had taken her and her sisters fishing, and she'd had to watch a poor fish gasp for air until it eventually stilled. She sat up, but the sound was still there.

She spotted Luna sitting on the kitchen floor, face buried in her hands. Amanda hopped up at once and rushed to her side. "Are you okay?" she asked, checking her over to see if maybe she'd fallen and hurt herself. "What's happened?"

Luna's head popped up, her face streaked red from crying. She wiped her eyes with the back of her hand and said, "I'm fine."

"You're clearly not."

She side-eyed Amanda as if she considered letting her in on whatever was going on. Clearing her throat, she stood up and insisted, "I'm okay, really. But, hey, listen. Mom invited us for dinner tonight if you're up for it."

"Yeah, of course." Amanda rose to her feet as well. She tried not to make it obvious how off guard the change in topic made her. Luna would appreciate it more if she went with the flow, but her questions were still alive in the back of her mind. "As long as it's not too late. I have—"

"To meet with your sister, I know," Luna interrupted. "You'll be back by then."

"Okay. Are you sure you're . . ." She would've finished with "okay?" But Luna had already disappeared down the hallway, Lucky yipping at her heels. A moment later, the *click* of Luna's bedroom door answered Amanda's question better than any words could.

She sighed.

Luna's strange moods weren't exactly *new*. They came in cycles as far as Amanda could tell. One day a week she would be solemn, stoic, but after that she would be energetic and enthusiastic. Over the course of the week, she'd slowly morph back into that solemn person until it came time to visit the hospital again. It was like the shift between Dr. Jekyll and Mr. Hyde.

Amanda didn't know what to do. Of course she wanted to cheer her roommate up, but that had never been the easiest task to accomplish.

She had a feeling this had something to do with the hospital situation. What really lay beyond those doors? Family didn't make someone feel like that unless something really bad had gone down between them. A few times Amanda had considered tagging along, but always lost the nerve when she caught that glint in Luna's eyes—the pure, unadulterated horror.

Amanda had assumed that with the closing of the semester, things would be better for them. But Luna seemed to have other plans.

Amanda's pager buzzed from the living room table. Her ex-boyfriend, Reese, trying to get ahold of her again.

She rolled her eyes. When would he give up? After the strange encounter with Luna, Reese's mind games were the last thing Amanda wanted to deal with.

She shot another glance down the hallway at Luna's closed door. Part of her wanted to go in there and needle her with questions until she opened up, but the other part reminded her that was a stupid idea. If Luna didn't want to talk, she wouldn't. From the day they'd met, she was always holding *something* back and that likely wouldn't change anytime soon.

I need a distraction, Amanda thought and eyed the nearly full trash can.

She plucked the bag out and tied the ends closed before putting in a clean one. Something about a tidy living space helped to tidy her mind. Until Luna decided to emerge from her room, she would expend all her nervous energy on cleaning. Focused, she carried the bag outside, hiking across the complex to the dumpsters.

With a grunt, she tossed the black bag inside and turned to go back to the apartment, gasping when she almost ran right into someone. A man. Skinny and tall, his angular features striking.

Amanda didn't think he was so handsome. Not anymore, at least. She grimaced. "Reese, what are you *doing* here?"

He tipped his head to the side. "Didn't you get my page? I was worried about you."

Amanda pressed a hand to her temple. They'd broken up months ago, but Reese wouldn't take the hint that Amanda wanted nothing to do with him, and she had done her best to get the point across. She'd stopped responding to his calls and didn't show up at the places where he liked to hang out. Their shared friend group had seen less of her as well.

Yet, he persisted.

"Yes, I've gotten *all* of them, and I never called you back for a *reason*." Reese frowned, but Amanda didn't wait for him to speak. She shouldered past him and headed back up the walkway to her apartment. "Go home, Reese!"

She almost expected him to jog after her and try to come into the apartment, but he stayed by the dumpster. She slammed the door, careful to engage all the locks for good measure.

Amanda had no idea what was troubling her roommate, but maybe it was for the best that she was keeping it to herself. Amanda had enough problems of her own to sort out.

Chapter Seven

LUCKY'S EXCITED YAPS were the only sound in the car as Amanda drove her and Luna to Rose's house for dinner that evening. Conversation fizzled out within the first five minutes of the trip, and they rode mostly in silence. Luna tried to seem upbeat, but after Amanda had caught her mid-meltdown in the kitchen, she doubted Amanda would buy it anyway.

So she gave up and wiggled in her seat, trying to get comfortable. One arm wrapped around her abdomen in an attempt to cradle her stomach without being noticeable to Amanda. Part of her worried the mysterious pain would sprout again if she moved wrong. The last thing she wanted was to start Amanda's barrage of questions, especially when she didn't have good answers for them.

Do you think your pain could've been from your gift?

Luna hated that question because it paved the way for harder to answer ones. It could be her gift picking up on something new, warning her, or it could all be a nasty coincidence.

Flicking on the radio, Luna searched for an uplifting song, something to take her mind off her anxieties. It worked for a few minutes. When the next song started, her heart sank.

"Every breath you take . . ."

Luna rushed to turn it off.

"Didn't like that song?" Amanda asked, chuckling. She sensed none of her roommate's darkness, and Luna envied her for that.

Amanda took over the controls, stopping on a pop song Luna didn't recognize. She watched the highway change to familiar territory. They passed by the park and the old home of her friend, Nazir. The *FOR SALE* sign remained stubbornly in the front yard after years of being on the market. It didn't come as a surprise. With the unsolved murders looming over the town, there were a lot of abandoned houses now. Amanda navigated through the neighborhoods until eventually stopping in front of Luna's childhood home.

A concrete path split the grass into two halves. The small white house didn't have much in the way of a front porch, which worked because neither her parents nor Luna were big fans of visitors anyway.

Luna went inside first. She was ready to see her mom again and put some kind of positive spin on the day. Like old times, her father, Abrahim, was seated on the couch watching television. He glanced at Luna when she opened the door but didn't get up to greet her.

"Hello, Luna," he said, then as an afterthought, "Amanda."

It wasn't often that Luna stopped by to visit. Mostly because she and her father didn't get along. When she'd moved away, she thought things would get better, but she was starting to doubt the tension would ever go away.

Amanda stayed silent, petting Lucky's head as a way to stay out of it. With a *woof*, she ran up to Abrahim and nudged his remote hand to get him to pet her. He ignored the dog completely.

"Hey, Dad," Luna replied, sitting down in the armchair in the corner. "Where's Mom?"

"Went to get groceries for dinner. Should be home any minute," he said, glancing up at the clock. "How've you been?"

"Great! We just finished another semester," Luna answered, trying to pretend she and her father didn't have an underlying loathing for one another.

"Well, that's good," he said, voice stiff in a way that made it clear he didn't care to pretend.

Luna and Amanda exchanged a glance.

The door popped open, and Luna could've melted with relief. Lucky broke into a series of barks as Rose shuffled in. She was a small woman with deep-green eyes and dark hair tucked under the cover of a black hijab. Her arms were full of groceries, but that didn't stop Luna from running up and giving her a hug.

"Mom! I'm so happy to see you," she said and took one of the bags out of her arms.

Rose rested her cheek on the top of Luna's head, then led the way into the kitchen. They set the bags on the counter and Rose said to Amanda, "Sweetheart, it's good to see you again." She wrapped her in a hug. Lucky trotted up and licked her fingers, and she added, "You too. You've gotten big!"

"She eats like crazy," Amanda said as Rose started sorting through the groceries.

"I bet she does," Rose agreed and pushed a bag of potatoes out of the center of the pile. She handed a peeler to both Amanda and Luna. "We have a lot of catching up to do. Help me get dinner started while you tell me everything."

Luna set the tool down. "Of course. I've just . . . gotta run to the bathroom first."

Amanda chattered, light and carefree as Luna made her way down the hall. Her gaze drifted toward her room, the door slightly ajar, and for a moment, it felt like time folded back on itself. She peered inside to find it looked the same as when she'd lived here. At one time, it had been her fortress, her sanctuary.

Luna glanced down the hall, using her ears to pinpoint where her parents and Amanda were. Confident no one was watching, she crept across her room and knelt in front of her dresser, hesitantly opening the bottom drawer. On the surface, it appeared ordinary, full of clothes. Her fingers brushed the familiar fabric, the beige wood beneath almost comforting.

Her fingers dove deeper into the drawer. *Where is it?* She pushed through the layers of shirts, a surge of panic flooding her chest. Her hand scraped against the side of the drawer, knocking into something hard. A small sigh of relief escaped.

She yanked the black notebook from its hiding place and set it aside, running her hands over the shirts to smooth the surface. Sitting on the bed, she clenched it in both hands, working up the nerve to read its contents. With shaking fingers, she opened it. On the first page was a paragraph she'd scrawled years ago:

The contents of this book are of true events.
I've written them down as proof, if only to myself.
If anyone finds this notebook,
then you hold in your hands an
eyewitness account of a serial killer on the rise.

Newspaper clippings, the paper yellowing at the edges, decorated the first few pages. They detailed the deaths of two cheerleaders, Kate and Susan, as well as Luna's best friend, Violet. Luna flipped all the way to the last page, dated June 1, 1989. Only a week after graduation.

In barely legible handwriting, she'd written:

Violet died. Max was close. Amy's traumatized, and the town worries about her. As for Chance . . . well, he's lost his memory forever, according to Max. I don't know what this experience has done to me, but the dreams have stopped. I don't want to say I'm free yet because it's kind of hard to believe. So much of this experience has been.
It might be the time to begin healing, but not to forget.
Never forget.

She had no idea how true the words were when she'd written *Never forget.*

Chapter Eight

LUNA WENT BACK to the kitchen and chatted with Rose and Amanda, her true feelings under wraps. They ate dinner and as far as her loved ones knew, she had a good time. Luna smuggled her notebook out of the house in her tote bag and kept it cradled on her lap on the drive home.

As Amanda drove out of Lima, the air between them felt thick with unspoken words. She remained quiet, but every so often, her eyes would flick toward Luna, as if sensing something simmering beneath the surface. Finally, the question she'd been dreading slipped out.

"Are you sure you're okay?"

Luna turned her gaze to the window, the motion giving her a moment to compose herself, but it didn't hide the frustration creeping at the edges of her thoughts. She exhaled, willing the irritation down. "I'm fine."

"That doesn't sound promising," Amanda replied, with a touch of concern.

"If it's all right with you, I'd rather not talk about it. You . . . wouldn't understand."

"Try me. You never know unless you try."

Luna's lips pressed together, a tight line of restraint. *I have a pretty good idea*, she thought bitterly. The things she'd lived through weren't the sort of happenings anyone could just *understand*. They weren't the kind of things most people would even believe. "Like I said, I'd rather not," Luna repeated, careful to keep her eyes in a spot inaccessible to Amanda. She didn't know what her roommate might see in them.

Amanda sighed.

Luna noted the disappointment but shoved away her resulting guilt. Max had said there were others using dreams to hunt him. It might be only a matter of time until they came after Luna too. If that was the case, Amanda could get caught in the crosshairs if she knew too much.

Arm's length, Luna told herself. That was the closest she would let herself get to anyone. Any closer than that would only end in heartache for both of them.

"Well, if you want to hang out, let me know. I'm sure Cassie wouldn't mind putting things off until tomorrow. We can watch a movie or something," Amanda offered.

Luna stared at her, grateful to have such a good friend. In a world where most people seemed wrapped up in their own lives, finding someone as selfless as Amanda was a rare gift. *It's too bad it's wasted on me.* "It's okay, Mandy, really. I know you've got things you need to do so go ahead. Please."

Amanda's response was flat, the concern still there but edged with resignation. "All right. Drop me off on the way, then. I'll catch a ride home later."

Luna agreed and went silent, staring out the window as Amanda continued down the highway. In Bowling Green, Amanda stopped in front of a house and said her goodbyes. Luna drove back to the apartment, Lucky letting out little excited yips every now and then. When she parked, she lingered in the car, her eyes locked on the endless stretch of night outside the windshield.

Lucky's whine cut through the stillness, a small, anxious sound that snapped her out of the haze.

"Tired, girl?" Luna asked, clipping the leash onto her collar. "Come on."

Lucky led the way up the path and into the apartment. Luna unhooked Lucky's leash and kicked off her shoes. The dog watched her with eager eyes, waiting, until Luna reached down to give her a gentle scratch between the ears. Luna couldn't allow herself to get close to other humans, but dog love was different. Stronger somehow. Lucky had a power no human did. No matter what was going on in Luna's head, when Lucky came around, things seemed brighter. She could hardly believe there'd been a time, not so long ago, when she had feared dogs.

Lucky whined happily and left the room. As soon as she disappeared down the hall, Luna's smile fell. With no other distraction, her gaze landed on her bag. She took out her notebook. Plopping onto the couch, she started to flip through it. The middle pages didn't have any words on them, but they didn't need to. A small plump bundle wrapped tight in packaging paper waited for her. Her fingers trembled as she eased it open, freeing a dagger from its paper coffin. It fell to the hardwood floor with a soft *thump*.

Luna stared at it. The very weapon that had flipped her life upside down. With shaking fingers, she bent down to scoop it up with the paper, afraid of leaving her fingerprints on it. A dried speck of blood marred the blade.

Is it mine? she wondered, picking up the faint, blurry outline of her reflection in the silver.

That was all it took to get the tears flowing again.

Chapter Nine

MAX GASPED BACK to consciousness, sweaty and terrified from another dream encounter with an assassin. His real life didn't give him a better experience. Footsteps in the hallway told him he wasn't alone. Which wasn't right because he *lived* alone.

As quietly as he could, he threw himself onto the floor just as someone burst into his room—another man cloaked in one of those black shrouds. The problem with this one, though, was that he couldn't wake up and be out of harm's way. This one had found his home. Most likely, the dream assassin had been sent to keep him distracted on the Other Side so he'd have no way to defend himself. As slowly as he could, Max slipped his blade from underneath his pillow and watched the shadow come closer.

Creak.

The man stepped around the bed, and Max launched himself to his feet. With one hand, he grabbed the man by the throat and with the other, he stabbed him in the side, driving the blade between his ribs. The man groaned and went slack. Max dropped him and took a step back, holding up the blade in anticipation of another attack. But the man didn't try to get back up. He held a hand to his side and peered up at Max through eyes glazed with terror.

"Come on. Is that all you've got?" Max taunted. His adrenaline was beginning to skyrocket. He was ready for whatever would come next.

The man said nothing as he dragged himself backward, inch by inch. Max loomed over him but didn't attack, curious to see what he would do next. When he picked himself up, Max braced, ready for round two.

The man sized him up, then ran.

Max let him go.

It didn't matter if he lived or not. The rest of them would find out where he lived if they didn't know already. This had been a coordinated attack and that meant nowhere was safe. Now, it was a numbers game. They knew where he was and what he could do. Next time, they wouldn't come alone.

I need to make sure I'm not alone either, he thought, and the awful feeling of dread wormed its way through his stomach. Luna was the only chance he had of having a partner, but she'd been unwilling to talk about it on the phone.

Guess I have to drop by in person. Make her understand.

He glanced at the clock: *10:03 p.m.* It was *sort of* late, but not so late that it would be weird for him to visit.

I have to do something, he thought. After washing his face in the sink and removing his bloody shirt to wipe himself down, he dressed in a clean outfit and ventured out into the night.

Luna lived a good ten-minute walk from him. He'd purposefully kept that in mind when he picked this place to rent. After everything that had gone down, it was in his best interest to not only keep an eye on the Chance situation but on his friend as well.

Now, he was glad for the foresight as he hurried down the sidewalk. A streetlight flickered overhead, casting long shadows as he ran. When he rounded onto Luna's street, the lights around the apartment complex perimeter guided him onward.

He pushed through a gap in the black gate, coming out not far from Luna's unit. Max stopped with the uneasy feeling that something was wrong. A shadow moved outside one of the buildings. Not just *any* building.

Luna's. Near her room.

He's here, Max thought, then pushed himself to run as fast as he could, which proved more difficult than it used to be. After losing his leg from mid-thigh down, he'd chosen to get a prosthetic to replace it. Though it had been three years, he still wasn't the best when it came to quick movement, but he put everything he had into it as he charged the figure.

Max grabbed him and heaved him to his feet, turning him around to see the man's face. He didn't recognize it.

Surprised, Max asked, "Who are you and what are you doing here?"

The man quivered in his grasp, shaking so hard Max thought he might faint. On closer inspection, he appeared younger than the others he'd fought. A new recruit possibly? "Please don't kill me," he begged, voice cracking like he was on the verge of crying.

The response caught Max off guard. "Then tell me why

you're here. How do you know this girl?"

"I *don't* know her," he said. "Honestly. I didn't do anything to her!"

"That better be true," Max warned, inching closer to see inside the window. From this angle, he could make out a lump in the bed, but through the darkness, he couldn't tell if it was Luna or if she was okay. He tried to get a little closer when his prosthetic leg caught in the mud. Max lurched forward. To keep himself from falling, he let go of the man.

Free, he sprang forward, scrambling on his hands and knees to get away.

"Hey!" Max whisper-yelled after him. "Come back here!"

Of course, he didn't. He sprinted out of the complex and into the night beyond. Max tore after him, each step frantic, until exhaustion stole his speed and he had to stop.

The man vanished into the night.

Chapter Ten

THE GROUND WAS solid beneath Luna's feet, but the haze made it hard to see where she was. She did her best to walk through it, but it grew thicker, choking her. Luna was only vaguely aware of the fact that she was in DreamWorld. Her primary focus was on escape.

In the distance, a faint blue light flickered, barely visible through the fog. It grew closer, slow but steady. Luna's instincts braced for danger. The light pulsed, brighter now, burning through the haze like a star tearing through the darkness. It surrounded her, searing her skin with its intensity. She squeezed her eyes shut, but it pushed through the darkness behind her eyelids, blinding her.

When the sensation dissolved away, she opened her eyes again. The field was gone, but she was aware that she was still within the confines of DreamWorld. This time a forest surrounded her. A very familiar forest. For a heart-stopping second, she thought the dreams that had haunted her years ago were beginning again. Then she spotted the sun. In those dreams, that had been impossible. A sigh of relief almost passed her lips when it lodged in her throat. At the other end of the clearing was a body.

This was worse than a nightmare. It was a memory.

Blood ran down Violet's face in two irregular lines from the bullet wound in her forehead. Her skin was pale and cold, limbs bent at the angle she had landed in the grass. Her eyes were closed, but they'd been open when she passed. Luna hovered beside her deceased friend. Unsure what to do, she stuck out a hand, meaning to touch her shoulder but stopped without making contact. She'd learned the hard way to keep her distance in dreams and in the Real World.

"I'm sorry," she whispered.

Violet's eyes flicked open, blue irises focusing on her best friend. "Luna . . ." she whispered, stretching a bloody hand toward her.

Luna jumped backward, just out of reach. When her feet hit the ground, the forest swirled away, and she opened her eyes in the safety of her own room.

I'm safe, she told herself but didn't feel it.

Darkness made it hard to see, but not impossible. Luna wiped away the sweat from her forehead, positive she'd suffered a panic attack, and tried to sit up to take in a sharp breath of air.

A figure stood on the other side of her room, rifling through the papers on her desk. If Luna *had* had a panic attack, then it was for good reason. The figure stopped and turned. Before Luna could move, it rushed toward her. A hand covered her mouth and forced her back down on the bed. She struggled, trying to break free and call for help, when blackness claimed her.

Finally, her eyes opened, and she was aware that time had passed. She lay in bed, listening to the thunder rumbling outside. Rain clattered against the roof like a thousand marbles tumbling down the siding and crashing to the grass below. It was still dark in her room. She shifted in bed, trying to convince herself to go back to sleep.

A terrible headache bloomed at the front of her brain, making it impossible to do anything but hurt. She switched on the lamp, instantly regretting it. Her head roared in protest. Stress was getting to her. Out of all her nightmares, the last one bothered her the most. It reminded her of the dream of the box. The glimpse she'd gotten of *his* eyes.

They were all creepy, but that wasn't what mattered. They were trying to tell her something. The flash of light held meaning, as did the memories of Violet that Luna had long buried deep within her mind.

Stop it, she scolded, swinging her legs over the edge of the bed. *They're just bad dreams.*

Mechanically, she wiped away a tear and saw her notebook on her desk, opened to the page she'd used to hold Chance's knife. She couldn't see the weapon. Panicked, she hurried across the room, flipped through the pages, but it wasn't there. She tossed the book aside and searched under her bed, beside her dresser, anywhere it could be, but there was no sign it had ever existed.

She racked her brain for a solution. Had Amanda found the book? A flash of that third nightmare came back—the one of a figure in her room rummaging through her belongings. Had someone actually been in her room? She shot the thought down at once.

There's a better explanation.

Lucky wasn't at the foot of her bed. Luna stumbled

clumsily to the threshold of the room and stopped to clutch the wooden doorframe, resting the roaring pain in her head against it. She forced herself to go down the hall. If Lucky had the dagger, she had to get it back before she hurt herself . . . or Amanda saw it.

Luna reached the living room, perplexed that her dog wasn't there either. She stumbled into the kitchen, scratching her head. Something wasn't right. Every day for the past year, she and Lucky followed the same ritual. Lucky would sleep at the foot of Luna's bed, and when she got up, Lucky would as well. The border collie would follow her as she went through her morning routine, barking all the while. That would serve as Amanda's alarm clock.

"Lucky?" Luna muttered, trying to gain her dog's attention without getting Amanda's as well. Her apartment was too small to have a dog Lucky's size disappear completely. "Where are you?"

A sharp knock echoed through the apartment. It wasn't the secret one that only she and Amanda used, so who was at their door at six in the morning? She stormed over to it, wishing it had a peephole. Taking in a deep breath, she wrapped her fingers around the knob and pulled it open.

No one was on the porch.

Rain splattered the ground, the sky cloudy enough that the light of the late sunrise barely pierced through. Luna's gaze dropped to the porch. A black mound lay there, soaked with rain. Gasping, Luna dropped to her knees.

It was Lucky.

A choked sob lodged in her throat as she scooped up the

dog's limp body, carrying her inside. Amanda stood in the middle of the kitchen, hair sticking up from her slumber and eyes wide with confusion.

"What's going on?" she asked.

"I don't know." Luna set the dog on the floor beside the table and ran her hand along her fur, searching for any sign of life.

"Is she dead?" Amanda asked, peering at Lucky like she thought the dog might rear up and attack.

Luna touched the front of Lucky's neck, noting the ripped skin. When she tugged her hand back, it was covered in blood. "Yeah," she said, raising the dog's limp head up to glance at the wound.

"How did this happen?" Amanda murmured. "She was fine yesterday."

"I don't know," Luna said, though she could vaguely remember Lucky curling up with her as she went to sleep.

"Oh God, did she get out when I came in?" Amanda asked, holding both sides of her head.

It was the most likely scenario. She had tags. Maybe someone accidentally ran her over and didn't know what to do, so they left her on the doorstep. Luna set the dog's head back on the white floor, running her thumb over the perfectly sliced strands of fur stuck to her skin.

Amanda made a squealing sound of grief. "Why didn't I double-check before I went to bed?"

Luna said nothing as she stroked the side of Lucky's face, savoring the feeling of her fur despite how cold and wet it was. She forced herself to stand and walk out of the room, steps stiff.

Luna went into the bathroom and shut the door. Collapsing beside the white bathtub, she cried.

55

Chapter Eleven

LUNA WIPED HER forehead with the back of her hand, then resumed filling the hole at her feet with dirt. She didn't want to think about her dog's body beneath the thin layer she'd already shoveled into it. Grit clung uncomfortably to her sweaty skin, and she longed for a shower followed by a nap, with the far-fetched idea of dreaming of happier times.

Overhead, the sky was heavy with clouds, but it had stopped raining for the time being. Luna didn't know how long Mother Nature would allow her to give Lucky a decent funeral, but she took advantage of the respite. She shoved a wooden cross into the ground as a grave marker to hang Lucky's collar on. Wiping her hair from her eyes, she stepped back from the grave.

Forgetting about the shovel, she ran through the apartment and into the bathroom, closing the door behind her. She cranked the tap as hot as it would go and stripped off her muddy clothes, telling herself she'd worry about the mess later. The water ran off her in brown rivulets, just starting to run clear when someone knocked on the bathroom door.

"What is it?" Luna asked, peering around the shower curtain. What did Amanda have to say that couldn't wait until *after* she'd finished her shower?

Amanda popped the door open a crack. "There's a boy on

the phone who wants to talk to you. He says it's important."

Luna could hardly conceal her annoyance. No doubt it was Max again. "Tell him to call back in twenty minutes."

"Okay," Amanda said and shut the door.

Luna tried to enjoy the rest of the shower, but the hot water no longer soothed her. Fuming, she climbed out of the tub and got dressed. She expected Amanda to be waiting in the living room, but she was moving around inside her own bedroom.

Luna paced the length of the kitchen, barefoot on cold tile, her thoughts spiraling.

The phone rang once.

She snatched it up. "Hello?"

"Luna." Max sounded calm. *Too* calm.

"What are you calling for, Max?" she asked as if she didn't already know.

"You know what." Luna opened her mouth, but he continued, "I know you don't want to hear it, but the darkness . . . it's there again. I can't do this alone."

Luna clenched her jaw. Her fingers tightened around the phone.

"I had another dream, Luna. Tell me if this sounds familiar: a field, a light. Feeling like your skin is on fire?"

Luna stiffened at the description. *No.*

"I'm convinced it's a warning that Chance has his memory back." Max continued. "Or that the people he's working with are up to something big. Either way, we can't ignore it."

Luna's throat felt swollen shut. No words would come out. She made an odd groan instead.

"What is it?"

"You've probably already guessed that I had the same dream," she forced herself to admit.

"There's your proof," Max said excitedly. "When we both had the same dream before you knew to take it seriously."

"Because people *died* before, Max."

"All cycles start somewhere. These people aren't going to go away just because you don't want to deal with them."

Luna hated the truth of those words. They made her want to scream. "I don't need this right now, Max, okay? I'm having a bad day."

Silence. Not the annoyed kind. The calculating kind. Reserved, he asked, "What happened?"

"Lucky died. We found her on the porch this morning. Whatever happened, happened during the night. Probably got hit by a car."

"Did you see it happen?"

"No," she snapped. "I was asleep."

"Then why assume it was a car?"

"She had a wound on her neck." Luna glanced at her hand, half expecting to see the blood still there. "It's the only thing I can think of."

"Uh-huh. Just one?"

"Yeah?"

"Do you really need me to spell it out for you?" he asked, punctuating his words with an exasperated sigh. "It's . . . happening . . . again. The evidence is right in front of us, you've gotta believe that."

"I don't *have* to believe *anything*," Luna snarled. Deciding she no longer had the energy for this call, she hung up and stormed down the hall to her room. Her eyes fell on her open notebook. Horror washed over her as she hurried toward it. Had Amanda seen it? What if she'd read it? *That's ridiculous.* Anyone who read it would have some questions . . . especially Amanda.

Luna picked up the book, balancing it on one hand as she plucked the torn paper off the carpet. The dagger was still missing. After discovering Lucky's body, she'd forgotten all about it. Little else mattered while she watched her precious puppy bleeding on the kitchen floor. Luna tucked the book under her mattress where it'd be impossible to see unless someone was searching for it.

She glanced at the clock. Most of the day had already been spent waiting for the rain to stop and the rest involved mourning. Alone in her room, the walls felt too tight. After high school, she'd read her share of self-help books. Almost all of them warned against isolation, against shutting people out. So, with effort, she pushed herself to leave the room and settled onto the love seat in the living room, unsure of what to do next.

A soft noise stirred down the hall. Moments later, Amanda emerged from her room. "Is she . . . buried?" she asked.

Luna nodded but didn't look at her.

"How're you holding up?"

"As okay as I can," Luna said. Trying not to remember her dead dog was taking every bit of her brain power, and if she managed to achieve it, the phone call with Max was waiting in the wings to hijack her thoughts and emotions.

Amanda went into her room after giving her a gentle

smile. The kind Luna imagined would say, "It'll get better with time." She wanted to scream about how impossible it all seemed, but she bit it back, reminding herself that what happened to Lucky wasn't Amanda's fault.

Accidents happen, Luna told herself, but she didn't fully believe it.

The image of the clean slash across Lucky's throat kept bringing her back to Max's warnings. She *wanted* to believe it was just a horrible accident, coincidentally timed. But the more she tried to hold onto that belief, the more it slipped through her fingers.

What if it wasn't?

If Max was right about something nefarious going on in the Other Side, it wouldn't stop on its own.

I need a second opinion, she thought.

She and Max weren't the only survivors of that day in the woods. There was one more person. Someone who could possibly give her some much-needed insight.

Amy.

Luna didn't know exactly what had gone down between Amy and Chance that day, but whatever happened had been enough for her not to show up to graduation. The last time Luna had seen her, Amy wandered into the woods to get help for them. After that, she'd disappeared.

Luna never reached out. Never checked in. Didn't give her a second thought. At the time, she'd been too consumed by Violet's death, and by the deep, festering wound she'd barely survived.

I'm a horrible friend, she thought.

Maybe she could find some answers by doing what she hadn't bothered to do three years ago—reach out to Amy.

Chapter Twelve

THE BIGGEST QUESTION Luna had now was: how could she convince Amanda to let her borrow her car without her wanting to tag along and hang out?

What's so boring that she won't be interested in it? Luna mused.

The immediate thought was school. Amanda *hated* her classes and hated homework. The only thing about school she had a vague interest in was the sorority parties.

Bingo.

Amanda was in the kitchen, spreading out a selection of fruits on the counter for a smoothie. "What kind do you want?"

"Uh, I'll have to take a rain check on that," Luna said as she approached her. "I was actually going to ask if I could borrow your car. Something's come up."

Amanda dropped a mango into the blender. "Is everything all right?"

"Yeah, yeah, it's fine. It's . . . apparently my parents forgot to drop off my tuition check for next semester, so I'm going to go handle that."

"Yeah, sure, no problem," she said, dropping another chunk of fruit on top of the first. "Keys are over there."

"Thanks, you're a lifesaver," Luna said, but avoided meeting her eye again, fearing that Amanda would pick up on her lie.

Outside, Luna allowed herself to finally take a deep breath. Years had passed since the last time she'd visited either Amy or her sister. Worse, she'd only been to their house once, and Chance had made sure to cut the visit short.

Signs blurred past as she drove, but Luna didn't read any of them as she focused on the open road. In her head, she rehearsed what she would say to Amy when she saw her again.

That depends on her state of mind, she reminded herself. Or what was left of her mind anyway.

Once inside Lima city limits, she stopped near the park, trying to remember the route she'd taken that day. It felt like a lifetime ago.

Luna crept down the streets, doing her best to punch through the haze she'd put over her memories and wound up in front of a white house. She almost passed it and had to slam on the brakes. At one time, it had been well taken care of—a beautiful, picturesque home that could've been in a magazine.

This house was not.

The lawn was brown and brittle. Flowers that had once thrived in the window boxes were long dead. Half the siding had fallen off to reveal the brown wood of the house underneath. The longer Luna stared at it, the more her plan started to unravel. Was it abandoned? If it was, Luna had no idea how she would get in contact with Amy.

Cautiously, Luna pushed away her doubts and made her way to the front door. She was almost positive no one would answer, but something drew her to knock anyway. The resounding thuds echoed inside the house, and she could picture it empty of furniture and life. Disheartened, she took a step off the broken porch, then a familiar *click* of the front door opening stopped her. Luna glanced over her shoulder, not knowing what to expect.

Hollowed cheeks and sunken eyes made up the face of the woman staring back at her. Her once long, vibrant brown hair had thinned considerably, appearing so brittle that Luna feared it would fall out in chunks.

She didn't recognize her at first.

"Luna? Is that you?" the sickly figure asked. Then it clicked. Amy's sister.

"Michelle, it's been a while."

Michelle nodded thoughtfully. "It has. Would you like to come in?"

"Please." Luna tried to offer a pleasant expression that would belie any of her shock.

Michelle stepped aside to allow her into the house, but she'd grown so thin it wasn't necessary. Luna could easily step past without her moving. Michelle closed the door and led the way into the cozy living room.

"What brings you here after all this time?" she asked, sitting down on the white sofa.

"I-I wanted to talk to Amy," Luna answered, unsure of her decision when Michelle's face bunched in grief.

"She . . . isn't here anymore," she said with an absence of the light that usually accompanied thoughts of her sister. For a second, Luna assumed she meant Amy was dead. Her face must've reflected that because Michelle added, "No, nothing like that." She raised a skeleton-thin hand. "I meant *not here* as in she doesn't live here anymore. Unfortunately, she had to be moved permanently to Brentwood Psychiatric."

Luna sank into the couch beside Michelle. "She went to a mental hospital? Why?"

"For almost a year, she refused to speak. She sat in her room, day and night, drawing and crying. We did everything to try to help her. We hired experts and saw therapists and tried medicine, but none of it was enough. Then she stopped eating, and I knew I had to do *something*."

"She didn't go to graduation either," Luna murmured, remembering the haunting line of chairs in front of the stage. Three for the dead girls. One for Chance. And one for poor Amy.

Michelle entwined her thumbs. "We tried so hard to convince her, but she didn't want to do it."

Luna knew why. Whatever Chance had done had been too much for her to handle.

"Do you know what happened to her, Luna?" Michelle asked so quietly that Luna had to strain to hear. "Do you know why she stopped talking?"

The words were an ugly lullaby, bouncing around inside Luna's head. Of course she knew. What happened was her fault. She'd dragged Amy right into Chance's path, and it was through dumb luck that she had been able to save her. Luna swallowed roughly, positive Michelle was onto her. She wanted to tell her the truth, but Michelle would never understand. How could she? Forcing away her guilt, Luna said, "No, I don't."

"Why visit now? No one has asked about her in years. It's

like the world forgot she existed."

Luna wilted a bit. In a few more years, all of it would be forgotten as people moved on with their lives. The cabin. The dead girls. The survivors. "No real reason," she lied, biting the inside of her cheek. "I was in the neighborhood and thought it might be fun to catch up."

The corners of Michelle's lips twisted up into a ghost of a smile. "Well, I'm sure she'd be happy to know someone misses her."

Confused, Luna said, "She knows you do," to which Michelle shrugged listlessly. Luna added, "I'm sorry she's been suffering."

"She's not the only one," Michelle added quietly. When Luna raised an eyebrow, she continued. "You might've noticed that I don't look the same."

Luna struggled with her answer. Would it be rude to agree if she wasn't the one who brought it up?

"I found out a while back that I have cancer."

"I'm so sorry," Luna said softly, reaching for the right words.

Michelle pressed on, as if she hadn't heard. "It was about a month after we sent Amy away. It went into remission, but recently it came back. I've had to start treatment all over again."

A cold shiver ran down Luna's spine. Could Michelle's illness be tied to something deeper than science? The timing of Max's warnings and Lucky's mysterious death all felt too connected, too deliberate. How far did the effects go?

"Want to see the pictures?"

"Huh?"

"Amy's drawings?"

"Oh. Yeah, of course." A picture was worth a thousand words, and if Amy hadn't spoken in years, then her drawings would speak volumes.

"Come on," Michelle said. The more she moved, the more her fragility became apparent. Several times, Luna had to fight the urge to reach out and steady her as she led the way down the hall. She stopped outside the only familiar door, using the jamb as support. "I haven't been in here in a long time. Forgive me if I get a bit emotional."

That was something Luna could understand. Three years had passed, and it was still tough to go past Violet's father's house knowing her friend had once lived there.

Michelle opened the door, letting Luna go inside. The room was musty and stale. There was no bulb in the socket, but enough light streamed in through the window for Luna to see. The last time Luna had been here, the walls had been delicate pink, dotted with giant pieces of paper that held cartoon drawings by Amy's own hand.

Now, the room was as abandoned as the lawn outside.

Paint had been chipped from the walls as if Amy deliberately dug her pencils into it. Most of the papers had been ripped away, leaving only bits stuck in the tape. Feathers from the ripped bedding dotted the dingy carpet and crayons littered the ruin like Easter eggs. Small pieces of paper with childlike drawings were taped to the headboard of the bed and the wall. Luna walked over to the nearest one.

On it was a drawing of a red sigil and next to that was a drawing of a snake. Fangs bared and eyes like hollow pits. Familiar in the worst way. It was the snake from the handle of Chance's dagger. Luna's attention darted to the next sheet of paper, desperate for more. A building made of stone. Chance's temple. Beside that, a wooden cabin. The same one from Luna's nightmares.

Chance hadn't only traumatized Amy. He'd driven her *crazy*.

"Well? Do you know what any of this means?" Michelle asked, clutching the paper Luna had dropped—the drawing of the sigil.

Luna had been so engrossed in the pictures that she'd forgotten Michelle was there. Slipping a mask over her surprised horror, she said, "No, not a clue."

Chapter Thirteen

LUNA SAT IN the parking lot for a long time. At the edge of the asphalt loomed a large building made of bricks and dark colors that reminded her of a mausoleum.

Slowly, she left the safety of the car and crossed the lot. Stepping through the sliding glass doors felt like stepping into the gaping maw of some great beast. The temperature dropped, and she reconsidered her plan as she approached the desk. Would Amy be happy to see her, like Michelle thought? Or would she only serve as a reminder of the things Amy hoped to forget?

A nurse appeared from an adjacent hallway to greet her. "Can I help you?"

"I'm here to visit Amy Jimenez," Luna said.

"Okay. First, I'll need you to empty your pockets. Then sign your name in the visitor log. Also, I need to see your ID."

As Luna scrambled to remove her driver's license, a door buzzed and slammed shut from somewhere deeper in the building. She scrawled her name in hasty scribbles on the sign-in page and emptied her pockets, watching the nurse put the items in a small plastic bag that she dumped into a bucket under the reception desk. She led Luna down a long white hallway, reciting the rules as they went. Luna barely heard her. There were a dozen doors along the linoleum corridor holding dozens of lost souls trapped by their own torment. She tried to picture their faces. The only difference between her and them was that she was still free.

They stopped in front of the last door. "You'll have twenty minutes. Remember, she's very frail," the nurse reminded, then swiped her ID badge. "So try not to say anything that will get her worked up or upset."

If only I could oblige, Luna thought. The sole reason she was here was to talk about Chance, and there was no pleasant way to do that.

Luna braced herself as the door opened, and she stepped through. It clanged shut, trapping her in the confines of white walls. A bed, much like one in a hospital, was positioned against the far wall. A barred window allowed a bit of light to stream into the room, and in the center of it all was a solitary chair. It faced the window, though Luna knew it didn't provide much of a view from that angle. A small figure wearing a knee-length white gown perched on it. Their back was to her.

"Amy?" Luna whispered, studying the tangled brown hair. A new thought came that she hadn't considered yet: what if Amy was too traumatized to speak? What if she hadn't made any progress at all? The figure twitched slightly but didn't move, and that feeling of dread hardened in Luna's stomach.

"Amy, it's me, Luna."

When Amy remained silent, Luna deflated.

This was a waste of time.

As if she'd heard the thought, the figure slipped from the chair in a graceful *swoosh* and faced her. Amy's skin was the color of porcelain. She was so thin, her legs strained to hold her up. Her brown hair, once long, now barely reached her shoulders, but her eyes held a traumatized gleam Luna recognized from her own reflection.

"Do you remember me?" Luna asked, clueless as to how to start this conversation.

"Of course I remember you," Amy replied, surprisingly lucid considering her appearance. "I'm not crazy. What are you doing here?"

Luna hadn't expected Amy to be ecstatic to see her, but the hostility caught her off guard. "I . . . came to see how you've been. I heard you were here, so I thought I'd drop in. What happened?"

Amy broke her gaze from Luna's. "It doesn't matter."

Luna bit her bottom lip, recognizing her own trauma response—denial. "It does to me."

"You wouldn't understand. No one does." She stared down at the floor, but Luna didn't have to see her face to guess what she was feeling.

Betrayed.

Alone.

Trapped in a box.

"I understand more than you think," Luna admitted. She used to think of herself as a close-minded person, and then she saw literal magic for herself. Now? She was open to everything.

Amy's mouth remained set in a straight line. It was impossible to tell what thoughts were in her head. "I know," she said. Luna smiled, thinking it was the right reaction, but Amy did not smile back. "I know about your gift and what Chance was.

What he tried to be."

The blood drained from Luna's face. Amy's words landed like knife blades driven into her chest. Ironic how only five minutes ago she worried that she would upset her. Of all her friends, Luna had always viewed Amy as the only *normal* one. That Chance had targeted her because she'd gone out of her way to help Luna and, for the most part, she fit his victim profile.

Maybe I don't know what happened as well as I thought I did.

"You know about DreamWorld?" Luna asked flatly, because she couldn't figure out which emotion to add with those words.

Amy clenched her hands into fists. "Yes, I know about *DreamWorld*. I know about *everything*." She stared out the bars on her window. "I have my entire life."

"Why didn't you say anything?" When Amy had saved Luna from Chance, she'd chalked it up to good timing; no other possibilities crossed her mind. How integrated was Amy with all that had transpired?

"I didn't know how much you knew," Amy admitted. "And it's not like I didn't consider telling you. I actually thought it would've been a good idea to have you in the loop, but that would've compromised my mission so I didn't say anything."

The room grew colder as Luna took in those words. "Your *mission*?"

"You. You were my mission."

Luna flinched as if she'd been slapped. A mission? Not a friend. Not an acquaintance. A *job*. A responsibility. "Your . . . *mission*?"

"It's pretty simple, really," Amy said matter-of-factly. "I'm a Keeper. Or I was."

The world spun again. Max was a Keeper, and now Amy too? How many Keepers existed in her circle? *And how did I not know?*

"What happened?"

Amy laughed, loud and maniacal. "What happened? *What happened?* Are you serious? You were there! I never wanted to be a Keeper, and then all that happened and I—" She paused to let out a deep exhale. "I couldn't do it anymore."

"So, the whole time you knew what could happen, what Chance could do, and you let it?" Luna asked, surprised to find coils of anger burning through her stomach. When she had entered Amy's room, she'd been filled with compassion and sympathy and guilt. All that was gone now. Amy wasn't a tortured victim of Chance's. She was complicit.

"My job was to study your gift. That's it. My partner was responsible for Chance. We were told not to intervene. Watch and report."

"Report? To who? For what?"

Amy tittered and shook her head. "Like I said, you'd never understand."

Luna narrowed her eyes to slits. "None of this makes any sense. If you know about the Other Side, then you know you're not crazy. Why the hell are you here?"

"It was the only way to escape," Amy admitted. "I didn't want to be a Keeper anymore, and everything I tried didn't work. This was my out."

"Your drawings made it seem like Chance traumatized you," Luna said. "Unless you faked it all as part of your plan, which frankly, is pretty fucked-up to make your family worry like that."

Amy again drew her lips tight. "You've talked to Michelle?"

With anger still flaring in her stomach, Luna didn't want to back down, but she'd never seen Amy angry. The last thing she expected to set her off was the mention of her sister. "I wanted to find you, and Michelle was the only point of contact I had. I didn't think you'd be upset about it. And I damn sure didn't think you'd be here."

"She sent me away."

"She was worried about you. She didn't know what else to do," Luna said, grimacing.

Amy continued, not seeming to hear Luna. "Sent me away like I was nothing."

"Besides, I thought you *wanted* to be here. You said it was your plan."

Amy grumbled something, then added louder, "It was, but it's more complicated than that."

Luna crinkled her face, not understanding. "She misses you, okay? At the end of the day, that should be what counts."

"Except it's not," Amy countered, slamming a hand against the white wall. "Because she *forgot* about me."

"I doubt it. She's got a lot going on. I mean, cancer isn't easy to handle *with* help, and without—"

"What?" Amy interrupted. She sounded suddenly small

and weak, as if all the wind had been knocked out of her sails. It was then that Luna remembered Michelle said she'd gotten sick *after* Amy had gone to Brentwood. Amy didn't know.

"She's sick," Luna said, watching Amy deflate in her chair. "I'm sorry. I thought you knew."

Exhausted, Amy asked, "Why have you come today, Luna?"

I shouldn't have mentioned Michelle, Luna realized in hindsight. *This* was the fragility the nurse had warned her of. Not any of what she'd seen before. "I wanted to see you. To catch up on what happened."

Amy narrowed her eyes.

"And see if . . . anything has been happening to you on the Other Side."

Amy scoffed. "What kind of friend are you anyway? We haven't seen each other in years. You come in and drop a bomb on me without so much as a how do you do, and expect me to help you?"

"I meant no harm, honestly," Luna insisted, trying to keep her desperation from seeping out. "It's . . . important that I know."

"Why?"

Luna tucked her lip in her teeth, unsure how to tell her that the danger she feared was still very much alive.

Maybe Amy sensed what she was going to say because a flicker of something went through her eyes but vanished before Luna could decipher it. "Get out."

"But—"

"I said *go!*"

That was much clearer.

Luna knocked on the door until her knuckles bloomed red. When the nurse let her out, she hurried down the long hallway, ignoring the woman's questions. If Amy wouldn't say what Chance had done to her, Luna would never know.

"Is everything okay?" the nurse asked as she grabbed the bucket with Luna's belongings.

Luna didn't answer, just hurriedly tucked her things back into her pockets.

"Have a good day!" the nurse called behind her as Luna hurried into the parking lot, hardly able to wrap her mind around what had happened.

Amy wasn't the girl Luna remembered. Not by a long shot. Whatever she'd gone through had hardened her.

Shaking her head, Luna ran to Amanda's car, shutting herself inside. That was when she let out the first full breath she'd taken since stepping out of the hospital. Snapshots of the interaction blasted through her. Amy was a Keeper, tasked with watching *her*, of all people.

Chance was the threat, not me, she thought, squeezing the steering wheel until her knuckles cracked. She couldn't decide if she was frustrated or defeated. *None of this makes any sense.*

If Amy and her partner had known how dangerous Chance was, why waste the time on observation? Why not shut him down at the first opportunity?

Unless they couldn't stop him, she thought. *Unless they were watching me because they wanted me to do it.*

Luna questioned her entire friendship with Amy as she started the car. Had any of it been real or was it all a cover so she could get information and report it? *Report it to who?* If that was the case, who was Amy's partner, the one responsible for studying Chance?

As she drove, Luna's mind went to Max. His entire DreamWorld involvement had been strange, and she couldn't forget the fact that he'd refused to answer when she asked how he knew so much about it. Then there was the information about Max's dream character, and the difference in his appearance.

A memory came to her: Chance's bitter eyes laced with jealousy. *He's in my way of getting to you*, he'd said. Luna had thought it was petty male rivalry at the time, but now, it made sense in a new, more terrifying way. *Max* was Amy's partner.

The world swirled, and she thought she was going to be sick. Luna slowed down as she passed her parents' house, considering going in for a little while, when Amy's words stopped her. *You come in and drop a bomb without so much as a how do you do.*

Disrupting her parents' day for the sake of a panic attack was right on brand with that assessment. Luna wouldn't make the same mistake twice in one day. She forced herself to keep driving. She would visit on a better day.

If there was such a thing.

She flicked on the radio, searching for something to lift her spirits. Glancing at the road, a truck headed directly for her. Not just *any* truck . . . a black extended cab. Luna gasped and jerked the steering wheel left and right, trying to keep the car straight. Tires tore across grass and rocks before she managed to line it back up on the narrow road once the truck had passed.

Gasping, Luna pushed her raven hair out of her eyes, counting her blessings that the near miss hadn't been worse. She watched the familiar truck receding in her rearview window, sick all over again. Someone she knew owned one similar.

Chance.

Chapter Fourteen

OVER THE COURSE of the next two days, Luna did her best to pretend that everything was fine, but her mind was a beehive of vicious thoughts, stinging harder and deeper. Lucky, the interaction with Amy, Max's frequent phone calls . . . hovering in her brain at all hours of the day. She needed to do something to take her mind off things.

That was how she came to the decision to get a job. Without classes and assignments, time was her biggest enemy. Working would keep her busy and ensure she was tired enough at the end of the day to get a good night's sleep. It seemed like a good plan until she actually applied to several places. None of her qualifications mattered because the answer was the same: "We're not hiring right now."

Luna knew it was a lie, for some of them at least. Did she seem desperate or was there something else they could see on her . . . or *sense?*

Luna wasn't the type to admit defeat, though. She sank into the couch, pondering more places she could try. Amanda wandered out of the hallway, calling a bright and cheery greeting. Luna winced.

She hadn't done anything wrong, but since Lucky's death, Luna didn't want to be around her as much. There was something about the pity in her eyes that got under Luna's skin. Avoiding her roommate was easier so she'd done just that, coming and going when she was sure Amanda was out of the apartment.

"Are you okay?" Amanda asked as she poured herself a cup of coffee.

Could Amanda see it on her, too, whatever *it* was? "I'm tired," Luna said simply. Emotionally, she was beyond that. She was wrecked.

Amanda tsk-tsked and folded her arms across her chest. "This is God's way of saying take a break."

Luna's eye twitched involuntarily. Amanda found comfort in her faith. Something Luna had never been able to do. Her parents had tried to raise her in their Islamic tradition, but she'd never taken to it. Never taken to *any* religion and couldn't understand how others found solace in it. Where others felt a sense of belonging, she felt only confusion. "No, I've had enough rest for a while," she said quietly.

Amanda shook her head, a hint of a smile playing on her lips. "You're an oddball, you know that?"

"I've been called worse."

Amanda placed her hands on her hips. "Whatever it is you're not telling me . . . it's starting to change you, Luna. You're acting different."

Luna shifted her gaze to the wall, wanting to escape from the conversation. "I . . . I don't think you'll understand."

"Yeah, you've said that, but you don't know unless you try, right?"

Luna sighed and propped her chin on her closed fist. "So

you've said."

"Okay, well, why don't you start by telling me where you really went when you left the other day?"

Luna stood up, surprised by the direct question. "I already told you, I went to get a check from my parents to pay for next semester."

Amanda followed her into the kitchen as she ran a glass under the tap, filling it with cold water. "That's a lie, isn't it? I called your parents out of curiosity, and Rose said she hadn't seen you since we had dinner together."

Luna sipped her water, trying to swallow her rage down with it. Amanda was keeping tabs on her now? "What are you, my wife? I don't have to tell you everything."

"You're right, you don't," Amanda said, holding out her hands passively. "But if you keep pushing people away, one day you're gonna find yourself in a place where you'll want help, and no one will be there."

"Noted," Luna said. "I don't want to think about what's bothering me. Can you understand that?"

"Yes, *that* I understand," Amanda said, bobbing her head. "But what I don't understand is why you can't trust me enough to talk to me."

"I don't feel like I should have to talk if I'm not in the mood for it," Luna snapped. This conversation was going in circles. Every time they spoke now, the words had no meaning. "My dog died. I don't really feel like having a heart-to-heart with anyone right now."

Amanda huffed but seemed to reconsider whatever she

had initially wanted to say. "I'll give you time to mourn, but I'm not going to let you sit in your grief forever. You won't ever get better if you spend your life moping. The walls will only get tighter."

Luna's gaze shifted to the floor. "I'm going out. I'll see you in a few hours, okay?"

Amanda didn't reply. Most likely, she thought Luna was foolish. Maybe she was, but Luna couldn't bring herself to care. As she walked out of the complex, her mind burned. She wished she had a place to go where she could be alone, where nothing and no one could find her. But no matter where she went, her thoughts were always there, ready to keep her company with their awful truths.

Right now, they reminded her of her final walk with Lucky, and she broke down all over again. Luna wasn't good at coping with death.

She was, regrettably, human.

A mourning dove flitted to the ground in front of her and sat there, feathers an array of soft browns and muted grays. It let out a soft *coo*.

Mourning indeed, Luna thought, watching it fly away.

By the time she got into town, she was exhausted, but not in the way she wanted to be. Her body felt heavy, but her mind continued to race with all the things she'd rather forget. A guttural yowl of frustration tore its way up her throat as she ran the last few blocks to the nearest restaurant, trying to get it all to stop for a while.

Inside the building, the air hit her like a wave. Sharp scents mingled with the hum of machinery and footsteps. Her eyes flicked over the kaleidoscope of colors: the crisp uniforms, vibrant posters plastered on the walls, constant motion. It was chaotic, alive. This was exactly the kind of energy she needed. She could thrive here. Maybe, just maybe, she might even enjoy it.

Luna stood behind the other customers, scanning the menu's faded letters and colorful pictures, weighing each option as the line slowly edged forward.

A blonde girl with a long ponytail flowing out of the back of her black hat worked the register, snapping her gum as she asked, "Can I take your order?"

Luna was about to speak when she studied the woman instead. Pale, narrow face, ice-blue eyes ringed with black eyeliner. Why did she look so *familiar?* The name tumbled from her lips before she could stop it. "Sarah?"

The woman's eyes darted from side to side, then narrowed as if she was just as uncertain as Luna. "I'm sorry, do I know you?"

The feeling that she was mistaken wiggled into Luna's stomach, but she pushed it away. "It's Luna, from Shawnee High School. You and your sister gave me a makeover for prom."

Sarah's face flooded with recognition, her lips curling up in a way that was very different from the Sarah Luna remembered. "Oh my God. Luna! Wow. How've you been?"

Sarah hadn't *technically* been Luna's friend, and really, her sister, Susan, hadn't been either. Chance had roped them into spending time with Luna and a slight bond formed as a result.

"I've been all right. What about you?" She tried to avoid any trace of emotion in her voice, fearful of igniting the same response from Sarah that she'd gotten from Amy.

"I've been making it," Sarah said. There was a smile on her face, but Luna could tell it wasn't real. None of her appearance seemed real. In high school, Sarah had been her sister's shadow, with dark hair and eyes that never lifted more than a foot off the ground.

She was a different person now. Chance's effects seemed to range from person to person.

Sarah leaned over the counter, close enough to whisper, "Are you in town for Chance too?"

Out of all the things Sarah could've said, Luna hadn't expected that. Sarah had never been one of Chance's groupies, and she didn't know a thing about the DreamWorld escapades. As far as Luna knew anyway. She was unfortunately in the middle of a situation that was much larger than her.

We all are, Luna reminded herself when she thought back to the twinkling grief in Amy's eyes.

"I'm here for college," Luna said.

"Hmm, okay," Sarah said, taking a step back. "Not me. I'm doing some private investigating. I've always had my suspicions about him."

You're right. Luna wanted to say it aloud, but stopped. How could she tell her? If she admitted the truth, there were a lot of layers of explanation that needed to go with it.

A throat-clearing sound came from the line behind her. Sarah peered around Luna. "Look, I gotta get back to work or the managers will give me grief, but I'll be in touch, okay? Did you want to order something?"

"No, but can I get an application?"

The idea of working alongside someone else who'd been tangled in Chance's web and survived was too tempting to pass up.

Sarah grabbed a thin stack of paper from beneath the register and passed a sheet to Luna. "Feel free to list me as a reference," she said, tugging on the front of her hat in farewell.

"Will do." Luna smiled and exited the line.

She might not be able to get Amy's part of the story, but maybe she could find some peace by finally giving Sarah the closure she desperately sought.

Chapter Fifteen

THE MOMENT THE door closed behind Luna, Amanda tried not to let their talk get to her. Maybe she *did* come on a little too strong, but every other approach she'd tried hadn't worked, and Luna's mental health was still steadily declining.

I need to give her space, Amanda decided.

Instead of hanging around the apartment and pestering Luna with questions, she'd hung out with her two older sisters. It wasn't fun, but she hadn't expected it to be.

Their favorite thing to do was tease Amanda about how young she was, how naïve. Not her favorite pastime by a long shot. Unconsciously, she slid her fingertip into her mouth, gnawing on her nail until a shock of pain lanced the quick. She drew her finger back, studying the remains of her chipped nail polish. She kept painting them, hoping it would deter her from the habit. One day she would stop chewing on them, but today wasn't the day.

I think I'll get a manicure. She was due for a self-care day, and since Luna seemed dedicated to spending time alone, she would too. She'd teach herself to enjoy solitary activities.

Amanda wandered into the kitchen, lazily skimming the cupboards for something to snack on. Her fingers hovered over a box of crackers when the familiar chime of the phone broke through the quiet. She glanced at the caller ID and sighed.

Max. Again.

She puffed out her cheeks and tried to ignore it, but the ringing grated on her nerves. It stopped, only to start again ten seconds later, more persistent this time.

Amanda hesitated.

Luna never seemed thrilled when Max called. In fact, her entire mood soured whenever he was mentioned. *What's his deal anyway?* Amanda wondered. She considered picking up—just to be helpful—but stopped. Luna had made it pretty clear that she didn't appreciate Amanda inserting herself into her business, and she'd been anything but pleased the last time she'd intercepted one of his calls. Answering another one would be pushing Luna's boundaries for sure, and that was the last thing she needed to do after their little spat.

The phone stopped ringing.

Amanda exhaled, relieved, and reached into the cabinet for a jar of peanut butter just as the phone started ringing for the third time. She stared at it. Then, with an eye roll, she muttered, "Screw it," and snatched it off the base. "Hello?"

"Amanda?"

"Yeah, Luna's not here."

"Sounds about right," Max said, obviously annoyed. "Do you know when she'll be back?"

"No clue. She left an hour or so ago."

"All right, well, let her know I called whenever she gets back."

"Wait," Amanda said, hoping to catch him before he hung up.

"What?"

"Why do you keep calling her? She's clearly going out of her way to avoid you, yet you call anyway. Why is that?"

"Because I . . . I . . ." Max tripped on his words, stumbling as if he couldn't decide exactly what to say. "I'm worried about her. And I know how stubborn she can be about asking for help."

Amanda waited for him to say more, but he went silent, waiting for her to contribute something. When she didn't, he asked, "Will you tell her I called?"

"Of course."

"Great." Max hung up without a goodbye.

Amanda frowned at the dead phone. Max sounded worried about Luna, sure, but it also seemed like he was hiding something too.

You're paranoid, Amanda told herself and grabbed her bag. She'd been in the house for too long. The walls were starting to drive her crazy.

Chapter Sixteen

LUNA SAT AT the table nearest to the counter and filled in the application. Focusing on the paper was hard. Like clockwork, her attention shifted to Sarah every few minutes. She couldn't help but wonder about the odds of so many of her classmates ending up in the same place. Bowling Green had a good university, sure, but Luna had never seen Sarah around campus. She had come out here solely for Chance.

From the day Susan disappeared, Sarah had always been her biggest advocate. If she'd spent the last few years investigating, she had to be following some kind of lead that brought her here. What all did she know about Chance? Did she know anything about the men he was affiliated with? How deep did that rabbit hole go?

Luna handed the completed application back to Sarah, who informed her that the manager would give her a call if interested, then went back to taking orders. Waiting for a call likely meant she wouldn't be hired for a while, if at all. Dejected, Luna said goodbye to Sarah and walked back to the apartment, thinking longingly of her bed. Tapping out the secret knock, she waited, hoping Amanda had gone out.

The door opened thirty seconds later, dashing that prayer. "Hey, girl."

Luna made a noncommittal grunt in return.

"Are you all right?" Amanda asked as soon as she let Luna inside.

"I'm fine," she murmured, crossing through the living room.

Amanda closed the door. "Max called while you were out."

A dozen emotions swirled through Luna's head. Max wouldn't dare tell any of the crazy stuff to Amanda, would he? "Did you answer it?"

"Yeah. He seems . . . worried about you."

"Thanks for taking the call," Luna said stiffly. She could've reinstated the boundaries issue but didn't have the energy. Instead, she took the opportunity to go into the kitchen.

Six missed calls waited on the answering machine. Almost all of them were from Max, with one from Amanda's ex, Reese. Luna deleted them all. The more Max harassed her, the less desire she had to ever talk to him again. Why couldn't he understand that? She downed some water, then placed the empty glass in the sink just as the phone began to ring. She expected Max.

It was her mother.

"Luna!" Rose cried into the phone, voice fading in and out. The car phone. She rarely ever touched that thing because it didn't have the best quality. Her using it meant there was an emergency.

Luna had never heard her mother in such distress and couldn't imagine what would cause it now. "Mom, what's the matter?"

"Your father is in the hospital."

"Wh-what happened?"

"He had a seizure, and it was bad, Luna. They had to put him into a coma to stabilize him. Doctors aren't sure what caused this. They have to run some more tests before they'll know anything concrete," Rose choked out.

"That's awful," Luna muttered, monotone. She loved her father, in a way, but when it came to his health, the downward decline wasn't a surprise. He'd struggled with it for years.

"Can you make a trip to the hospital?" Rose asked.

"Yeah. Yeah, of course."

"I'll see you in a bit." Rose hung up with a stifled goodbye.

Luna closed her eyes and tried to focus on her breathing to keep herself from spiraling. Lucky was dead, and her dad was sick. Like an unpleasant alarm, Max's words played again.

I woke up with the worst feeling this morning. It's familiar, Luna, too familiar.

Amanda came closer, but Luna kept her gaze on the phone. Neither of them moved for the longest time.

"Did something . . . happen?" Amanda asked, placing her hand on Luna's shoulder.

"Dad's in the hospital," Luna replied, struggling with the words as she set the handset on the base.

"What happened?"

"Mom said a seizure, but they need to run some tests to find out why. She wants me to come down to see him," Luna recited, toneless as if she were reading from a script.

"That's awful, I'm so sorry!" Amanda said. "Do you want

me to come with you?"

Her eyes were filled with warmth and sadness and concern—all traits that made her a good friend. And right now, Luna needed a good friend more than anything.

WHEN LUNA AND AMANDA arrived at the hospital, Rose was waiting beside the sliding glass doors of the emergency room. She'd stopped crying but red torrents marked both sides of her face. Luna ran up to her, anxious to be filled in, and Amanda trailed behind. Rose hugged her daughter tight. When she let go, Luna was ready to unleash her entire collection of questions.

"Do they know what it is yet?"

"Not yet, no," Rose answered, dabbing her eyes.

"I'm so sorry," Amanda said, holding a hand to her chest. She really meant it.

Rose focused on her as if she'd only just noticed she was there. In her grief-stricken state, she probably had. "Hello, sweetheart. Thank you for coming."

"Of course," Amanda said.

They entered the hospital, and as they walked through the lobby, Luna found herself glad she hadn't told her mother about Lucky yet. A person could only hold so much grief at a time.

"Can we see him?" Luna asked.

"We can, but he's still unconscious." Another tear trailed from the corner of Rose's eye, as if saying the words out loud made it all come flooding back.

"I want to see him." Luna wouldn't add that she wanted

to see him *alive*, but her tone made it clear.

Luna trailed behind Rose and Amanda as they navigated through the halls, head bowed to block out the images of the sick people around her. Being in the hospital had always made her uncomfortable. *This* hospital especially. Her head throbbed as they entered and exited an elevator, then gathered outside a room.

"First, I want to say your father is in pretty bad shape," Rose said. "If he's woken, which honestly, I doubt, please try not to make his condition obvious."

Luna and Amanda were both smart enough to know that anyone who had a grand mal seizure wouldn't present well. Luna also didn't mention that if her father was awake, that meant he would be okay. She wouldn't think to criticize him, she'd be happy he was alive.

Rose opened the door. Entering the room, Amanda kept pace with Luna, her face drawn tight as if she had something to say but wouldn't.

Abrahim was still unconscious, and Luna was glad because, prepared or not, she flinched. The two women beside her did too. Her father had deep black half-circles under his eyes and his cheeks were hollow. The veins in his forehead and throat bulged with a deep bruise color, as if he had embossed tattoos running the length of his neck. Each hand was clutched in a painful bind at his side, and Luna guessed they had been stuck that way since his seizure.

Luna was too numb to speak.

"Oh my God," Amanda whispered and put her hand over her mouth. "Is he going to get better?"

"Eventually, yes. He'll have to be kept here for a while, though," Rose said, stating the obvious. "So they can monitor his vitals."

There was hope in the words, but Luna couldn't bring herself to feel it. Hope had always been too dangerous in the past because it made someone let their guard down. And that was when the worst always crept in.

Chapter Seventeen

THE HOSPITAL CORRIDOR at night was mostly quiet except for the occasional beeps and dings from the equipment inside the rooms. With the patients asleep and only a few nurses on duty, there was an odd sort of peace, of stillness, that was absent during the chaos of the day.

A shadow slunk down the corridor, reveling in the darkness and the silence. His steps were quiet but swift as he carried himself with purpose up a flight of stairs, stopping outside one of the rooms.

He glanced over his shoulder, left and right, down both sides of the hallway. No one was around. He was alone in his misdeeds. Gently, he eased the door open, careful to make no sound, and slid inside, leaving it cracked for easy departure.

The light from a monitor highlighted the bed. A man lay on it, though he could've passed for dead. The shadow slunk to the side of the bed and grasped the IV line, holding the thin rubber tube between gloved fingers. He slipped something from his sleeve. Hours ago, he'd snagged it from the supply closet in preparation.

The wrapper crinkled as he unsheathed the fresh, sterilized syringe. Not that it mattered whether it was clean or not for what he had in mind. The silver needle gleamed in the light as he inserted it through the wall of the tube and pushed the plunger down, forming an air bubble in the liquid. It swirled through the line, getting closer to the man in the bed.

Tucking the syringe up his sleeve, the shadow crept back out into the corridor, listening to the *squeal* of the heart monitor as the man flatlined.

Chapter Eighteen

THE NIGHT PASSED in a flurry of anguished nightmares. When Luna woke in the morning, she was more exhausted than when she'd gone to bed. After a meager breakfast, she sat in her room folding laundry and doing her best not to think. She tucked her clothes into her dresser, reorganizing them several times until she was satisfied. The phone started to ring from the kitchen. Luna plucked the last shirt from her hamper and folded it, waiting to see if Amanda would answer it.

When she didn't, Luna sighed and made her way down the hall to scoop the phone off the base. "Hello?"

"Hi, this is Tim Raven, manager at Burger World, calling. Is this Luna?"

"Oh. Yes," she said, forcing herself to perk up, to sound normal. After her night, it proved a harder task than usual. "It's nice to hear from you."

"I'm calling regarding your application. Can you make it down for an interview today at three?"

Luna glanced at the clock. It was already two, but the restaurant was only a fifteen-minute walk from the apartment. It wasn't like she had anything else to do. "Yes, I can."

"See you then."

Luna hung up and called down the hall for Amanda, unsure if she was home or not.

Her friend's blonde head popped out of her room. "Yes?"

"I got a job interview so I'm heading out," Luna said, tossing a thumb over her shoulder.

"Good luck, girl. I hope you get it!"

She couldn't tell if Amanda was being sincere or if she was being sweet because she knew Luna was going through a lot. Luna didn't ask. She left the apartment, shooting Lucky's grave a disgruntled glare as she walked across the complex. The cross cast a shadow over the lawn, highlighting the bare patch that concealed her beloved dog. Her mind translated it into a warning of things to come.

Stop it! Luna shouted inside her head.

When something went wrong, most people could brush it off, but not her. No, she assumed the absolute worst.

I'm not a victim. I'm not being targeted, she chanted inside her head. No matter how many times she repeated the phrase, she couldn't fully believe it.

THE INTERVIEW SEEMED interminable. The past hour and a half had been one of the most uncomfortable moments of Luna's life. On the outside, she was positive none of her true feelings showed.

But that came at a price.

By the time she stood and shook Tim's hand at the end of the interview, she felt like she would crack and it would all come spilling out. He promised her a job starting the following Monday, so at least her acting hadn't been for nothing. Luna was on her way out of the restaurant when she saw Sarah mopping the floor by the door.

"Hi, Sarah. What's up?" Luna greeted, not surprised when her voice came out flat and toneless. She'd used up everything she had in the interview.

"Luna," Sarah said and continued mopping. She seemed distracted, overworking to take her mind off it. Luna narrowed her eyes, wondering if Sarah had gotten a job for the same reason Luna wanted one. "How'd it go?"

"I got the job. Your recommendation helped, thank you." Luna forced a smile she didn't feel.

Sarah must've sensed it because she asked, "Are you okay?"

"Fine," Luna replied automatically. It was a reflex now, requiring no further thought.

Sarah observed the distance in her eyes. "We'll talk more about things, but not now. There's too many people here," she offered, as if she thought that to be the reason for Luna's standoffishness.

Luna nodded, surprised at how quickly Sarah could swing from casual to serious. Sarah dipped her mophead in the bucket and Luna waited, expecting her to chime in with something else, but she continued her work in silence. Luna gave up and left the restaurant.

The walk home was plagued by the image of her father's body in the hospital. *He has to recover.* She wouldn't consider the other possibility. Not unless she had to.

When Luna entered the apartment, the phone was already ringing. Her shoulders slumped. Every time she heard that sound, only bad news followed. Luna trudged over to it, expecting to see Max's number, but it was her mother's. Luna's entire mood shifted. "Any word, Mom?" she asked, crossing her fingers. She needed good news more than anything.

"Oh, Luna. It's horrible!"

Luna winced, holding the phone away as her mother sobbed on the other end. A minute later, she brought it back to her ear and asked, "What happened?"

"Your father is dead!"

The words didn't sound real. "What?"

"He had a heart attack."

Luna held her hand over her mouth the same way Amanda had when she'd first seen Abrahim in his hospital bed. This had to be a mistake. Her mother was wrong. They were *all* wrong, and she would show them.

"I'll be there as soon as I can."

Another heavy sob escaped Rose as she hung up. The corners of Luna's eyes burned with a familiar tingling sensation, but she had no desire to cry. The world was fuzzy like an out-of-body experience or a bad bout of dissociation.

Luna cleared her dry throat and called for Amanda.

"Hey, girl! How'd it go?" she asked cheerfully as she stepped into the kitchen.

Luna smiled, wide and inauthentic, hardly able to push everything down beneath it. "I got the job."

"That's great."

"Yeah," Luna said, then let the deranged smile fall. Why bother to keep up the façade when her life was in shambles? As soon as she told Amanda the news, she would know Luna wasn't okay. And really, didn't she already know?

Amanda's eyes went wide. "What is it?"

"Dad . . . didn't make it through the night," Luna forced herself to say, wondering how close to Rose she sounded as a sob punctuated that sentence.

"I'm so sorry, Luna."

Those words broke any resolve Luna had left, and she cried harder. Amanda drew her into a tight hug until she gasped for air.

"Do they know what happened?" Amanda asked when Luna broke out of the embrace.

Luna shook her head and blew her nose into a tissue. "Mom was crying too much to really say. Can you drive me to the hospital?"

"Of course." Amanda grabbed her keys off the counter. "Let's go."

Luna was stoic as she followed her friend to the car. Amanda's expression was mostly neutral. Nothing to hint at what was going through her mind. Maybe it was because she didn't know how to react. After the way Luna had blown up at her, Amanda must've sensed she was a walking bomb that could, and would, explode at the slightest inconvenience.

The car ride was silent as Amanda wove in and out of traffic, Luna silently sobbing the entire way. When they made it to the hospital, Amanda parked as close to the door of the emergency room as she could. Luna switched into autopilot as she followed her to the building. Every few feet, Amanda shot her friend worried glances and Luna pretended not to see. Like last time, Rose was there waiting for them.

"Luna!" she cried as soon as she spotted the two girls.

Luna let her mother wrap her in a tight hug.

Rose pulled back to study something on her daughter's face as she brushed a lock of raven hair out of her eyes. "You look unwell."

You too. Luna wanted to say it aloud but it felt cruel, so instead she said, "I haven't been sleeping well lately."

Rose smiled, the expression painful. "Yeah, me neither."

"What happened to Dad?"

"Apparently, he was in worse shape than they thought."

"Aren't they supposed to watch for that?" Luna asked, outraged despite her grief. If a hospital could mess up so severely, could she trust anyone?

Rose either didn't hear the question or chose not to engage. "Would you like to see him?"

Luna's automatic instinct was to say no. It would help both of them process their grief if Luna paid her respects, but the thought of seeing her father's corpse brought back flashes of when she'd seen Violet's dead body in the woods. Seeing him like that meant facing the reality that he was gone, and all that remained was a shell.

"Come on," Amanda said, breaking Luna from her thoughts.

Rose had already begun walking inside the hospital, and Amanda was right beside her, grasping her gently by the elbow to steady her. Luna followed but felt very far away. When they reached Abrahim's room, Luna wasn't sure how to process the scene. A nurse and doctor were already inside. Rose rushed to Abrahim's bed, holding his hand and crying. Amanda stayed by the door, a hand over her mouth to hide her expression.

Luna stood in the middle of everyone, staring at her deceased father as if he were an otherworldly creature. His ghostly color yesterday had been nowhere near his skin tone today. He was nearly *translucent*, the greens and blues of his veins shining through his skin.

The doctor grasped her shoulder. "I'm sorry. We did everything we could."

Luna's lip twisted into a snarl. If they had done everything they could, her father would still be alive. Not wanting to listen to another lie, she smacked his hand away and ran from the room. She held a hand over her mouth, stifling the sounds of her wild sobs as she hurried down the hallway. Tears scoured her cheeks. From behind came footsteps as Amanda did her best to keep up.

Luna didn't give her a second thought as she approached the door she'd seen every week for the past three years. She flung it open and dashed inside. Then stopped. The bed was empty. Horror spread through her. She ran over to it, tossing the covers aside in her search for some sign of Chance. When that provided no results, she twirled around, surveying the entire room before crumpling to her knees in defeat.

He was gone.

Chapter Nineteen

THE WOODS WOULD always be Chance's favorite refuge. It was a sanctuary of solitude; the only spot where he could truly be himself. Whether he was awake or asleep, he could escape within them. This part of the forest lay not far from his cabin. It should've been secure, but when Chance spotted eyes the color of pine needles staring back at him from a familiar strip of trees, he knew things would be different this time.

"You found your way back," the man said as he disconnected himself from the shadows.

There was something unsettling about the way Cody looked, both menacing and innocent at the same time. His face still held traces of boyish youth, but the heavy leather jacket and the darkness in his eyes told a different story. He was a few years older than Chance, but in that short time, he'd done far more damage than most managed in a lifetime. It had been a long time since Chance last faced him. He'd done his best to ensure he never would.

Nothing gold can stay, he thought. "Yeah," Chance said out loud. "Magic works. Who woulda thought?"

"As I told you it would."

The sessions they used to have were always intense. Cody

was intense with everything he did. He'd been the one who taught Chance how to destroy and manipulate this plane without setting off the alarms that would trigger Keepers. All of that was information he used daily. For that he was grateful, but there was no other reason to associate with Cody. He'd been a good friend of Chance's at one time. Problem was, he was second-in-command within the group. He would be leader soon enough.

That made him enemy number one.

"I guess you've grown tired of waiting," Chance said with a dry, bitter laugh. "Finally come to finish me off?"

Cody huffed through his nose. "You oughta know better than that. Who do you think helped you come back?"

"*Myself*," Chance said, emphasizing the word.

"Going solo was *your* choice," Cody reminded him. "And now it seems as though you don't have any option *but* to rely on us." Chance's eyes darted away. "Disagree all you want, but your healing will take time. Are you confident you can survive on your own until then?"

"How *much* time?" Chance demanded through gritted teeth.

"Considering the fact that you essentially DIED in DreamWorld, I'd say it's best to give it a few days," Cody said sharply, his eyes narrowing with frustration.

I don't have that long.

He often had nightmares about the group catching up to him and making him pay for running away. They had eyes and ears everywhere, and the fact that he'd made it this long was nothing short of a miracle. He would've kept running if Luna hadn't trapped him in the coma and left him a sitting duck for all his enemies to close in on.

Chance's gaze dropped to Cody's hands, waiting for him to summon a weapon. "Whatever."

"Whenever you decide you're ready to stop pouting and talk to me like a man, we've got your truck ready for you at the compound. Your dagger too."

Chance narrowed his eyes at Cody. This was a truce, a peace offering, and a threat all wrapped into one. He still had a place to go if he wanted to. Cody wouldn't kill him, *yet*, but how long would the offer last?

I don't have magic anymore, Chance reminded himself. Until his reserves regenerated, he was vulnerable. He knew that and so did Cody. If he didn't take him up on his offer, he would likely be killed on the spot.

With a wave of hopelessness, Chance thought, *I'll never get away*. His best hadn't been enough. "What do you want in exchange?" he asked as emotionlessly as possible. It was better than letting Cody see how afraid he was. How angry.

"You back in service. Ever since your . . . *escapades*, the Keepers have been on us, and we've lost some good men. You owe us, owe *me*, for keeping them from finishing you off a long time ago."

Chance's head throbbed with the phantom pain that always came from time spent with Cody. He was an energy vampire, literally draining those around him. Of course Cody's men could help Chance get out of his bind, but it would come at a price. His help, *their* help, always did.

Chance weighed his options. He wanted to lie and have Cody believe that he had some plan in action, but he didn't. Cody would be able to see through anything he came up with anyway. This was the man who had, at one time, flipped Chance's world upside down by showing him that there were others like him. That magic was real.

"Okay," he conceded. "But if I'm going to help you, these are my demands . . . "

That had been his transition back to life.

The days since had been filled with activity on this side and the Other. He'd done what he could to lay low. There were *a lot* of enemies now. Cody wasn't lying about the Keepers, but Chance did his best work under pressure.

Always had.

He had been lucky for his good looks, his charm. Without magic they were the only tools he had left, and used well, they could help him just as much. That was how he'd gotten his hotel room—a swanky little place that charged about sixty bucks a night. He'd charmed a nurse into giving him enough money to make it for a few days. But that money wouldn't last forever. Now that Cody knew his location, there was no telling when he would come for him.

At least the benefits of following their orders had already started to pay off. They'd gotten him a job as a nurse's aide at the hospital. It was desperately understaffed, and the paperwork was easy enough to forge, so they'd asked no questions. Chance was sure Cody's men had a few members working administration at the hospital, too, which of course, didn't hurt.

Now, I wait for him to change his mind, Chance thought bitterly.

It was as if the last few years had taken him on one giant loop and brought him back to their doorstep, desperate and alone.

All I need to do is kill a few Keepers, he told himself. *I can do that.* There were a few he planned to kill anyway.

Plus some other people.

That brought to mind the image of Luna's face, and his stomach clenched with an odd mix of longing and hatred. It was her fault he was in this situation, but that obsessive limerence was still very much alive. He didn't know *what* it was he wanted to do with her, only that he wanted to make her pay for doing this to him.

His first night out of the hospital, he'd tried to track her down. Without magic, the task was harder but not impossible. He'd gone to Lima, starting his search at the house she used to live in with her parents. She hadn't been there so he'd focused his attention on her parents. More specifically, her father.

With a little bit of poison, he became bait.

Luna had shown up at the hospital with her mother as anticipated. He'd planned to snag her wallet when she wasn't paying attention, jot down her address, and make his way there later. What he *hadn't* anticipated was how seeing her in person would stir the strings of his infatuation. She was more beautiful than the pictures in her childhood home gave her credit for, and it had taken considerable effort to get out of there before being seen.

Not yet, he told himself. *Chess not checkers.*

The blonde girl she'd come in with was new. He didn't know her but made a note to find out more about her. As they visited, he busied himself with changing the linens in the nearby rooms, waiting for the opportune time. When the blonde girl left the room to go to the vending machine down the hall, he approached her and got her number.

He was in.

Good looks are as good as magic, he mused. The smile fell when he pulled a picture of Luna from his pocket, stroking the edges.

Good looks couldn't solve everything.

Setting the photo down on the nightstand with care, he got out of bed and made his way to the bathroom. The shower steamed quickly, and he stood beneath the hot spray, letting it wash over him like a reset. For a few minutes, the heat dulled his muscles and his thoughts. When he finally stepped out, he dried off and put on a clean pair of black jeans, feeling more like himself with every layer of routine.

Using a towel, he wiped steam off the mirror. A sculpted face, made more dramatic by his time in the coma, a small nose, blue eyes. The most recognizable thing about him was his bright blond hair. One of his first moves had been to change it. The ends of his hair were now dyed black, shining dark against the blond. He loved it, the combination of light and dark like a blend of Luna and himself. He picked at his black hair. It wasn't nearly the same shade as Luna's, but natural beauty was the best kind because it couldn't be copied.

A familiar smile crept onto his face. The same one that

always surfaced when he thought of her. The anticipation of their reunion played like a film reel in his mind, scene after imagined scene unfolding. He pictured her expression when she saw him again. Anger? Fear? Probably both. The thought should have thrilled him. Instead, it left a hollow ache in his chest.

It didn't matter how many women wanted him. None of them were *her*. And wanting someone who wanted nothing to do with him only sharpened the edge of his frustration.

Why was he so easy for her to discard?

His thoughts darkened as he remembered how fiercely Luna protected those she cared for. She'd saved Amy. He'd found that out by reading old newspapers at the library. That's also how he'd discovered Max had survived.

That bitter knowledge had come like a kick to the gut. He hadn't done any of the things he'd wanted to. All of that work had been for nothing. But not this time.

This time would be different.

If he had to take out Keepers to both placate Cody and build up his magic reserves again, those two would be the ones to start with.

And this hunt would be his favorite.

Chapter Twenty

AMANDA FOUND LUNA first, followed by Rose a few minutes later. They sprinkled Luna with questions, none of which she could answer. Her eyes refused to move from the bed. Rose escorted her out of the room and sat her down in the waiting area, but Luna continued to see the empty bed.

The world filled with a dull tone, blocking out all sounds other than her heartbeat. Dread swirled through Luna's brain in a kaleidoscope of her worst fears. She didn't remember getting in the car or making it home, but came back to herself as Amanda guided her into the living room.

If he's not there, where is he? It was a harrowing thought. The world was enormous. The dream version of it even more so.

Amanda tried again to get her to talk, but Luna was silent as she went to her room and closed the door. On autopilot, she focused on putting an overnight bag together. Tonight she needed to go home. Mom would expect her help over the next few days to wash, shroud, and prepare her father for his funeral. Luna's hands shook as she grabbed a few T-shirts and stuffed them in her bag.

The entire time, she thought, *Where is he?*

Soft knocking on her door made her jump.

Amanda carefully stepped into the room. "Sorry, didn't

mean to scare you," she said. Then, after an uncertain minute of silence, she added, "Where . . . did you go? Earlier. What was that about?"

Luna closed her eyes. She knew Amanda would ask, but she expected to have more time to prepare an excuse. "I wanted to be alone."

Amanda's eyelids drooped. "But . . . why that room? Why not go outside?" Silence, then, "Does it have to do with your weekly visits?"

Luna pressed her lips together, barely managing to hold it together. She closed the zipper on her bag, purposefully avoiding eye contact. Outside, a car honked twice—Rose waiting for her.

"I'll see you when I get back," Luna said.

"All right." Amanda sounded defeated, as if there were a million more questions she wanted to ask but she knew it would be a waste of energy to do so. "I'm sorry about your dad."

"Me too."

"Is there anything I can do to help?"

"No. There isn't anything *anyone* can do," Luna said, then slung her bag over her shoulder.

"I'm here, okay?" Amanda offered, eyes landing on the bag. "When do you think you'll be back?"

Luna shrugged, noncommittal. Amanda walked to the door, stopped, then continued down the hall.

Unconsciously, Luna clutched her stomach at the sight of the ugly scar Chance had left there. When she realized what she was doing, she dropped her hands and looked up, spotting her leather-bound notebook on her desk. She felt as if she were watching herself from outside of her body as she opened it to a page toward the end.

A rugged sketch of the cabin she'd drawn from memory. On the next page was the temple, which made her shiver in a way the cabin did not. Next to the picture, she'd written a scratchy line about the final confrontation between herself and Chance.

Rereading it now, she could remember the hopeful version of herself who had written those words. The one who believed Max's promise. The one who believed in happy endings. The one who was ready to live her best life. Picking up a pen, Luna scrawled the date her semester had ended, since she wasn't exactly sure when he'd broken free from the coma. She stared at the numbers, the last day her life had been normal. Below that, in handwriting that was shakier than her original entry, she wrote *The day Chance woke up.*

Two honks sounded outside again. Rose was increasingly impatient. Any minute now, she would start calling from the car phone. Sighing, Luna closed the notebook and stuffed it under her mattress. She didn't see Amanda on her way out of the apartment and thought maybe that was intentional.

As soon as Luna climbed into Rose's car, she expected *something,* whether it be sobbing or an endless barrage of chatter, but neither happened. No words passed between them, only the hum of the tires over the highway. The stillness was thick with everything they couldn't say. When Rose parked in front of her house an hour later, tears dripped down her face. As soon as they stepped inside, the trickle swelled into a flood.

"Twenty years, Luna. We were married, living together in

this house for twenty years," Rose said, staring at the family portrait on the wall. She swallowed once, nostrils widening, and added, "I still can't believe he's gone."

"I know," Luna said. Until that point, her shock had been able to keep the sorrow at bay. Hearing the raw grief from her mother broke through it, and her own tears started to come.

"This has been my home for most of my life. Without your father . . . it's empty. I'm alone. The home I loved is now just a house. Cold and lonely like I am."

"I'm here. I'll always be here."

"And I appreciate that, Luna, but you have to understand, it's not the same. You've got a life of your own while I'm sitting in the middle of mine with an empty bed to greet me at the end of each day."

"I miss him, too," Luna said, picking at a loose piece of skin on her thumb. She'd always had a complicated relationship with her father. They bickered more than anything else and leaving home for college had been a relief. But at the end of the day, he was still her father, and she loved him. This grief was layered. "Whatever you need, ask. I can move back home for a while to help out. I mean, at least until things get easier."

"I can't imagine things ever getting easier. Everything I always feared is coming true, and nothing I do will stop it."

Luna could understand that feeling well. It had been more than three years since Violet died, and thinking about her, even for a short period of time, was nearly impossible without wanting to break down in tears.

Luna was out of comforting words so she wrapped her

mother in a hug. She was essentially dead inside, but she could play a role just fine. Today, she'd be the shoulder her mom could cry on . . . if only for a little while.

It's better than nothing.

A sharp knock at the front door startled Rose, her body tensing before she forced a quick, apologetic smile and hurried away to answer. Luna stayed close, a few hesitant steps behind. From the doorway, she caught fragments of voices from the men who had transported her father's body home from the hospital.

She slipped quietly into her old room, the door clicking softly behind her. Pressing her ear to the wall, Luna listened to muffled footsteps. She pictured them moving down the hall, loss filling the air as they lay her father gently in her parents' bed. A fresh wave of grief hit her, cold and crushing.

She would have to pull herself together soon and step into that room to help her mother prepare him for the funeral, but it was going to be hard. Maybe the hardest thing she'd ever had to do.

A soft knock came from the hall. "Luna?" the person called.

"Nazir?"

He stepped inside, looking slightly older than the last time she'd seen him, but there was warmth in his eyes that hadn't faded.

Luna hugged him. "What are you doing here?"

"I heard about your father," he said when they separated. "I wanted to help. After how much you guys did for Sidra, it's the least I can do."

Gratitude blossomed inside Luna. She blinked back tears

and managed a small, shaky smile. In the midst of all this darkness, Nazir's presence was a light. When he'd moved out of town three years ago, she didn't know if she would ever see him again. But here he was, a lifeline when she needed one most.

Chapter Twenty-One

EARLY THE NEXT morning, Luna took her seat in a stiff foldout chair. The ceremony hadn't started yet, but Luna had no desire to talk to anyone. Nazir sat in the seat beside her, not prodding, not asking questions, just offering silent companionship. Luna stared at the hole at the end of the clearing, fidgeting in her chair to forget the awkwardness of her uncomfortable black skirt. Rose was on the other side of the clearing, catching up with distant family. She tried to wave Luna over several times, but she pretended not to notice.

The *Imam*, a small man dressed in a black *thawb*, took his place beside the pit. He called everyone to attention, and they made their way to their seats. By the time he began to speak, Luna's face was drenched. The chairs could've remained empty, and Luna likely wouldn't have noticed.

Abrahim, her sometimes hardheaded father, was really gone. Rose passed her a handkerchief, and Luna took it to wipe her face, not realizing that her neck and collarbone were also wet with tears. Rose grasped her hand and squeezed, then stood and crossed the congregation to start the *namaz e janazah*.

Nazir gave a sympathetic smile, and she offered half a smile back in an attempt to try to calm the tears.

"Luna!" someone hissed from the distant line of trees.

Over her sniffles, it was easy to dismiss. *It's all in your head,* she thought.

Then heads swiveled in unison. Luna followed their cue, spotting someone running across the open field toward them. Face red with exertion, Max came closer. He waved his hand, signaling for her to come toward him.

Sniffling again, Luna stood, moving through the rows of mourners. She whispered a dozen apologies and earned as many dirty looks in exchange. When she reached the end of the chairs, Max grabbed her wrist and dragged her across the field, out of earshot. She stumbled behind him, confused, and did her best to keep up. He didn't slow until they made it to the other end of the cemetery.

"Max! What are you doing here?" Luna asked.

He let go and turned to face her. "In case you've forgotten, we need to have a serious talk."

"Tell me you didn't seriously come all the way here to talk about your Keeper shit. I'm kind of in the middle of something, if you haven't noticed."

"*Our* Keeper shit," he corrected. "You somehow keep forgetting how much you're a part of all this."

Luna snarled. "Really, Max? You're going to do this now? What is wrong with you?"

"Hello? Have you heard *anything* I've said? I am fighting people on a *nightly* basis. These deaths around you aren't bad luck, Luna. Someone wanted this to happen," he said, chin lifted in defiance. "There's only one person out there who would target us like this."

Luna stilled.

Max raised an eyebrow. "What? Cat got your tongue? I know everything that's been going on. Amanda filled me in. She also told me where you'd be since you never answer your damn phone." When he caught the expression on her face, his tone softened slightly. "She's worried, too, you know."

Luna drew her eyebrows together to hide the hurt. It was bad enough that she couldn't trust her oldest friend, but now it seemed she couldn't trust her roommate either. "But not you, though. You're not *worried*, Max. You're desperate."

"Whatever label floats your boat."

"Enough!" Luna snapped. "Stop it, okay? Let me mourn. I'll talk to you some other day about this shit if you promise to leave right now."

"No, you won't. You're going to blow me off again."

Luna let out a frustrated groan and started to walk back toward the service. She'd given him a chance to change her mind and now she was only angrier for wasting the time.

"I caught one of them sneaking out of your room."

She stopped mid-step, like her body forgot how to function. One foot dangled in the air, trembling. The world around her blurred, sound collapsing into a high, ringing silence. Her chest tightened. A memory crashed into the present, a rupture so violent it rooted her to the spot—the dream of the man in her room. Had it not been a dream after all? Slowly, ever so slowly, she faced Max.

"Wh-what?" she asked in a scratchy whisper. Her voice refused to come out louder.

"I wanted to tell you when it happened," Max started, the words falling rapidly from him as if he feared that if he spoke too slowly, he'd lose her interest again. "But you've been avoiding me."

"It wasn't . . .?" She couldn't bear to finish the end of the question. It would only make it real.

"It wasn't him," Max assured her. "But does that really matter? It was *someone*. I don't know what he was there for, but he probably won't be the last."

Luna would've much preferred that Max punch her in the stomach than drop a bombshell like this.

The man was really there. She replayed the terrifying image of him rushing toward her. He'd really been there and now Chance's dagger was missing.

Fat tears rolled down her cheeks, and Max's expression softened. "I know," he said. He reached into his pocket, fishing out a scrap of paper to pass to her. "But hey, go finish up what you need to do. We'll finish this talk later, okay?"

Like an obedient child, she sniffled and bobbed her head, taking the paper. Max wrapped her in a hug as she looked at the address scrawled on it. "We're going to be okay," he assured her.

The words were meaningless.

Dread settled like a rock in her stomach. All she wanted was to be normal again, but what did that mean anymore? Normal life had waved goodbye to her when she learned magic existed. She needed to find a way to move her life forward, incorporating both parts of herself. If she lived with the constant thought that Chance was always watching her, she would endure that fear forever. And that wasn't a life. Certainly not the life she'd fought so hard to keep.

But how could she go on when her closet was full of skeletons who threatened to drag her inside every time she opened the door?

Chapter Twenty-Two

THE FUNERAL SEEMED to last an eternity. Luna had always considered herself lucky that she had parents who stayed together and were happy, or at least their version of it, for over twenty years. Now that a component of her family was gone, she feared the entire structure would fall apart.

Luna wasn't sure how she made it through that hour of her life, but she didn't come back to herself until she bid Nazir goodbye. By the time Rose dropped her off at her apartment, she was in a daze again and thought longingly of her bed.

"Amanda?" she called as she stepped into the apartment.

Her roommate wasn't there. A wiggle of irritation blossomed in her stomach. She could guess the reason behind her friend's disappearance. She had known Max would make an appearance at the funeral, so she was steering clear until Luna could cool off.

Then she exhaled. Luna had been gone all day. Most likely, Amanda had things to do with either her sisters or her friends. She wasn't intentionally avoiding her, even if it felt like it.

Luna sat down on the couch, taking off her shoes. With nobody else in the apartment, the day's events pressed down on her. Her mind volleyed between Abrahim's wrapped body in his grave, what Max had said about the intruder in her room, and the missing dagger.

The familiar triple tap startled her. She jumped up to open the door, eager to get to the bottom of what had happened today. Amanda nearly radiated happiness, and Luna squinted, taking her in. Amanda didn't seem to pick up on her mood as she stepped into the apartment and tossed her ridiculous silver purse onto the floor. She collapsed on the sofa, placing the back of her hand on her forehead like a melodramatic princess from some medieval film.

Luna closed the door, running her tongue along her teeth as she contemplated what to say. Her throat burned with questions, but there was something about Amanda's mood that made Luna hold back. Just because she'd had a bad day didn't mean she wanted anyone else to.

"You seem . . . really happy," Luna said at last.

"Yes! I am." Amanda shot upright, dropping her hand from her face. "I had the most amazing day."

Luna bit the inside of her cheek, fighting the bitterness clawing its way up. *It's not her fault*, she had to remind herself.

Amanda's smile faltered, guilt flickering in her eyes. "Oh, I-I . . ." she stuttered. "I'm sorry, I forgot. How was the funeral?"

"It was a *funeral*, Mandy. It wasn't good," Luna snapped, annoyed at her sudden concern. "Max showed up and made a mess of things, but other than that, it was okay, I guess."

Amanda bit her lip, smearing her red lipstick across her teeth. "What did he do?"

"Exactly what you're probably imagining he did," Luna said. "Or did you not think about that when you pointed him in my direction?"

Amanda peeked at Luna through her lashes. "I'm sorry, all right? He seemed so concerned about you, and I thought maybe if you wouldn't talk to me, you'd talk to him. I didn't know he'd totally crash your dad's funeral."

Luna's shoulders slumped with guilt. Amanda wasn't the type to have bad intentions. It was entirely possible she *didn't* know what Max would do and that her heart was in the right place. "Look, I'm sorry too. You're allowed to be happy, you know. Don't like . . . take my bad mood personally or anything."

"I know," Amanda said. "I understand." She simpered and sat down on the couch.

Luna waited, giving her another opportunity to start a conversation, but she was quiet as she turned on the TV. Luna took her leave and went into the kitchen, Chance's empty room at the front of her mind.

I need to hear Max out. I need to hear exactly what it is he's been so desperate to say. She scooped up the phone, dialed his number, but he didn't answer. *Of course not.* She went to her room, plopped on the bed, and stared at the ceiling.

Somehow, she fell asleep. Morning came and with it, her first day on the job. The part of her brain that was used to faking her way through life was alert, warning her that she needed to get herself together and get through it, but it took effort. There was nothing on the answering machine. No indication Max had tried to call during the night.

Luna tried to talk herself down. Just because Chance came out of a coma didn't necessarily mean things would take a turn for the worse. Max had mentioned that there was a possibility his memory would be gone, that he'd have to learn things all over. That could be the case . . . or maybe he'd been moved to another facility. There were several possibilities.

When something sounds too good to be true, it usually is, she reminded herself. The other men Max kept encountering, why were they here? Were they helping Chance?

It's the only way to escape from them, Chance had told her.

It made sense that they would search for him, and in his state, he wouldn't have been hard to find. If they brought him back, they could've restored his memories too. If they did . . . like a moth to a flame, he would chase her even if it led to his own destruction. Images flashed through her mind of the night of Lucky's death and the stream of new nightmares. She closed her eyes, trying to make it all go away. It was speculation. All of it. The only thing that was real, that she could count on, was that her father was dead, and somehow, life had to keep going.

Luna blew a lock of raven hair out of her eyes as she rummaged through her closet for her uniform. The shirt was hot and bulky, and nothing she did assuaged her discomfort. Picking at it uncomfortably, she left the apartment, deciding to walk. It was easier than asking Amanda for her keys, considering she would have to navigate another attempt on Amanda's part to get her to stay home.

Hands in her pockets, Luna kept her gaze on the sidewalk to avoid meeting anyone's eyes. The black uniform hat didn't sit quite right on her head, but at least it blocked the sun from her eyes. Somehow, she was able to plaster on her normal mask as soon as she stepped through the doors of the restaurant. For most of her coworkers, this would be their first impression of her, and she wanted to make it count.

Tim greeted her, brought her to the back of the restaurant, and gave her a basic tour of the store. Then they killed a solid hour on paperwork. After that, Luna waited for him to grab someone to train her. Dread gurgled in her stomach at the idea of having to shadow a stranger. When Tim came back with Sarah, she instantly felt better.

"You're in good hands," he said, smiling as he went to the front of the store and left them alone.

Sarah waited for him to be out of earshot, then said, "I'm gonna be honest with you. This isn't a fun job. People are mean when they're hungry. But you're smart, so you should get the hang of things pretty quickly." She led Luna over to the register, explaining the buttons and what to push for each customer's order.

Luna was embarrassed at how long it took her to get a handle on it. She always prided herself on her above-average intelligence, but this took a different skill set: social skills she was sorely lacking. About an hour into her shift, things started to get easier. They picked up a rhythm with Sarah repeating a customer's order to Luna and her working through the process of entering it into the register.

When a lull in customers came, Luna let herself relax. She and Sarah went on break together, sitting at a table by the window. "How're you liking your first day so far?" Sarah asked, taking a sip of water from her cheap paper cup. "You're doing a good job."

"It's all right. Better than I thought it would be," Luna admitted, keeping her eyes on the table.

Sarah scrunched her face. "Are you okay?"

Luna sighed. Could she open up without everything coming out? "Honestly, no. It's been a tough week. I had to bury my dad over the weekend."

"Oh, wow. I'm sorry to hear that," Sarah said, dark eyebrows shooting upward. "And you still came to work today? That takes strength."

"Wasn't sure what else to do."

"I get it," Sarah said, setting down her cup. "Thoughts can be loud sometimes. Especially when you don't want to hear them."

Luna swirled her cup, watching the liquid move inside.

"I'm sorry if I'm crossing a line here, but your father's death wasn't an accident, I'm guessing," Sarah said, pinning her with the intensity of her ice-blue eyes.

"No, that's not—" Luna swallowed down her reservations. "He's been sick for a while now. He had a seizure the day before, and I guess it was too much for his body to handle."

Sarah humphed and stood to her feet. "If you're sure that's what happened. I'd look into it if I were you, though. Make absolute sure."

"He was sick," Luna reiterated. "That's it."

Sarah's shoulders slumped. "I'm sorry. I'm probably not helping."

"It's fine. I know you mean well," Luna said. But did she?

It seemed as though Sarah also saw the world through trauma-tinted glasses.

The door dinged as a customer walked in. Luna crumpled her empty cup and rose from her seat, ready to greet him and end the conversation. Sarah's hand on her elbow stopped her. "Do you know where that old cabin in the woods is back in Lima?"

A horrifying twinge twisted Luna's stomach as if someone had liquefied her guts. Every day was a struggle to forget about it. To forget about Chance. For a long time, the cabin had been Chance's dirty little secret born from a literal nightmare. When news of *that* day leaked, speculation followed about who owned it and where it had come from. Luna hated the fact that she was one of the only people who knew the truth.

"Yeah, I know exactly where it is," Luna said, trying not to show how shaken she was. Was this Sarah's idea of a test? "Why?"

"We should meet there sometime this week and search it," Sarah suggested. "I've been meaning to go, but am afraid of going myself so I keep putting it off."

Luna was torn. She wanted to help Sarah, but could she handle seeing the scene of the crime again?

"Yeah, we can do that," she agreed, words laced with a confidence she didn't feel.

Going back into the cabin, the scene of her old nightmares, would bring it all flooding back. But maybe that was what she needed. After all, the best way to get over a fear was to face it head-on.

Chapter Twenty-Three

PHYSICALLY, LUNA WENT home a few hours later, but mentally, she was stuck in the conversation with Sarah. She couldn't get the image of her father in the hospital out of her mind. The struggle with his health had been long, arduous. She hadn't expected him to fight forever, but what if Sarah was right? What if someone had done something to him? The single slash across Lucky's throat came to mind. The kind of injury that didn't come from an accident.

We should've had an autopsy.

Abrahim had requested a traditional Islamic funeral. Fast burial, no autopsy, nothing to desecrate the body for burial. Luna was all for carrying out her father's last wishes, but what if that had been a mistake?

She stared at the phone and thought about calling her mother to tell her those thoughts. Maybe if she could get her on the same page, they could have her father exhumed, then do the autopsy and find proof. She stopped herself. Proof of what exactly? Then she reminded herself that her mom was in the middle of *Iddah*, the mourning period of a widow. She would be in it for a total of four months and ten days, leaving the house only when absolutely necessary so she could focus all her time on remembering her deceased spouse.

She didn't need unnecessary stress and worry. If Luna was wrong, that's all she would cause her mother. Reluctantly, Luna jettisoned the idea as she put on her sneakers, carefully tying the laces into double knots. Maybe a run would help her clear her head and better consider her options.

Amanda's soft humming drifted down the hall from the bathroom as she excitedly readied herself for her date. Though they were in the same apartment, Luna felt like they were a million miles away from one another.

A knock sounded at the front door. Luna tilted her head in Amanda's direction, expecting her to rush to it like a laboratory rat to cheese in a maze.

Amanda peeked out of the bathroom as she stuck an earring in her ear. "Luna! Be a dear and get that for me? I'm not quite ready yet, and I won't let him see me till I'm absolutely perfect!"

"Yeah, sure," Luna replied, getting up from the kitchen chair. She opened the door, pulling on her fake mask to greet the man on the other side. "Amanda will be out—"

She stopped.

As Amanda had stated, the man was tall, face beautiful. But his eyes were full of hatred, of evil, like the face of the Devil himself. His lips cracked into a grin, exposing all his perfect white teeth.

"Luna, baby," Chance said, his smile so wide it looked painful.

"No," she whispered, nearly choking on the word. In her head, she screamed at herself to close the door and lock him out, but couldn't move a muscle.

"So good to see you again," Chance whispered, taking a step inside. His hand dipped into his pocket to reach for something unseen. The gesture was enough for Luna to open her mouth, desperate to scream, cry, anything to alert Amanda that something was wrong. That she was in danger.

Chance pushed open the door with a slight *creak* and backed her against the dividing wall between the kitchen and living room, perfectly out of Amanda's sight should she happen to glance down the hallway. "What's the matter, doll?" he asked, eyes not leaving hers as he pulled a small red pansy from his pocket. "Didn't you miss me?"

Luna couldn't breathe as he brushed her hair aside and set the flower on her ear. When his other hand came to rest against the wall, she was trapped beneath him.

He bent his face close to hers and whispered, "I've missed you."

Before his lips could touch hers, a strangled sound made its way up her throat, and she pushed him away. He stumbled back a step, and she ran out the open door, not looking back for fear of seeing him behind her. She recognized his truck in the parking lot, and that was enough to power her stride, keeping her going. Outside the apartment complex, she ripped the flower from her ear and ground it on the concrete with the sole of her shoe, then continued her frantic rush, flashes of blue eyes in her mind. Her muscles burned and her eyes blurred. She lost her footing, collapsing to the ground, elbows burning from the scrapes.

The pain was nonexistent over the roaring in her head.

Chance had *recognized* her. No delay, no hesitation. His memory was *fine*. Suddenly, she was seventeen again, struggling against a tide of anguish. Blinding pain erupted in her stomach, crippling her. It reminded her of a knife slicing its way through her tissues and organs. Cradling herself, Luna was almost glad she'd already been on the ground when it started. Gasping, she tried to keep herself from falling apart. A stiff breeze buffeted her, oddly cold for the start of summer.

Suddenly aware of her surroundings, she picked herself up and started to walk without any real plan of where she should go. She just felt it necessary to keep moving. *Why did I leave the apartment?* It solved nothing and it meant she'd left Amanda with him . . . *alone*. Chance's favorite victims were small, pretty females. Girls he was physically stronger than. People he could overpower.

I have to go back, she thought. *I can't let her meet Violet's fate.*

The last thing she wanted was to see Chance's face, but she would stand toe-to-toe with him if it meant putting an end to things. Lesson learned. When Max had something to say, she should always listen. And where *was* Max? She debated going to his apartment but faltered.

Time's a factor, she reminded herself, and that gave her the necessary oomph to pick up the pace.

When Luna approached her apartment door, she trembled and pounded on the wood, hoping Amanda would let her in or at least wouldn't lock her out. After a moment of nothing, Luna tried the knob and the door opened. Inside, the lights were off. She stumbled through the living room and switched on the lamp, convinced she would walk into a crime scene.

Everything was in its place. No signs of a struggle.

"Huh," she murmured.

Maybe Amanda would be okay for a while. She was a pretty girl. Maybe she reminded Chance of someone he had known in high school. He might keep her around, if for no other reason than to rub it in Luna's face.

Luna moved into the kitchen, eyes falling on the note placed at the center of the table. Heart fluttering, she grabbed it and read the looping handwriting.

Luna,

Amanda wanted me to write a note to tell you we were leaving for our date. Kind of unnecessary since you probably figured that out. That's blondes for you. I won't waste your time with something trite. I have my own things to say, dear Luna.

You broke my heart. Did you know that? Maybe it's my fault that things didn't go to plan. I tried to use you for your power, but that was a big mistake. You are too smart to be a pawn, and luckily, I am the type to learn from my mistakes. Overcome and adapt. You're probably wondering what that means for you.

Well, I'll give you a little hint. I'm not going to use dreams this time. Maybe if you pray, I'll show you mercy.

Sincerely yours,
Your Worst Nightmare

A sickening sensation of falling coiled through Luna's stomach, and she hugged herself as her body threatened to shut down. Her worst fears were coming to life. He would kill her just as he'd done to Violet. Except her death wouldn't be as quick. He'd make her suffer, drag it out if he could. Luna tucked the note into her pocket and began to pray.

Pray, as her worst enemy had suggested.

Chapter Twenty-Four

THE DATE WITH Amanda had been long, much longer than Chance intended it to be. Although Amanda was pretty, she reminded him too much of Luna's friend, Violet. He didn't need to speak. Amanda would talk for long gaps of time and answer her own questions without giving him a second to himself. To her, all his charm was in his appearance. That had been a wonderful thing to learn on their first date, but now, he was tired of it.

When the night came to an end, Chance couldn't be more relieved to get rid of her. He kissed her on the lips and waited for her to leave his truck. Blowing strands of multicolored hair out of his eyes, he prepared to drive away when movement from across the complex caught his attention. A small figure hustling through the shadows. Moonlight bounced off black hair.

Luna.

Watching her in her normal routine, not paralyzed by the fear he instilled in her, pleased him more than it should. As he had been at the hospital, he was captivated by the very sight of her. When had she gotten back? Had she found his note?

A few hours ago, standing on her doorstep, he had wondered how she would react to him. Then, much to his chagrin, he learned nothing had changed. Her face had been stoic. If anything, she was *afraid*.

Most of all, she still hated him.

Moonlight illuminated her face as she retrieved a bicycle from the bushes beside her apartment. She zoomed away, oblivious to him lurking nearby. He hadn't expected to see her again tonight and didn't know what to do now that the opportunity presented itself.

Luna had always had a strong effect on him, but it was different now, more powerful, and if it came from hatred or admiration, he couldn't tell. His body could, though. The sound of her terrified whimpers played in his mind, bringing a twisted sneer to his face. Part of him wanted her to make those noises again.

Curious, he followed. Where was she going this late at night? She was alone, which wasn't strange for her, but she seemed to be up to something. She disappeared around a corner, moving too quickly not to have a destination in mind.

When she crossed the street, Chance hung back, waiting to see her next steps. She threw her bike down on a long patch of grass. He traced the lawn to a building in a different apartment complex.

Who in the world was she visiting so late?

He squinted as she jumped onto the nearest porch and pounded on the door. Chance recognized the person who opened it.

Chapter Twenty-Five

LUNA TOOK A deep breath as she stared at the hardwood of Max's front door. She was surprised to see how close he lived. Now that she was here, she wasn't sure how he'd react to her visit.

We promised to talk, she reminded herself. Not only about Chance and the strange men who were helping him, but she also had the new information from Amy to ask about. The inside of the apartment was quiet. Maybe he was already asleep.

She stayed on the porch and knocked again, louder. At last, the door opened. Max's eyes narrowed to slits as he studied her from her face to her feet. "Look what the cat dragged in."

"Very funny," Luna said, rolling her eyes as he stepped aside for her to enter the apartment. "We have a lot to talk about."

Max shut the door, then hobbled over to the couch, plopping down. It had been years, but she found it odd to see Max's new gait, to know he was missing a piece of his body because of Chance.

"You're a Keeper," she stated unequivocally.

Max blinked once, twice, three times. "Yeah, and . . .? I thought that was obvious."

"I visited Amy," she said, then paused, realizing that information would be all but useless to him. "Your partner."

"Yes?" he prompted, sounding like he was losing hold of his patience. "What's your point?"

"My *point?* Max, how could you not tell me Amy was a Keeper too? This whole time, I thought she was traumatized by what happened. Turns out she knows more than me!"

"I didn't think I had to spell it out for you, Luna." He crossed his arms and sat back in his seat. "Why'd you decide to track her down now?"

Luna smiled but not from happiness. It was his tone, that reprimanding edge that made her feel as though she had done something wrong. "I wanted to talk to her about . . ."

Max leaned toward her slightly, eyebrows raised with anticipation. "Chance?"

Luna huffed through her nose. "Yes. I wanted a second opinion about what you told me at the cemetery. And I also wanted to know how Chance found her back then and why it was her that he wanted me to kill."

"Now you know."

Luna shook her head. "I don't *know* anything. Who was the man you caught in my room?"

"Dunno. He got away before I could get any answers out of him."

"But it wasn't . . ."

"Chance? No. I told you that."

"Well, he showed up on my doorstep today. He's dating Amanda," Luna said, then dug into her pocket. She didn't make eye contact as she passed him Chance's note. "He's got his memory, too, it seems."

"What's this?" Max asked, then read it. With a snort, he passed it back to her. "He thinks he's a Bond villain or what?"

Luna took the paper, carefully tucking it into her pocket. "Whatever he thinks, he's got a point. He's a literal dead man walking if those people catch him. Unfortunately for us, people are the most dangerous when they've got nothing to lose."

"Yes and no," Max said, then glanced at the open spot on the couch beside him. "You can sit down."

"I'm fine," she said, waving a dismissive hand at him. "How did this happen, Max? You said his memory loss was permanent, but you knew he could've, and probably *would've*, found a way out?"

Max was silent.

"And why the hell would you not tell me?"

Guilt flitted across his face. "My reason for being a Keeper is not my proudest moment, if we're being honest with one another."

The words lingered, unsettling in their quiet weight. She'd been under the belief that Keepers were the good guys. Could it be possible that that wasn't always the case?

What did Max do? she wondered, not for the first time. "I can't go on blind faith anymore," she said. "If I'm going to be any help to you, I need to know everything you know. Even the stuff you're not proud of."

Max curled his lip, aggravated. "I don't think a lesson on recent history will help us right now. Especially when I've been busy trying to figure out how to get us out of this alive."

"And *I'm* trying to figure out why that hasn't been your

number one priority this entire time." She folded her arms across her chest, bristling. Max caught the edge to her tone and stood up with an uncertain wobble. Luna stared at the leg, not wanting to make eye contact as a new question passed her lips. "Why isn't he in jail?"

"I never told the police he was the one who shot me." When Luna's face twisted in a mix of anger and horror, Max held up his hand. "Remember the situation you left me in. I wish I could've taken my opportunity to get him locked up, but I couldn't. I was injured—badly, I might add—and Violet was dead. Chance was unconscious in a temple next to what was left of a decomposing girl's corpse. I couldn't make up an excuse that would explain all of that, and you know I couldn't tell them the truth. They wouldn't have believed me, Luna. They would've taken me to an asylum."

"So, what *did* you tell them?"

"I told them I got shot by a stray bullet and fell into the bear trap. That I didn't see where it came from, and I didn't know who was responsible."

"And they believed you?" Luna asked. The story sounded so hollow. Such an obvious lie. Then she thought of the condition he'd been in. The police likely wouldn't have been willing to press him hard at the scene, chalking up anything strange to his physical state.

"More or less. I was the only witness they had at the end of the day." The irritated twitch of his nose was enough to know that he was upset with her for taking off rather than staying to help him piece together a story.

"But you weren't. What about Amy?" Luna asked. "She went to get help."

"She didn't come back, Luna," Max said, careful to catch and hold her eyes as he did so. "She called in an anonymous tip from a pay phone in town."

Her hands trembled, fingers curling into fists. "She fled?"

"Apparently. And the cops never followed up with her to get her story."

Luna buried her face in her hands. For years, she'd been upset with herself for her cowardice, but Amy seemed to have far more than Luna.

"She's not contacted you?"

Max shook his head. "I wish, but I haven't heard a word. I didn't come to you first about things, you know. I just didn't have any other options."

Luna swallowed down her reservations, forcing herself to ask the question she dreaded the answer to. "So, the cops think Chance is a victim?"

Max shrugged. "They don't know *what* to think of him. He was another piece of a weird situation."

"That's great!" Luna laughed and threw her hands up, collapsing into the armchair behind her. "Just wonderful. You did your job as a Keeper, all right. Except you did it too damn well. You helped him get away with it, and . . . and you never thought I should at least know about this?"

"It wasn't as if you asked," Max huffed. "And you're just as much to blame. Don't forget you were there with him when he was unconscious. You could've ended all of this!"

Luna pictured the scene: Chance slumped against the wall, eyes closed, paler than he'd ever been. At first, she thought he was dead, but she'd detected the faintest pulse. He'd been vulnerable. Maybe the only time he truly had been. She could've pulled the trigger and ended it, but she'd been unable to do it.

"I am *not* a murderer, Max," Luna said.

"Let's agree to disagree that we both made mistakes."

"Fine. What do we do now?"

"Honestly? I'm not sure," Max admitted.

"Are you serious?" Luna asked, dumbfounded. "You were *hell-bent* on getting my attention, barging in on my father's funeral, and now you're gonna tell me you have no plan? You don't know how to fix any of this?"

Max licked his teeth, clearly as frustrated as she was. "Hence, why I need your help."

"You are beyond infuriating."

"I'm sorry for the funeral thing, okay? I was backed into a corner. You wouldn't listen to me, and I was concerned when I caught that man sneaking out of your house and worried they might come back and hurt you. What we need to do now is come up with some kind of preemptive strike. Something to stop them before they can further whatever it is they're trying to do. I mean, Chance admitted he's not about to use dreams and these men seem not to be using them as much either. No dreams means no magic."

"So what?"

"He'll be easier to beat without the smoke and mirrors. We have a window of opportunity here. He might have his memory back, but his magic will take time. Three years of not exercising it? It's bound to have atrophied like any muscle that's neglected for too long. He'll come after us Topside while it recharges, and if you ask me, that's a hell of a lot easier to combat. Especially now that we know what to watch out for."

Luna ran her fingers through her hair. It wouldn't do any good to point out that while that was true for Max, it wasn't for her. Luna was tiny compared to Chance. In hand-to-hand combat, she wouldn't stand a chance. A faded memory came to her of him pinning her down in his truck, sinking his knife into her stomach, and she recoiled, folding her arms around herself. Blinking back the thoughts, she focused on Max's warm, brown eyes.

"Okay, let's say you're right, and he decides to come at us like a regular psychopath," Luna said, calm tone belying her true feelings. "Most of his victims died only seeing that side of him. They never knew he had magic, and it didn't matter."

"You're right, but you forget something. Chance killed those girls because they meant nothing to him. He had no reason to keep them alive. Just a carnal desire to sate his own bloodlust. That's not the case with us. You'll be the last one he hurts, *if* he hurts you at all. Remember the reason he's fighting this war: he wants you, and he wants to get back at me."

Luna tilted her head. "Get back at you? For what?"

Max's face twisted as if he'd suddenly tasted something unpleasant. "Nothing."

"Bullshit. You're still not telling me everything, are you?"

Max's gaze was trained on the carpet at her feet.

Anger flitted in her stomach for a second, then smothered

itself. She felt cold and numb. What could be so bad that Max didn't want to share it with her?

Is this why Amy fled and hasn't gotten back in touch? she asked herself.

Max patted his thighs once and forced himself to his feet. When Luna peered up at him through the fringe of her black bangs, he said, "Go home and make sure Amanda is okay. Since these men only attack at night, it stands to reason that they'll be back later. I can't say for sure whether they'll come for you or me. Maybe both of us. I'll swing by in an hour or so and we can figure out next steps from there, okay?"

Luna closed her eyes. Everything that had been bubbling at the surface wanted to come out, and she was ready to let it. Chance wasn't the only one with nothing left to lose. Letting her eyelids flutter back open, she said, "I thought I knew you, Max, but I can't get over the fact that things don't add up. That you're lying to me. There's clearly more between you and Chance than you've told me, and I don't understand why you would hold back after everything we've gone through."

Max tightened his jaw, frustrated. "If it'll balance our friendship, I'll tell you everything later tonight. Okay?"

Luna tapped her foot once, anxiety prickling at her. She was on the verge of a massive discovery and didn't want to stop drilling, not when she was about to strike oil. "What's wrong with right now?"

"It's a long story," he said. "And you need to get your ass back home and make sure you still have a roommate. If Chance starts adding to his body count, it's going to make things a hell of a lot harder for us."

"Fine," she huffed, her mind a tornado of doubts. She had the unmistakable feeling that he would somehow get out of telling her the truth.

Chapter Twenty-Six

THUNDER RUMBLED. Lightning tore across the dark night sky. Rain poured in bucketloads from the weeping heavens and splashed to the ground with enough force to bounce before the grass could fully absorb it. To most people, it was the type of weather too overwhelming to leave their warm houses. To Chance, however, it was the perfect night to accomplish those things society frowned on.

Sitting in his truck, he was perfectly dry. He took a silver Zippo from his pocket and flicked it open, watching the tiny orange flame. His anger was very much like it, devouring everything inside of him and leaving nothing behind. With a flick of his thumb, he shut the lighter and squinted through the darkness. Tonight had been a long time coming. He held up his snake-handled dagger to study the blade in the faint moonlight. It would finally taste blood again. He brought the silver to his lips to kiss it, then tucked it back into his pocket.

Chance slipped out into the night, the raging storm covering the sound of his slamming door. Rain soaked through his hair to his scalp and plastered his black clothes to his skin, but he paid no attention to his discomfort as he crossed the street. Overhead, thunder rang out. When he reached the apartment, lightning followed, giving him the briefest glimpse of his reflection in the window. With the blinds drawn, he couldn't see through it and ducked down, uncertain if he'd been spotted.

A dull light glowed from somewhere within, but no sounds of life could be heard. Chance took his dagger out of his pocket, wedging it into the window frame. The screen popped loose, and he ducked down again. After another minute of silence, he was sure his advance had gone unnoticed. He peered over the lip through the crack in the blinds.

The coast was clear.

Chance hauled himself into the warm room. Rainwater ran off him, ruining the yellow floor with dirt and muck. He crept through the house, leaving muddy footprints on the linoleum tiles. He'd have to clean them later, but at the moment, he had only one goal in mind. Until he accomplished it, everything else wasn't important. He tucked his blade between his fingers as he crept to the edge of the room.

The apartment split into two paths: one leading to a hallway and the other to a darkened living room. Where would his target be? Napping peacefully in front of the TV in the living room after a long, hard day or curled up in bed in a room deeper in the apartment? Chance decided to cover all his bases and checked the living room first. The recliner had a decent-sized lump on it, illuminated by flashes of the TV. Was it his target or someone else?

Do other people live here?

Chance chuckled softly to himself. If there was anyone else, he would use them to his advantage the same way he had used Violet to get to Luna.

Chance crept closer to the chair, one silent footstep at a time. He hovered over it, holding his breath, and sank the blade into the lump, laughing in triumph. But there was no fighting, no screaming, no blood. His laughter died away. If he had killed his biggest rival, then the lack of a struggle was a shining disappointment. Chance tugged the knife free to survey the damage. A feather drifted from his blade.

He had fallen for a decoy.

Max was far too smart to be taken by surprise, and Chance was mad at himself for thinking he could win so easily. According to Cody, he'd been holding his own quite well. Unlike Luna, who'd been surprised at his reappearance, Max expected this. He'd likely been counting down the days. Chance's grip on his knife tightened. He didn't know why Luna had visited Max tonight, but after Chance was finished, he wouldn't have to worry about their relationship ever again.

With a careful glance around the room, he retraced his steps to the hallway. His laugh had been loud, and he wasn't sure if he'd alerted anyone to his presence. Pressing his back to the wall, he crept down the hall. Outside, the thunder roared and shook the skies. Zeus was clearly as angry as he was. It was too dark to see ahead of him, and he had no idea where Max was waiting. The door nearest to him was cracked open to reveal dim light inside.

Chance smirked. *Maybe this will be easy after all.*

He crept toward it, hand almost on the knob, when someone grabbed him from behind and shoved him to the ground. Chance jumped to his feet, dodging a blow aimed for the side of his head. He could make out the outline of his attacker and ducked, elbowing him in the gut. Max towered over Chance.

He couldn't rely on brute force to win this one. He'd need his wits. Max moved to punch him again, and Chance swiftly ducked out of the way, his speed a perfect match to Max's strength. Max's fist collided with the wall behind Chance, and he roared in pain as a crack raced up the drywall.

"I wondered how long it would be until you showed up here." Max seethed as he shook his hurt hand. "None of your friends could handle me."

Chance chuckled, thinking idly that this monster of a man reminded him of Luna. "I have something they don't—dedication."

"Is that why you're back to your old tricks, stalking Luna?"

Chance stormed toward Max until they were almost nose to nose. "Why do you keep fighting? Nobody gives a fuck about you. If you went missing, who would care? If you died, who would come to your funeral?"

Max smiled coyly. "Luna would."

Chance smirked. "Don't worry, she'll get over those feelings by the time I'm finished with her."

"Leave her out of this!" Max roared, lunging for his throat. "This is between us."

Chance ducked to the side again, enjoying the fury on his face. "You're so right about that."

Max charged forward to ram his shoulder into Chance, but missed and stumbled into the wall instead. He wobbled on his prosthetic, struggling to regain his balance.

"Come on, Max. You didn't need to give me a *standing* ovation!" Chance tilted his head back to exaggerate his laughter.

Max growled and tried to swipe him in the face. Chance slid to the side, coming to a stop behind Max. He sank his dagger into Max's lower back. The motion was met with resistance at first, but he shoved harder, plunging the steel through muscle and into guts. Max wobbled unsteadily then toppled forward. Chance darted out of the way as Max fell against the door. Had it been closed, he would've been able to get up and continue the fight, but it had been cracked a bit too wide. It swung open to its full extent, and Max tumbled swiftly into the basement. Chance crept to the door, watching with a sadistic smile as his enemy rolled down the stairs like a carpet.

That had been a stroke of serendipity. He'd thought beating his enemy would take much more strategy and effort, but it seemed that Lady Luck shone on him.

Chance stared into the darkened stairwell, listening for movement or groans, anything that would alert him to signs of life. A bolt of lightning ripped across the sky, shedding its light through a ground-level window at the top of the basement wall. It illuminated the foot of the stairs where, at the edge of the last step, there lay a crumpled body, limbs twisted at awkward angles.

Max was finally dead. After all the time Chance had spent plotting his death, it was over in less than five minutes. Triumph ran through Chance's veins as he crept down the stairs. With an unnecessarily forceful kick, he nudged the body with his heavy boot. A puddle of blood poured from the wound in Max's back, staining the gray basement floor. His neck was twisted at an unnatural angle. Chance wondered which injury had killed him. Another bolt of lightning lit up the dark room, and he found his dagger, yanking it free from the pile of flesh.

"Goodbye, old friend," he said, then started jogging up the stairs.

Whistling a happy tune, he mentally crossed another enemy off his list. Cody would be pleased with his quick progress, and he buzzed with the surge of energy that would help recharge his magic.

One down, two to go.

Chapter Twenty-Seven

THAT NIGHT, LUNA followed Max's advice and went home, cuddling under a pile of blankets on her bed. Amanda was already asleep by the time Luna returned. Relieved, she went to her room, anticipating Max's arrival.

Chance's evil face was burned into the back of her mind. The triumph in his eyes. After three years of being free, he'd found her, and she couldn't stop replaying the scene. She'd spent a lot of sleepless nights like this one, pondering what she would do if he happened to show up on her doorstep, but for all her worries, she never thought it would happen in such a literal sense.

Luna turned over in bed, the shadows surrounding her, haunting her. The red letters on her clock glowed in the darkness. It was late, and there was still no word from Max.

Did something happen?

Carefully, without disturbing Amanda, she crept into the hall and out to the kitchen. There was no indication on the answering machine that anyone had tried to call. Luna scooped up the handset and dialed Max's number, but there was no answer.

Maybe he's on the way, she told herself, and went back to her room to wait. Time passed, and she fell into a fitful slumber. She woke not long after and jumped up to check the phone. Still no call. Luna peeked in Amanda's room, worried she would accidentally wake her roommate, but she wasn't there.

Must've left during the night.

Luna suspected it was to see Chance again. Poor, sweet, naïve Amanda had no idea what forces she was trifling with. All she saw was a beautiful face, not knowing what evil lurked underneath it. Luna had seen the monster so many times she no longer saw the beautiful veneer. He barely registered as human to her. He was more of a force, a deep dark evil that was everywhere and nowhere at once.

Luna collapsed onto the hard kitchen chair and put her hands over her face. Her last conversation with Max blazed through her brain. He was hiding something from her. Something that connected him to Chance. *What could that be?* Could it be the reason for him avoiding her now? Had he changed his mind about coming clean?

He owes me the truth, she thought, and she would force it out of him if she had to. She tried again to call, but after six rings, there was no answer. Luna was disappointed but not surprised.

Maybe he fell asleep, she considered. If he'd been as hard pressed as he claimed, she doubted he was getting much sleep at night. *He'll call back when he wakes up.*

A FEW HOURS later, Luna's shift ended. She punched out and headed to the door, considering what to do with her evening. Sarah hadn't been at work today, but being in the building made her think of her anyway, especially when she thought of what she'd said about the cabin.

Maybe I should bring Max, she thought, but an uneasy rock settled in her stomach when she remembered his sudden silence. She ran all the way to his duplex, the pain in her muscles and tightness in her chest not helping her erratic state of mind. She pounded on his door. No answer. Pressing her ear to the wood, she listened, desperate to pick up any noises from inside, but it was quiet. She searched for a key to let herself in but stopped when she spotted a neighbor peering at her from behind their curtains. Wary of having the police called on her, she left.

Defeated, she made her way home, knocking three times on the door. Amanda answered, stepping aside to let Luna in. One step into the apartment, and she froze. Chance sat on the couch. Between her run and the unpleasant surprise, she choked on the mouthful of air she'd taken.

"Perfect timing," Amanda said, resuming her place on the couch. Face glowing, she placed a hand on Chance's knee. "I didn't get the chance to introduce you to my date last night."

Luna bristled as she met Chance's eye. To see him in such a normal scene, acting as if he were an ordinary person, gave her the feeling of uncanny valley. He wasn't human. He was a monster in a mask. "It's okay, Mandy. We've met."

Amanda's eyes volleyed between them, eyebrow raised curiously. Chance stood, taking a step toward Luna. She searched his hands for weapons. Surely, he wouldn't try something with Amanda right there . . . would he? There was a menacing gleam in his eyes and in his stance, but he managed to pull a puzzled expression over his face.

"I think you have me confused with someone else. I'm

Malcolm," he said, holding his hand out to her.

Her fear morphed into anger. She'd forgotten how wonderful an actor he was. "The. Hell. You. Are." After all he had done, he was going to pretend he didn't know her. That they were strangers.

I wish we were.

He smirked, his outstretched hand reaching subtly closer as if he wanted to grab her.

In her mind, she was inside the cabin, wrapped in a blanket in bed beside him. Jolting out of the memory, she shouldered past him and hurried to her room, collapsing on her bed. What was the word for the exact second a person's world fell apart? She didn't know, but she felt it. This was the lowest moment of her life.

Footsteps came from the doorway. Amanda glowered, arms folded over her chest. "Um, Luna. What the hell was that?" she asked, glancing toward the living room.

Luna could imagine how the scene must've looked from Amanda's point of view. Luna had snubbed her date, and she had no way to explain herself. Why couldn't Amanda hear the pain and accept it at that? "I can't be around him."

"He was being polite, and you were so rude. That was hella lame," Amanda said. "I think you should apologize."

"I'm not going to do that," Luna muttered, pressing her face into her pillow.

"What is actually wrong with you? I have been so patient with you, and this is how you repay me?"

"I have my reasons," Luna said and forced herself to sit

up.

"Which would *be* . . .?"

"Remember how I don't like talking about my past?"

"Yeah?" Amanda impatiently shook her head.

Luna locked eyes with her roommate. "Well, it has something to do with him! I knew him . . . years ago."

"I think you're wiggin' out cuz he doesn't know you."

"He's *pretending* he doesn't know me to make me seem crazy. This is what he's always done," Luna said. How many times in senior year had he done little things to prank her father, to prank Violet, to make people think she was something she wasn't?

"I don't believe this," Amanda said, rolling her eyes. "Are you so jealous of me that you've resorted to sabotaging my date?"

Luna could only stare. How did Amanda draw *that* conclusion? "How could you say that?"

"I've tried so hard to be sympathetic, to be a *friend*, but it's like you hate me for that, Luna. You hide away from me any damn chance you get. Now you're going to get mad at me for hanging out with other people?"

"As if! No. It's not like that. I'm not mad. In any other case, I'd be happy that you're happy," Luna insisted. "But he's *not* any ordinary man. He's dodgy. I'm worried for you."

"Well, don't be," Amanda said, flaring her nostrils.

Luna got up off the bed and plucked Chance's note from its place on her dresser, purposefully shaking it in Amanda's face.

"What is this?" Amanda demanded, staring angrily past the piece of paper at Luna's face.

"Just read it."

Amanda snatched it, skimming it over. Crumpling it in her fist, she asked, "Is this your idea of a joke? It's not funny."

"It's from Chance. He's *making fun of you*. Come on!"

"*Who?*"

"Your date! That's his real name. He is *not* Malcolm!"

"I don't believe this," Amanda said, dropping the paper. She stormed out without giving Luna any more time to speak.

Luna stared after her, hurt by the quick dismissal. It had taken so much nerve to tell Amanda, and she hadn't given so much as five minutes to listen. It was senior year all over again. Luna bent down to pick up the note, uncrumpling it. Like it or not, Chance had some brains. He'd purposefully left his name off it so it couldn't be traced back to him. Luna laughed with a mixture of nervous irony and frustration as she tossed the note on her dresser.

Making a move for her bed, she heard more footsteps in the doorway, expecting Amanda's return with another snippy remark.

Chance stood there instead.

Chapter Twenty-Eight

"YOU," LUNA SAID. She wanted to stand to her full height, confident and strong, but her legs shook, and she feared her knees would buckle.

"Yes, me," he said and stepped inside, closing the door behind him.

The room swirled around her as she searched for an escape. With the door closed, she felt very small, and the room even smaller. It was too easy to remember how easily Chance had overpowered her in the cabin, how seemingly simple it had been for him to pick her up and carry her around as if she weighed nothing. He'd been younger then, smaller too.

"You're looking well." He crossed the room in two strides.

Luna scoffed, eyes on his hair. "You look ridiculous, *Malcolm*."

Smirking, he grasped a lock of her short hair. "You cut it." He paused, eyes drifting across her face. "Not only that, but you also wear makeup now, I see. Things have changed." He let go of her hair. "Not everything, though. You were so surprised to see me last night. Almost as if you'd forgotten about me."

"You weren't supposed to find me."

"And yet I did. Imagine that," he said, grinning wide

enough to show off his sharp white teeth. "I guess it's true what they say. When something is meant to be, nothing can stop it from happening."

"We're *not* meant to be," Luna spat, daring herself to meet his eyes. "You should've learned that from what happened last time. Or was that the only part of your memory that was erased?"

"Ouch, darling," he said, displaying mock hurt. "You throw knives, and yet, I'm back thanks to you."

Luna curled her lip, remembering all Max had said about the men he'd been fighting. The men who had broken into her room to steal the dagger. If anyone was responsible for his seemingly miraculous recovery, it would be them. He was trying to get under her skin, and it was *working*. "That's not possible. I would never help you."

"Remember the Rosebone, Luna?" She winced at the word. The Rosebone was a contraption of Chance's that consisted of a worn, rotted old femur entwined with a long-stemmed red rose. He never told her what the purpose of it was, but she'd assumed it was another part of the ritual he had tried to do to Amy. The one she'd put a stop to. "It was a fail-safe option if something went wrong. Our magic is bonded. When everything went down, you didn't zap away my powers like you thought you did. I was suspended in a kind of stasis between worlds. I just had to find my way back."

The pains, the nightmares, the feeling of being watched. It all made sense. He'd been with her all along, waiting to break through the veil and find her. Her knee buckled, threatening to give out, but somehow, she kept herself steady. "What do you want?" Luna challenged. She was angry. *So* angry that all her effort had been for nothing. That her best hadn't been enough.

"I haven't quite decided," he said. "Because you see, I'm in a *predicament* thanks to you. So it's an eye for an eye type of thing, you understand."

"Yeah, I understand. You want revenge because I bested you."

"I want something a little *worse* than revenge," he said, taking his snake-handled dagger out of his pocket.

The blade glinted in the light. Luna could nearly see her reflection in it.

"They stole it for you," she said.

Chance smirked. "They did. Gave me my truck back too."

"Get in it and fuck off, then. I'll give you a head start before I call the police."

A hearty laugh tumbled from Chance's lips. "And tell them what, exactly? I've not done a thing as far as the law is concerned."

Luna wanted to argue but couldn't. Max had exonerated him of what he'd done in Lima. It was her word against his. Her shoulders slumped at the realization.

Chance jutted his bottom lip out in an exaggerated pout, mocking her. "Oh. It's sinking in now, isn't it? What you've done. What you set free."

"I never wanted to be involved with any of it. You ruined your own plan by bringing me in on it. If you had left me alone, you would've succeeded," she pointed out. "So really, you only have yourself to blame."

"I needed you then. With your gift? You were part of it, a big part. But if I'm stuck with them, I don't need you anymore," he said, pointing the tip of the blade at her.

It should've scared her. "Kill me, then," Luna said, holding her hands out to either side of her. "Part of me died on that day anyway. Everything since has merely been survival."

Chance's smirk intensified, a predator closing in on prey. "That'd be a little too easy, don't you think?" he asked, softly trailing the blade over her exposed throat.

Through clenched teeth, she said, "Depends on how you plan to kill me."

He laughed softly and pressed the blade a little rougher into her skin. "You were always so good with semantics, weren't you?" He bent toward her. Luna shivered at his closeness, trying to keep calm despite the knowledge that she wouldn't be able to escape even if she tried. "You're so brave. All the damn time. You forget that I'm dangerous. You know this blade has tasted blood, and that I feel no remorse for that fact."

"Get it over with, then," she taunted.

"There's not a great deal of sport in that, is there? I could kill you right here, right now, but then what? I like this game. I like to play with you," he said softly. "I couldn't do that if you were dead."

"You are such a creep."

"Am I?"

She smacked the knife away, not caring if she got cut. "Get the fuck out of my room."

He brought his face close to hers, breath fanning across

her lips. "You have no idea what hell I went through in that place . . . because of you. What hell I have to deal with now." His nostrils flared, but the absence of emotion in his sapphire eyes convinced her he would slash her throat as soon as he finished his speech.

She narrowed her eyes and pushed him, relieved when he moved back a step. "Yeah, well, it hasn't been peaches and cream for me either. Because of you, I had to bury my friend."

"She deserved it," he hissed.

Luna reared back, ready to slap him, but he caught her wrist and grinned. "You're going to have to be quicker and smarter than that if you think you can stop me. I have more power than you give me credit for, love."

That was a lie. At least for the moment, he had no magic, but how long until it was back? How long until the nightmares started again? Luna watched him through exhausted eyes. Where was Amanda? He had to have been in her room for a good ten minutes, at least.

She sent him in here, Luna realized. *She meant it when she said she wanted me to apologize to him.*

"Instead of torturing me, why don't you run away?" Luna asked. "Get away from everything if things are so bad." It was a long shot, but how fantastic would it be if he did it?

He smiled, big and wide, but his eyes were sad. "It's too late for that, and if there's no escape for me, there's no escape for you either." He dug in his pocket, and Luna braced herself.

He plucked out a small hypodermic needle and tossed it onto her bed. She stared at it, at first not understanding. Then she remembered something she'd learned in biology class about the fragility of the circulatory system. What havoc a single air bubble could cause if it was in the wrong place at the wrong time.

Her father's sudden heart attack.

Horrified, she whispered, "You killed him."

"Of course. Did you think his death was natural?"

I did, I really did, she thought, still staring at the needle. Abrahim had suffered seizures in the past. He was an older man, and the years were taking a toll on him. A heart attack was the logical next step.

"I needed to find you. It was nothing personal."

It was to her. How could it be anything less? Frustrated, she asked, "How could you get close to him? There's security at the hospital."

"Paperwork can be forged. It wasn't hard for them to get me in there," Chance explained as if he were talking about the weather. "And the rest? Well, you know what DreamWorld can do."

"Who are they?" she asked in a small whisper. "Who are these men who are helping you?"

There was no triumph in his eyes, just cold defeat as he said, "Max knew them." He pulled out a wad of white fabric and tossed it on the bed. "Open it."

With trembling hands, she unwrapped the cloth as carefully as she could. It was a white T-shirt. Across the chest were two brown streaks in the form of an X. Marks left by cleaning off a bloody knife.

Horrified, she stared without seeing as things fell into place. Max hadn't been avoiding her. He'd never showed up because he never left his apartment last night. He was dead.

"No!" she started to say but it caught in her throat, burning like acid. Her fingers curled around the fabric, and she brought it close enough to her face to smell the blood. "You're not going to get away with this."

A wicked smirk graced his face. "Who's going to stop me?"

Struggling to get hold of herself through her sobs, Luna said, "I can call the police and tell them you told me you did it."

"Sure, love, you could do that if you want pretty little Amanda to end up like Violet."

Defeated and overwhelmed with grief, she sank onto her bed beside the discarded items, numb.

Chance reached out, hooking a finger under her chin and said, "Don't worry. When I've made things right, the pain will stop for both of us."

Chapter Twenty-Nine

AFTER CHANCE LEFT the room, Luna didn't move for a long time. Back stiff, she studied the items he'd left behind, wary of touching them. If he was telling the truth, they were evidence. They could help her, but not if she contaminated them. Tears welled in her eyes. If they were evidence, then that meant Max was dead and her father had been murdered.

Luna wanted to try calling Max again but going to the kitchen meant the possibility of bumping into Chance. Plus, if the items were evidence, that would give him the opportunity to take them back.

She eyed the shirt. It *looked* like Max's. Same size. Same cut. But white shirts were everywhere. It could be anyone's. Chance was probably playing with her head again, like he always did. He'd spent years trying to put space between her and Max.

Max is fine, she thought. *He has to be.* He's too smart. Too careful. Chance couldn't have—

No. She wouldn't accept that.

He's fine, she told herself. *I'll go back to his house. I'll make him answer the door this time.*

Sickness twisted deep in her stomach as she crouched over Chance's "gifts." To avoid contamination, she pulled her shirtsleeve down over one hand and shoved them into a plastic bag. Her hands trembled as she tied it shut, the rustling sound too loud in the silence. Her next move felt both impossible and important.

The television blasted from the front room, and she guessed Amanda and Chance wouldn't be going anywhere anytime soon. Chance would likely monitor her for the rest of the night to see what she would do.

I need to take these to the police, she thought. But how would she get out of the apartment without Chance noticing? She eyed her window. Not great, but better than the front door. Grabbing a fistful of quarters from her bedside table, she stuffed them into her pocket. Then, with the plastic bag clutched to her chest, she slid the window open and eased outside.

The grass was cool and wet beneath her bare feet, but she forced herself to ignore it. The gate around the complex had a gap in it. Luna wasn't sure if that had been done intentionally or was the result of weather over time, but the bushes around it hid the opening from almost all angles. She slid through it. Across the street stood a pay phone, and she hurried over to it, shoved the coins in, and dialed the police.

"911, what is your emergency?"

Her voice caught in her throat until the woman repeated the question. Then, finally, Luna whispered, "I . . . I need to report a murder."

***

THE INTERROGATION ROOM was as sterile as a morgue

with its white walls, hard surfaces, and no warmth. A fluorescent light buzzed overhead, casting a sickly pallor over everything. Two officers sat her there while taking the evidence she'd presented and told her to wait. In the meantime, they'd given her shoes to wear. They were two sizes too big, stiff around the edges, and they made her feel like a child playing dress-up.

With every minute that passed, her anxiety grew stronger. *There's no way he'd leave real evidence,* a tiny pessimistic voice piped up. He was too smart to do something so careless, but on the other hand, he was cocky enough to believe he could get away with anything because so far he had.

The door finally opened, its *creak* startlingly loud in the quiet. An officer stepped inside, face unreadable as he shut the door behind him. He moved slowly, deliberately, and took the seat across from her, folding his hands on the table.

Luna sat up straighter as she waited for the confirmation that it *was* blood and that they were en route to arrest Chance at the apartment.

"We didn't detect any blood," the officer said flatly, eyes locked on hers. "Just corn syrup and some kind of dye. Looks like a prank. And a bad one."

Luna searched his face for any sign of a joke, a smirk, a flicker of uncertainty. There was none. "But what about the needle?" she asked, grasping for something to prove she wasn't losing it.

He rolled his shoulders, unconcerned. "What about it? No fingerprints. Nothing inside it. No way to tell it was ever even used, let alone part of a crime."

Her stomach dropped. She felt like a balloon with the air let out, crumpled and weightless. Unable to meet his eyes again, she stared at the tabletop.

"Look," he started, "we can connect you with someone. Mental health services. A counselor, maybe."

A counselor. The words bounced inside Luna's head. She curled her hands into fists in her lap. *They think I'm crazy.* "No. I'm fine. Thank you."

He nodded, his voice softening. "I understand. When I lost my father, it was the lowest I've ever been. Grief can do strange things to a person. But . . . you gotta remember that life is worth living." He reached into his pocket for a business card and handed it to her. "Just in case."

Luna took it, barely glancing at it. When the word *Counselor* stood out, she shoved it into her pocket and pushed back her chair. "Sure."

He watched her walk to the door. "We can arrange a ride for you."

"Don't worry about it. I'm sorry for wasting your time," she said, and stepped out into the hallway. She ignored the curious looks from the woman at the front desk as she hurried through the lobby and out the front door.

Humiliation burned beneath her skin, crawling like fire ants on the walk home. Every step felt heavier than the last. She replayed the conversation in the interrogation room, wondering where she'd gone wrong, rehearing the officer's condescension, the pity. *Mental health services.*

No one will ever believe me, she thought, and it could've

destroyed her if there had been any hope to begin with.

Her walk took her past Max's apartment complex, and something in her flared to life. Desperate, she hurried to his door, pounding on it until it felt as if the sides of her hands and wrists were bruised.

Empty silence swallowed her hope.

Crushed, she trudged back to her own building, slipping through the same fence, the same window. Everything was the same. Except her.

She collapsed onto her bed like a puppet with its strings cut. Her chest heaved, and she buried her face in her hands, trying to muffle the broken sobs clawing their way out of her.

Chapter Thirty

THE TEARS EVENTUALLY dried, and Luna lay in bed staring at the wall. She wiped her eyes and glanced into the hallway, trying to figure out how much time had passed. Her door was partly open, enough for her to lock eyes with Amanda as she walked down the hall. The look she returned was cold as she slammed the bathroom door.

It's one problem after another.

Usually, she would let time fix this situation, but she couldn't afford that now. She wanted to ask Amanda if she'd heard from Max recently, but Amanda wouldn't want to talk to her when she was still upset. Luna would have to pacify her first.

She waited for Amanda to walk back down the hallway and followed her. Chance sat on the love seat, arm draped along its back as he flicked aimlessly through the channels. Amanda plopped down and curled up into a ball beside him, comfortable, as if they'd known one another for ages rather than a few days.

He's still here, Luna thought, studying him. Audacity was nothing new for Chance, but she'd forgotten how much of it he possessed.

Amanda's face filled with bitterness as soon as she spotted Luna.

Panic settled on Luna's shoulders. She couldn't exactly ask

Amanda what she needed to know with Chance sitting right there.

If I turn back now, I'll look weak, she told herself. *Improvise.* She approached the couch, putting on her best friendly face though her movements were quick and tense.

Amanda scowled, and Chance's eyes sparkled with interest. An awkward silence hung in the room, pressing down on them like an invisible weight.

Amanda seemed to be the most bothered by it. "What do you want, Luna?" she snarled.

"I-I . . ." Chance smirked, enjoying every minute of Luna's internal torment. It hardened something in her. "I wanted to apologize to you both," she started, locking eyes with Amanda, "for my behavior earlier when you introduced me to your date. I was rude, and I'm sorry."

Amanda's expression softened. Caught off guard, she said, "Oh, um, apology accepted."

Chance's eyes volleyed from Amanda back to Luna, visibly confused. *If he wants a game, I'll give him one.* She took two steps closer to him. Her heart fluttered, but her nerves were calm as she stuck her hand out, preparing herself for a handshake. "Hello, I'm Luna."

Slowly, he slid his large hand into hers, the skin-on-skin contact sending an unpleasant jolt to her stomach. When Luna tried to take her hand back, he clutched for a second too long before releasing. Amanda gave Luna an approving nod, who forced a smile in her direction. Free, she moved to the kitchen and collapsed onto one of the dining chairs. Being so close to Chance, *touching* the hand that had once been covered in her blood, made her physically ill. But she couldn't hide anymore, that much was clear.

Sounds of channel surfing stopped. Luna tensed, cautious of whatever Chance was searching for, especially in front of Amanda. He had a habit of watching the news to see when they broadcast his crimes. Would he have the urge to do that in front of his new date? Amanda didn't matter to him. She was a means to an end. This game was for Luna's benefit alone.

"In recent news, a local twenty-one-year-old was found dead in his home. Police have found clues of foul play."

Luna nearly flew out of her chair to watch the story. Amanda didn't pay her any attention, but Chance did. He watched her every expression. Luna blocked out her peripheral vision, focusing on the picture of Max's apartment complex.

"Police are unwilling to release the victim's name until the family has been contacted."

"Max," she whimpered.

Chance hadn't been lying. If he was telling the truth about Max, it stood to reason that he was also being honest about her father.

Amanda watched the news story to completion, then asked, "Luna, was that your friend? The one I spoke to on the phone?"

Luna moved her chin up and down once, words failing her. Amanda hopped out of her seat, hugging Luna tight. She hugged back, unable to drag her eyes away from Chance. He wore such a smug, self-satisfied expression that she wanted to erase it with a blunt object.

Look what I did, he mouthed so Amanda wouldn't hear. *I killed poor old Max, gutted him like an animal.*

"I'm so sorry, Luna," Amanda whispered in her ear, holding her like she was a precious gem.

Sorrow burned Luna's throat like acid, and without meaning to, she let out a sob. No tears came with it, but after that, there was no holding it in. She cried against Amanda's shoulder, unable to see the cold, mocking gaze of someone who hated her so much that they thrived on her misery.

LUNA STOPPED CRYING a short time prior to Chance leaving for the night. She was mad at herself for letting him see how sad she truly was, but Max had meant the world to her, and Chance knew it. Without Max, she was vulnerable, *helpless*. She had no special knowledge and no way of obtaining any. Worst of all, Max would hold onto his secrets forever.

As Luna lay in bed that night, one thought circled her brain: if a Keeper couldn't stop Chance, what could she possibly do to stay safe?

A light knock on the door drew her attention. She sniffled, wiping her face with the back of her hand, and expected to see Chance. Amanda peeked in instead.

"Hey, how are you holding up?" she asked softly.

Luna didn't know how to respond. She wasn't okay, didn't think she would ever be close to it again. "I-I'm fine."

"It's okay to be sad sometimes, Luna. You don't have to be strong all the time."

Luna didn't know how to respond to that either.

"I'm sorry for being mad at you earlier," Amanda said and sat on the bed. "It was petty, and I was frustrated. It wasn't right."

Luna nodded, silently accepting the apology.

"Talk to me," Amanda prompted.

Luna forced her words out. "I could've helped him."

Amanda's face twisted in surprised confusion. "Who? Max? His death was *not* your fault."

If only she knew. "I think Max knew who wanted to hurt him, and . . . I did nothing about it."

"Who is it, Luna?" Amanda asked, staring into her eyes. "If you know, you should go to the police."

Luna closed her eyes, trying, unsuccessfully, to block out her trip to the police station. "They won't believe me," she said and slumped over onto her pillows.

"This is really serious. Why wouldn't they believe you?"

Luna stayed silent.

Amanda sighed and stood, scanning the room as if searching for another way to convince her. "Well, I can't make you do anything you don't want to do."

Luna stared at the wall on the other side of her room.

Amanda pursed her lips, uncertainly. "Do you want something to eat?"

"I'm not hungry, Mandy." She couldn't remember the last time she'd eaten, but food held no interest for her.

"Some food in your stomach will make you feel better," she insisted. "Come on."

Luna didn't protest as her friend grasped her hand and led

her down the hallway. She sat on the same couch Amanda had shared with Chance earlier, positive she would throw up anything she managed to get down. Amanda moved about in the kitchen, clattering pots and dishes as she worked. Luna wished she would drop the idea.

A tear dripped onto her knee, leaving a subtle wet patch on her jeans. As she stared at it, she knew the time to talk had come. "Do you really want to help me?"

The sounds of dishes stopped, and Amanda appeared in the entrance of the kitchen, eyeing Luna as if deciding whether she had said that or not.

"Of course."

"Okay. On one condition."

Amanda sat down beside Luna, clutching her hand. Her blue eyes were wide, anticipating. "Anything."

"You have to believe me when I say he's dangerous," Luna whispered, hoping her words wouldn't enrage Amanda again. She avoided eye contact, not wanting to see the mood swing that would surely make an appearance.

Amanda yanked her hand away. "Are you still on that? What's your damage, honestly? He's been nothing but a gentleman."

Luna chose not to comment on that, but it wasn't easy. "I'm sure you've wondered about my hospital visits."

"Yeah," she said, a little less bitter.

"Well, I lied to you. I never had a sick aunt. I was visiting Chance. Did he tell you he recently woke up from a three-year coma?"

A bitter laugh tumbled from Amanda. "He works there, he's not a patient. You're completely mental!" she gushed, throwing her hands into the air."

Luna noted that information as a horrifying fact. "Am I? How well do you really know this guy? Has he shown you where he lives yet?"

"We've only been on a couple of dates. He doesn't have to show me anything!" Amanda exclaimed, jutting out her chin. "We're just having fun."

"Maybe. Or maybe he's been careful about what he *does* show you so you don't find out the truth."

Jaw tight, Amanda said, "I wanna be patient with you because I know you're going through a lot right now, but you better be going somewhere with this."

"You asked me whose room it was that I went into the day my dad died. Believe me or don't, but I'm telling you it was his."

Amanda stood up, and Luna reached out, grabbing her wrist. "Please don't go yet." Amanda stopped, watching her warily as if she were a wild animal, but she waited for her to speak. "Would you be willing to read something for me?"

"What do you want me to read?" she asked, relaxing in Luna's grip as her curiosity won out over everything else.

"Hold on." Luna let go and went into her room.

She reached under her mattress and grabbed her notebook, staring at it for a full minute. It was a long shot letting Amanda read it, but the newspaper clipping about Chance would be particularly hard to ignore. With the book tucked under her arm, she went back into the kitchen, ready to hand it over, when she paused.

"This is a record of everything that happened to me. You'll see for yourself that I do know Chance . . . Malcolm . . . whatever the hell he calls himself, even if he acts otherwise. Please read all of it."

"But—"

Luna cut her off, "Don't argue with me." For once, she wanted Amanda to *listen*. "Read this book, cover to cover. Then tell me how you feel. Can you promise me that?"

Amanda still eyed her as if she wanted to argue, but she swallowed it down and said, "Okay, I promise."

Luna stared at the notebook one more time. *It's a bad idea*, she told herself but dismissed the thought. This was the last one she had. She passed the book to Amanda's waiting hands, feeling as if she was passing part of herself with it.

"You want me to read all of this now?" Amanda asked, tilting the book sideways to gauge how many pages it had.

"Yes, please, Mandy."

Amanda tucked a strand of blonde hair behind her ear and opened the cover. "Okay," she said and started to read.

Luna sat beside her, hardly able to breathe. Each time Amanda flipped a page, it felt like a fresh stab to the chest. She anxiously skimmed each page as Amanda did, wondering what she thought of it all. She'd been awfully quiet so far, and Luna wasn't sure whether that was a good or a bad sign.

At last, Amanda closed the book, staring at the back cover, eyebrows knitted together in thought. "You're saying this really happened?"

"Every word. I kept the newspaper clippings to show that I wasn't crazy."

"I remember watching the news when those girls went missing. It was a big story for a while," she murmured, the crease between her brows getting deeper. "They never found who was responsible."

"Because the truth was insane."

"I'm so sorry."

There was that line. The line Luna hated more than anything else. "Don't give me that. Do you believe me or what?" Luna asked. The room went silent. Luna jittered in anticipation, unsure what she would do if Amanda didn't believe her. If she couldn't save her friend from certain doom.

"I believe this happened to you . . ."

Luna closed her eyes, waiting for the bomb to drop. *"But?"*

"But the part about Malcolm," Amanda said slowly, and opened the book to one of the newspaper clippings. She tapped her finger on the picture. "The boy . . . in the photos. He's similar but . . ."

Luna parted her lips. There was an easy explanation for the difference in appearance. When Chance had kidnapped her, he'd been younger, a teenager, but he wasn't a dumb kid anymore. He had grown into a man, his face hard and chiseled. There was still an inkling of familiarity to his gangly teenage self, but the change was striking enough that he could pass for a different person to someone like Amanda, someone who had never known him during his high school years. "That was a few years ago."

"People change, they do . . ." she started, thumb stroking the edge of the black and white picture. "But there are some features that are *too* different. And not only that . . . he's got a different name."

Luna rolled her eyes. "He could be *lying*, have you thought of that?"

"I've seen his driver's license."

The muscle in Luna's jaw twitched. "He made a point of showing it to you?"

Amanda scoffed. "Of course not. I saw it when he took his wallet out to pay for dinner."

Luna reached up to pinch the bridge of her nose. There was so much innocence in her that it almost made Luna feel dirty for trying to convince her otherwise, as if she could corrupt Amanda simply by telling her the truth.

"He acted like he didn't know you."

"It's a game. I can't tell you what he's done if you don't think we've ever met."

Amanda stared at her, and Luna knew she wasn't speaking because she *did* think Luna was crazy. And why not? Everyone else did.

Luna's hand hovered over her stomach. She'd never shown anyone her scar, but she was growing desperate. *Amanda can't ignore this*, she thought, and grabbed the edge of her shirt, lifting it to expose her stomach. A heavy purple scar marred her light brown skin down one side, rugged with enhanced ugliness from Chance's botched stitches.

Amanda's gaze locked on the scar. "Oh my God."

"That's from Chance's dagger." Luna glanced down, making herself see it. If it was ugly to her, it would be worse to Amanda, whose viewpoint wouldn't be dulled by familiarity. "He kidnapped me. Did you read that part? Said he wanted to keep me there and . . ." she trailed off, lowering the hem of her shirt. That was the most she'd ever said about her experience in Chance's cabin out loud.

It hurt to talk about.

"I'm sorry, honey," Amanda said, searching her friend's eyes. "You went through something horrible, and trauma isn't easy to deal with."

"It's not."

"But you can't take your pain out on other people," Amanda said carefully. "Malcolm didn't hurt you. He only looks like the man who did. It's an unfortunate coincidence, is all."

Luna's mouth went dry. "He's killing again . . . torturing me and using you to do it. Max tried to warn me that he was back, and Chance killed him to silence him."

"Chance is gone, sweetheart," Amanda said, rising from the couch to cautiously place her hands on Luna's shoulders. "Malcolm will not hurt you. I promise."

"Someone murdered my dad, Mandy," Luna whispered.

"No, girl," she said, looking suddenly sad as if she'd crossed from uncertainty to pity. "I thought it was a heart attack."

"It was, but what if someone *made* him have it?" Luna asked, desperate to get Amanda to see things as she did. To make her understand the looming danger.

Amanda's shoulders drooped. "Have you been sleeping

okay?"

Luna was speechless. She'd given it her all, but Amanda wasn't listening. She wasn't *hearing* what Luna had to say. And if she wasn't going to listen, nothing would change. She would seal not only her own fate but Luna's too. "You're not going to stop seeing him, are you?"

"You know I love you, and I'm sorry about what happened to you in high school, but Malcolm is innocent," Amanda said, handing the notebook to Luna and shattering her hope with it.

"But—" Luna started, then stopped. If Amanda had made up her mind, there was no changing it. Luna calmly gathered the contents of her journal and tucked it under her arm. She slapped Amanda across the face and left the room.

Chapter Thirty-One

HOURS AFTER THE encounter with Luna, Amanda was still rattled by it. They'd never had a fight like this. Bickering about who left a cupboard open or not replacing the toilet paper? Sure. They'd had tons of those. Putting hands on each other? That was new.

As she lay in the hotel bed, watching Malcolm flip through a magazine, the what-ifs wouldn't leave her mind. *What if he was lying? What if Luna was right?*

He seemed so normal, but the things she'd read in Luna's journal were hard to ignore. And so was the scar on her roommate's stomach. Amanda's face burned where Luna had hit her. She was sure there was a mark, but Malcolm hadn't commented on it. The violence of the reaction further convinced her she was telling the truth. Luna was afraid of this man.

But she's not scared of him, she reminded herself. *She feared a man who* looked *like him.*

Amanda tilted her head. It was true she hadn't known him long, but he'd not been unkind to her or anyone else. There were no cross words or anything to suggest he was anything less than the perfect gentleman she believed him to be.

"I'm sorry about the way Luna was toward you today," she said, gauging his reaction.

Malcolm clicked his tongue. "Don't worry about it. You said she's going through a lot right now. I can't hold that against her."

Amanda forced a smile. Did he sound . . . strained? "What do you think of her?" Amanda prompted, trying to read his face. "My other friends think she's strange."

Malcolm closed the magazine and studied her. Was that interest she saw in his eyes? "I don't know her well enough to say," he answered at last.

Amanda stayed quiet. Not the response she'd wanted, but really, what had she expected him to say? He probably thought she was weird for asking.

He passed your stupid test, she told herself. *Let it go.*

Chapter Thirty-Two

MANDA STAYED THE night with Chance, and in the morning, he tagged along with her back to the apartment. The day passed by in an almost wordless blur. He waited patiently for her to tell him to get lost, but she was quiet. Icily so. He suspected it had something to do with Luna. The slap was no doubt still on Amanda's mind. Chance couldn't say he blamed her; with a slap came the additional element of humiliation.

He tried to play up the sympathy card, acting as sweet as he could to try to get more information out of her. Violence was unlike Luna. What had happened between them to incite it?

It has to do with me.

Amanda mostly ignored him, too worried about avoiding Luna. And Luna seemed to be doing the same, as if their lives depended on not breathing the same air as one another. Luna stuck to her room, much to his disappointment. The one time she came out, it was to leave the apartment altogether. Amanda was a bit more complicated. She floated around, dusting and wiping away grime in harder to clean spots. He guessed she was the type to focus her anger into a task, which for her, happened to be cleaning.

He sat on the sofa, watching television and listening to Amanda move around furniture in her struggle. When dinnertime came, he offered to cook just to make her sit down. If he was honest, the entire situation aggravated him. Almost left him uneasy.

Luna came home not too long after that. With a scathing glance at him, she resumed her place in her own cage. He expected her to come back out for dinner, but she never did. He gave up, adopting Amanda's cleaning techniques to busy his mind when she went to bed. As he threw away the dirty rags and sponges from the day's cleaning spree, all he could think about was that the entire day had passed, and Amanda never asked him when or if he planned on leaving the apartment.

She wants me here, he mused, throwing a wet dishcloth into the sink. *And I can use that.*

AN HOUR LATER, Chance stepped out of the shower and threw on a pair of red plaid pajama pants. He ran his fingers through his multicolored hair as he admired himself in the mirror. There was a fullness to his cheeks and abdomen from steady meals. Tossing the towel into the hamper beside the counter, he scowled. The scars on his arms seemed darker, the purple lines glowing against his skin. Why had he given himself so many and in places so noticeable, at that?

I really was a dumb kid.

There were multiple ways to siphon his magic, but he hadn't known that then. He poked at a particularly nasty scar on the inside of his left wrist. While he wasn't ashamed to show them off, he found himself unlikely to tell anyone the truth of why he had them. Amanda believed them to be the result of an old restaurant job. Anyone with a brain could tell that didn't make sense, but Amanda hadn't called him on it. Rather, she'd gone along with it as if it made perfect sense.

With another quick study of himself, Chance headed to Amanda's room to see that she was already asleep. Relieved, he settled himself into her bed, doing his best to get comfortable. Her chatter was mind-numbing, and tonight, his head was cluttered enough already.

Whimpers and yells started from the other side of the apartment. Chance jumped to his feet, rushing to Luna's door in a blind panic. He had no plan of what he would do when he got there, he only wanted to see what it was that was making her sound like that. When the door swung open, he expected to see one of Cody's men, but she was alone, writhing in her sleep. Walking toward her slowly, he glanced around her room, confused. He placed a hand on her shoulder, impressed with her strength as she fought her imaginary demons. Dropping onto her mattress, he stared at the sleeping girl.

Night terrors or was it Cody at work on the Other Side?

Being around her for only a few days had taught him so much. Outside, she put up a good front, but the extent of the damage he'd caused was clear. Chance used his thumb to swipe a stray lock of hair out of her eyes. In the moonlight, she appeared peaceful, and he was struck by her beauty when the creases from her frowns were gone. The bags under her eyes told him she'd been crying over Max's death, and that thought filled him with a surge of jealousy. He stroked her cheek gently, and she stiffened at his touch, then relaxed a few seconds later.

So beautiful.

Chance stuck his tongue in his cheek and lifted his feet to lie on the mattress beside her. He wrapped his arms around her, bringing her close to his chest. He didn't consider what might happen if she were to wake up and find him holding her. Instead, he reveled in the moment. Luna exhaled, her trembling lips brushing the bare skin below his collarbone.

A small smile crossed his face. *I could get used to this.*

He dreaded the thought of trudging to Amanda's room and putting that mask on again.

I can't stay here, he reminded himself. *I can't let Amanda suspect anything.*

Did it really make a difference if she did? It was only a matter of time before things with Cody soured, and he would have to leave anyway.

Holding onto Luna, he dozed off, and when his eyes opened again, it was to the sound of Amanda calling for him in the hallway. He didn't know how much time had passed, but Luna was still asleep. Gently, he disentangled himself from her and climbed off the bed.

"I'm in here!" he whispered, loud enough for Amanda to hear.

She pushed open the door with a scrunched face, waiting for Chance to join her in the hall before she hissed, "What were you doing in there?"

"She was screaming. I thought someone broke in,"

Chance admitted.

Amanda's face softened. "I'm sorry. I should've warned you that she has night terrors." She paused to ruffle her blonde hair as she stared through Luna's dark doorway. "She's had them almost the entire time I've known her. I thought she got better, but I guess I'm so used to it, I've stopped hearing her."

Chance was unsure what to think. "Well, she seems better now. If she keeps having fits, I could get her some medicine to help her sleep through the night."

Amanda placed a hand on his upper arm. "You're such a caring guy."

Chance hid his nervousness behind his smirk as he kissed her. Lady Luck had shone on him yet again by giving Luna a roommate who was so easy to manipulate, so clueless. When it came to him, no one was immune to his spell . . . except for Luna.

Chance followed Amanda to bed, his body heavy with exhaustion, desperate to shut down and escape the day's chaos. His subconscious had other plans. When he opened his eyes again, he was on the Other Side. He stretched, muscles tight. The woods wrapped around him, shadows shifting between gnarled trees. A shared haunt with Cody. At the thought of him, he glanced over his shoulder but didn't see anyone. For now, he was alone.

Since I'm here . . . he mused.

Fingers trembling, he reached out, watching the air ripple like water around his hand and arm. With his other hand, he mirrored the movements, closing his eyes to feel the strange, electric wiggle coil deep in his gut. Taking out Max hadn't restored his magic, but it had sparked it back to life. If things got desperate, he had some power. But for now? He'd hold on to it.

Just in case.

"Is that progress I sense?" Cody called from the woods behind him.

Chance winced but faced him squarely. How long had he been watching? Chance masked his flicker of doubt behind a grim smile. "I took out the troublemaker."

Cody bobbed his head, a spark of approval in his forest-colored eyes. "Good. What about his partner?"

Chance let out a short, bitter laugh. "Don't get your panties twisted. I'll get around to it."

A sneer curled Cody's lips, dripping with warning and something darker. "For your sake, you better."

Chapter Thirty-Three

MAX'S FUNERAL CAME a week later. His family scraped together what money they could for a proper ceremony, and Luna borrowed some from Amanda to help with the remaining costs. Until the day came, Luna spent most of the time in her room, moping and upset. She only left to go to work, and then it was right back to her dungeon for the rest of the evening. Things were tense between the roommates, but ultimately, it seemed Amanda had decided that she deserved the slap because she didn't mention it again.

Neither did Luna.

The time in seclusion hadn't left Luna feeling any different, but whenever she saw herself in the mirror, she appeared frailer. Amanda must've noticed her unhealthy glow because she'd tried to draw her into conversation a few times, but Luna had replied with only a few words, if any.

Luna couldn't consider her a friend anymore. At least not on the same level she used to. Amanda had read and believed every bit of Luna's past, yet she wouldn't stop dating the monster who had caused it. She was stuck in her own fantasy world, and that place would spell doom for their friendship. Luna hadn't realized how much life Amanda had breathed into her until she no longer had her support.

Chance surely knew how sickly she'd grown too. She had caught him watching her several times and wondered when he would make good on his words and finish her off. Part of her readily welcomed it. If she were dead, she'd no longer have to live as a ghost of herself.

Amanda peeked in her room. "You ready to go?"

Luna glanced down at her black skirt, the same one she'd worn to her father's funeral. A bad feeling warned that Max's wouldn't be the last one she'd wear it to. "As ready as I'll ever be."

"Come on."

Luna got off her bed, limbs as heavy as weights. She walked with Amanda to the car, not understanding why she insisted on tagging along to Max's funeral. Amanda claimed it was because she wanted to pay her respects, but Luna suspected it was guilt about the entire Chance thing, and this was her way of trying to make up for it.

If only she understood that there is no making up for it.

They drove in silence. When Amanda parked at the cemetery, Luna nearly threw herself out of the car. Amanda followed, holding a bundle of long-stemmed white roses, and grabbed her arm.

"Wait for me," she said. Luna turned on instinct and glared at her. "And stop making that face. You know I'm worried about you."

Luna tugged her arm free and muttered the simplest answer she could, "I'm fine."

"This is because of the whole Malcolm thing," Amanda said flatly.

In her head, Luna shouted, *Yes!* But out loud said, "My best friend died," and resumed her walk across the lot.

"Oh."

Wind whispered through the nearby trees, carrying with it the faint scent of damp earth. She stepped carefully over uneven stones, their gray faces etched with names and dates long forgotten. It seemed fitting that Max would be buried only a few feet away from Violet. She could imagine Chance filling the entire lot with her loved ones.

Except for Dad.

A group of white lawn chairs had been arranged around the open pit. Luna sat down on one of them, feeling the legs sink into the grass beneath her. Amanda stood behind her, fidgeting awkwardly like a lost puppy. Luna watched people line up beside Max's casket to pay their respects and forced herself to acknowledge it, knowing it contained the remains of her best friend. She hadn't searched for details about his death. Knowing wouldn't make it easier to stomach.

Amanda made a move to sit in the chair beside Luna but stopped, her focus trained on something behind her.

"Hey, babe," a familiar voice purred.

Luna's blood chilled as Amanda and Chance embraced. *Amanda* invited *him?* Betrayal twisted inside her chest, fighting the grief. Footsteps. A shadow loomed over her. She peered up into Chance's blue eyes. "Sorry about your friend," he said, exaggerating his fake sorrow.

Luna didn't reply. Instead, she threw her anger at Amanda. "How dare you?"

Amanda twirled the flowers in her hand, offering one to Luna. She scoffed and stormed away, mingling in the line beside Max's casket. As she inched toward the front, her anger morphed into something else. Sorrow. She pressed her fingertips on the rich mahogany surface, surprised how cold it felt, and stared down at Max. He was dressed in a nice black suit, lying on a white casket lining, eyes closed, and brown hair carefully coiffed. For a split second, she could believe he was at peace. Having been murdered by his worst enemy, he hadn't been in this condition when he was found. "I'm so sorry that I didn't listen to you sooner, Max."

She rushed from the casket, hovering near the edge of the clearing. She wanted to run from the entire funeral altogether, but there was nowhere she could go that would allow her to escape the feelings inside her. It took effort to force herself to sit back down, this time in a chair far from Amanda and Chance.

The pastor began to speak, and Luna tried to comfort herself by imagining that Max was in a better place, but it didn't work. What if a better place simply didn't exist?

At the end of the ceremony, Max's casket was lowered into the pit. Luna, Amanda, and a few of Max's relatives lined up beside it and dropped their flowers atop the casket, one by one. Luna didn't see Chance drop anything in, and she was glad for that small mercy. He had no right to be there, let alone pretend to care.

Amanda hugged Luna unexpectedly, twining her fingers through Luna's. It was supposed to be a comforting gesture, but Luna didn't feel it. She broke free and went back to her chair. Thankfully, Amanda didn't follow. A few people started to make their way to the parking lot and others split into groups around the field, talking.

Luna stayed in her seat, comatose. A hand touched her shoulder lightly and she jumped, expecting it to be Amanda or Chance, but a blonde girl in all black greeted her. At first, Luna thought it was one of Max's relatives until the girl's bright eyes met hers.

"Sarah," Luna said, surprised.

She nodded once, her gaze drifting across the field. "Is that Chance?"

"Yeah."

"I think we should get out of here."

That was something Luna readily agreed to.

As the two crossed the field, no one paid attention to their departure. Sarah glanced over her shoulder, no doubt pinning Chance with her glare. "It should be him in that coffin."

Luna hugged herself tighter as she said, "It should." To keep the silence from swallowing them alive, she added, "What are you doing here?"

"Max was a cool dude. He was my buddy for a while back in elementary school."

Max always had a lot of friends. With all the stress between them, Luna forgot about that part of him.

"Let's go get something to eat. I'm buying," Sarah offered.

"I know what happened to your sister," Luna blurted out. She hadn't planned to say it. Not so hastily, at least, but it was out now.

Sarah stopped, turning to her as if she wondered if she'd

misheard her. "Y-you do?"

"I've . . . known. For a long time now."

Sarah's brow furrowed slightly, as if trying to force the right words to the surface. Her lips parted, then closed again, pressing into a thin, uncertain line. Her eyes shifted, and she opened her mouth once more, but no sound came.

"Did you drive here?" Luna asked.

"Yeah," Sarah answered, twisting her lips into a frustrated scowl. "But forget about that. What happened to Susan?"

"I'll tell you. It's . . . it's a long story. Can you drive me home first?" Luna asked, trying to keep her tone calm despite her rising anxiety. It wouldn't be long until Chance noticed her absence, and he would search for her. She wanted to be long gone by then. "I need to show you something or else what I tell you won't make sense."

Sarah's eyes flashed like she wanted to argue, but her shoulders slumped instead. "All right. I parked over here."

They got into her car and drove back to Luna's apartment. She was glad she'd had the foresight to keep the key earlier. Sarah stayed in the car while Luna hurried into the apartment, taking her black notebook out from under her mattress. She searched for the part about Susan and reread it. How would Sarah take the info?

This needs to be done, she told herself. No matter how hard a conversation it would be. She tucked the journal under her arm and hurried back to the waiting car.

Sarah eyed it as Luna climbed into the passenger seat. "Let me see it."

"Not yet."

Sarah dropped her hands into her lap. "To the cabin we go, then."

Luna didn't want to go anywhere near that place, but ironically, she couldn't think of a more sheltered location for them to talk. Sarah weaved between both lanes on the highway, motivated to get there as quickly as they could. At the edge of the forest, Sarah parked on a patch of dried grass. It took effort for Luna to convince herself to climb out, and when she did, her world swirled.

Together, she and Sarah made their way through the trees. Sarah didn't know the way, so by instinct, Luna led them. It wasn't long until they reached a familiar clearing, leaving Luna sick with memories of Violet's death. She did her best to avoid the spot where her body had lain. After it was behind them, Luna didn't fare much better. The paranoid part of her brain swore she could still hear Chance creeping through the foliage. More memories threatened to cripple her: the truck ride to his cabin that had knocked her unconscious, and the wound he'd inflicted upon her when she refused to obey him.

Sarah wasn't affected as she waltzed through the trees. Luna envied her carelessness, but she held her tongue. As soon as Sarah found out what had happened to her sister, some of her light would be forever changed. They followed the ashen path until it dumped them at the clearing with the cabin and stone temple. Luna stood where the undergrowth changed to grass and found it incredibly hard to move another step. Sarah continued onward, leaving Luna no choice but to follow.

Dark brown walls. Plants growing through the cracks. A

small porch and windows painted black. The cabin was the stuff of nightmares. Literally.

Sarah placed her fingertips on the door. The wood was so warped that it swung open gently, revealing the darkness inside. Luna stared into the mouth of the beast, waiting for it to swallow them both. Sarah was the first inside, and after mentally composing herself, Luna followed. As soon as she stepped foot in the foyer, she swayed on her feet, flashes of her last experience flooding her mind. When she glanced up, her eyes caught the shackles hanging from the wall. They were rusted now, but they hadn't always been. At one time, they'd been pristine silver.

Chance had used them to hold her prisoner.

After her initial survey of the room, Sarah whipped around and faced Luna. "Tell me all of it now. Everything you know. What happened to my sister?"

Luna barely heard her, her voice an unpleasant jolt back to reality. Numb, she handed over the book and said, "Read it. Cover to cover."

Obediently, Sarah plopped down on the dirty floor and began to read. With Sarah distracted, Luna found herself drawn to the chains. She knelt beside them, running the rusty metal between her fingertips. The floorboards beneath were stained with dark flecks. Her blood. She clenched her stomach, still remembering the pain. Remembering the way Chance had sat beside her, reviving her when she'd fainted and telling her the awful truth of his plans.

Luna stood up. Moving on autopilot, her feet led her down the hall and past a closet. It was overgrown with ivy now, but at one time, that closet had been Max's prison. At the end of the hall was a bedroom. Luna slowly pushed open the door to see it. Chance had lain her in that bed to recover a few hours before she'd been able to stop his fusion. Nauseous, she took a few steps backward.

"All of this is true?"

Luna jumped, worried she had traveled to the day of her flashbacks, until she remembered it was only Sarah. "Yes. That's why I wanted you to read it. I figured it was the easiest way for you to understand." Sarah was silent so Luna added, "You got to the part about your sister?"

"Chance killed her. Just as I thought."

"I-I wanted to tell you but—"

"The body, the burnt one in the nameless plot, is Susan?" she asked, enunciating each word.

Luna nodded.

"Skip Day, when I went to school and Susan stayed home . . . that was the day he killed her?"

"I think so."

"Why? Why would he hurt her? She worshipped him. Would've done anything he wanted her to do," Sarah whispered.

"She found out what he did to Kate," Luna said, but she couldn't say for sure why Chance did any of the things he did. That was the only logical reason he could've had. Everything else was senseless. But murder always was.

Sarah sniffled. "Sounds about right. Susan was so upset those days before she disappeared. Now I know why."

"I tried to help her." Luna offered a comforting hand to

Sarah.

"If that's the case, why didn't you go to the police?"

"When it comes to Chance, conventional methods don't work. I think he knew people in the department. Max thought there were others."

"A cult?" she guessed.

Luna shrugged. It made sense, though. Rituals. Death. Powerful men. It all seemed culty. She asked, "Y-you believe me?"

Sarah drew her eyebrows together and stared down at the dark, dusty floor. "If I had read this from anyone else, no. It's crazy. Hell, it's downright insane, but . . . I believe you. I get this strange feeling that you're not lying. If Susan knew what you think she knew, it made sense that she would've tried to help. In its weird way, this answers every single question I've had."

"Maybe now you can find some closure."

"All I can do is try," Sarah said, taking another glance around the room. "How could you be here after everything that happened to you?"

"I didn't have a choice."

Sarah glanced over her shoulder. "Those shackles were yours?"

Luna blinked, a haunted gleam going over her eyes.

Sarah's eyes widened, her mouth opening into a slight O. "That's what was going on in high school. Chance was abusing you."

Luna refused to comment on that. It reminded her of something Violet had said so long ago.

"He didn't hurt you . . . like *that*, did he?"

Luna flinched as if she'd been struck across the face.

"I'm sorry," she added quickly. "It's just . . . I mean, he took you here. You were alone with him and hurt." *Vulnerable* was the word she didn't say but it hung in the air anyway.

Luna couldn't be sure that *that* hadn't happened. She'd passed out and woken in his bed, half undressed, with him beside her. Those were the parts of her memories she refused to revisit.

"I need to get out of here."

Chapter Thirty-Four

SARAH FOLLOWED LUNA back through the trees to the road. Before they got in the car, she said, "I'm going to make a stop at the cemetery before I drop you off, if that's all right."

"That's fine," Luna agreed, her voice a raspy wisp.

She wasn't in a rush to return to the apartment and deal with Amanda's antics anyway. The drive back to the cemetery was silent, the devastation clear on Sarah's face and in her posture. *It's better that she knows*, Luna told herself, but was it really? It wouldn't lessen her pain. If anything, it might add to it.

Most of the crowd from Max's funeral had cleared out by the time Sarah and Luna returned to the cemetery, Amanda and Chance included. Luna kept an eye out for him, regardless, as Sarah walked through the graves, mumbling to herself so faintly that Luna couldn't make out what she was saying. At last, she came to a cheap, plastic tombstone at the back of the lot. There was no name on it, but there didn't need to be. Sarah fell to her knees beside it, fingers digging into the dirt as if anchoring herself was the only way to keep from toppling over. "Luna, I . . . I thought it'd be a relief to come here and say goodbye to Susan, but it's not."

"I know," Luna said softly. Seeing Max in his casket would

always remind her how she'd let him down.

Mascara streaked Sarah's cheeks as she looked up. "Chance needs to pay for what he's done. We need to go to the police."

Luna knelt beside her. In the back of her mind, she remembered the pity in the officer's eyes as he watched her leave the interrogation room with her tail between her legs. Help wasn't an option, and there was no gentle way to break that news. "Sarah, as much as it sucks for me to say, the police have no evidence that he was the one who killed Susan. They couldn't so much as ID her when they buried her, so what are the odds they'll make the connection now?"

A torrent of tears made their way down Sarah's face. Luna hated knowing her exact feeling. All the wishing in the world wouldn't be enough to change things.

"Could you . . . I mean, would you be willing to take me there? To DreamWorld?" Sarah asked as she rose to her feet. "I want to see it for myself."

Luna startled at the request. Was that something she could do? She'd never tried. Luna met Sarah's eyes again, those glittering, ice-colored orbs that seemed more fragile every time she looked into them. Sarah believed her in a way that Amanda did not.

"Okay, I'll try," Luna said softly. She owed her that much. "Thank you."

Sarah led the way to the car, and Luna imagined the fresh pain that must be in her heart. Luna had been in her position before. Hell, she was still there, wishing someone would swoop in and ease her pain. It wouldn't happen for her, but she could be that person for Sarah.

Sarah's car was a small red SUV with a hatchback. She opened the back door, pressing the seats down to create enough space for them to both lie flat comfortably. She was the first to crawl inside and plop down. Luna followed a long, hesitant minute later. Sarah didn't seem bothered by their proximity, but Luna was uneasy being so close to anyone. It broke all of her rules, but she pushed that away. Sarah was a *friend* . . . or the closest thing she had to one now.

"What do I do?" Sarah asked, studying Luna expectantly.

Luna reached out and grasped her hand. "You go to sleep," she said, "and I'll be right there with you."

At least, that was what Luna wanted to believe. She'd never brought someone else to the Other Side. It had always been Chance who could pull off that kind of thing.

They went silent, Luna's gaze was trained out the rear windshield, watching the cloudy sky above. Sarah fell asleep first, Luna never releasing the grip on her hand, scared of the possible consequences of breaking contact. When Luna drifted off, she woke by Sarah's side. Their surroundings weren't somewhere she'd ever been. A tiny room with transparent walls stretched into black nothingness. Each step they took echoed, the room stretching to accommodate their travels.

"Where are we?" Sarah wanted to know, wonder in her eyes.

Luna pulled her hand from Sarah's, not sharing her friend's amazement. The lack of knowledge made her afraid.

"Newcomer!" a great Voice bellowed from the sky. Luna was particularly rattled. In her time in DreamWorld, she'd never heard a voice unless it came from another person.

"Hello?" she called to it.

"You have brought an outsider!"

Sarah's eyes went wide as she met Luna's gaze, searching for answers she didn't have. "What's going on?"

Luna was at as much of a loss as Sarah, but she didn't want to let her know how little control she had of the situation. That she could've potentially upset something she hadn't known existed.

The Voice continued. "Sarah Cross."

Sarah's back went ramrod straight. "Yes . . . *sir?*"

"Initiating memory wipe."

An earsplitting alarm blared out, and Luna clamped her hands over her ears. What was *happening?* Max hadn't told her anything about a situation like this.

There's so much I don't know.

"You . . . you can't do this!" Luna pleaded, searching for a face in the nothing, some indication that she was being heard. "There's bad people coming, and she's the only one willing to help."

"She knows nothing of this world and thus has nothing to contribute," said the Voice.

The words struck a nerve. How much had Luna endured in this place of nightmares with no clue how she fit into it all? Why was Sarah the exception? "Neither did I at first."

"You belong here."

A chill ran down her spine, but she didn't focus on the cryptic statement. "You're not going to stop Chance. You haven't so far. Sarah is the only one willing to take on the job. Why not let her?" Luna asked.

"It's a dangerous quest meant only for the most capable Keepers."

"Your Keepers are dying!"

"There is still one handling the task."

"Amy," Sarah said. "The coward."

"The natural order of things must be maintained," the Voice insisted.

The screeching noise started again. "No!" Luna screamed and wrapped her arms around Sarah, unsure if the contact would save her or make things worse for both of them. An orange veil seeped from her, enveloping them.

The overbearing noise halted.

"Sarah?" Luna asked. "Are you okay?"

Her eyes snapped open. "I'm . . . fine, I think."

"See that?" Luna howled to the sky. "She does belong here!"

The Voice was silent for so long she assumed the being had disappeared completely. Finally, it said, "Very well." The alarm cut off and left them in eerie silence.

"I think I want to go home now," Sarah whispered.

Luna nodded and closed her eyes, trying to force herself to wake up and bring Sarah with her. The invisible walls gave way to the back of Sarah's car with a disorienting *pop*.

Sarah sat up, rubbing her palm across her forehead. "That

was . . . crazy.”

That was an understatement. Luna sat up beside her, drawing her knees to her chest. What had that Voice been, and what did it mean that she could win in a fight against it? Had she really won anything or had it been some type of test?

“Now I know for sure that your book wasn’t full of hot air,” Sarah said. “Which means the part about Chance should be right, too, but it seems that he never lost his memory.”

Luna stared out the window. “Apparently, and that’s the worst part. Those men are helping him.”

“So we’re both probably on their list now. Others too.”

“Probably,” Luna agreed, resting her chin on her knees.

“Are you scared?”

Luna closed her eyes halfway. That word had taken on such a different meaning over the years. “Scared” used to mean uneasy, nervous. Now, she associated it with death and torture. Pain. “I’m terrified. It’s worse not knowing what will come next. If he’s not using magic, I can’t take him out the same way I did before.”

“He killed Max, huh?” Sarah asked.

“Yeah,” Luna confirmed. “After what happened in Lima, Chance’s people put a target on his head. He made it on his own for a while, but I guess they sent Chance to finish the job. Without Max, I have no clue what to do.”

Sarah’s lips rested together, not tight but closed, as if she was holding back a thought. A faint crease formed between her eyebrows. “Maybe you don’t need him. You’ve got magic and brains. Study Chance’s routine and see what you can learn. He was with a girl at the funeral. Who is she?"

"My roommate," Luna said flatly.

Astonished, Sarah asked, "Are you serious? Have you warned her?"

All the rage from Luna's previous interactions with Amanda came flooding back. "Yes, but it hasn't done any good. She thinks I'm mistaking him for someone else."

"She knows about everything?"

"Yes, but as far as she's concerned, he's a nurse's aide named Malcolm."

"Let's hope she finds some sense while she still can." Sarah glanced at the book sitting between them. "The Voice mentioned Amy . . . and your book does, too, but where is she now? She wasn't at graduation."

"She's in Brentwood."

"The mental hospital? That's a shame," Sarah said, chewing on her bottom lip. "If we went there, do you think she'd be willing to talk to me?"

Luna remembered her visit with Amy. How sudden and all-consuming her anger had been. *Maybe she's had enough time to cool off.*

"We can find out."

∗∗∗

HALF AN HOUR later, Luna and Sarah parked at the back of the lot outside Brentwood. Luna had her black book tucked under her arm as they went inside. The nurses took their jewelry, wallets, and anything else they had on their person. After a five-minute argument, they allowed Luna to hold onto her book as long as she promised not to leave it with Amy when she left.

Then they were escorted down the familiar long, white hallway to Amy's room. "I'll be back in twenty minutes," the nurse said, then took her leave.

Luna wasn't excited to see Amy again. She stayed by the wall, unsure what this visit would bring. Sarah, having no previous interactions with her, didn't hesitate to step into the middle of the room. Like last time, Amy sat in a chair facing the window with her back to her visitors.

"Hi, Amy," Luna greeted hesitantly.

Amy's shoulders tensed. "Why have you come back?"

"I wanted to talk to you," Sarah said.

Slowly, like something from a horror movie, Amy rose from the chair and faced Sarah. She was tiny, her frame frailer than the last time Luna had seen her, but she strode right up to Sarah as if she was ready to fight her. "I remember you. You were one of those pretty, popular girls. Susan's sister, right?"

Sarah gave a sharp nod, eyes wide with uncertainty.

Amy waved a hand and took a step back. "Say whatever you've come to say."

"I'll be as simple about this as I can. Chance woke up. Did you know he remembers us . . . remembers everything?"

Amy raised her eyebrows, amused. "You told her the truth?" she asked Luna. Then to Sarah, "My condolences."

"He's not working alone this time," Luna chimed in. "Without your partner, there's no other Keeper to take care of this."

"Chance killed him," Sarah added.

Amy's nostrils flared. "It was inevitable. That's what happens when people get themselves involved with something they can't handle." She pinned Sarah with her glare. "You'd do best to stay in your lane."

"So I've been told," Sarah said, folding her arms across her chest.

Luna's grip on her journal tightened. "Help us stop him."

Amy laughed. "Even if I wanted to, I can't. If you haven't been paying attention, I'm a little locked up."

"You don't have to leave this place to help," Luna said. "You can scope the Other Side and tell us what you find out about his friends."

"And jump in front of the firing squad?" Amy stuck her hands in her pockets. "I don't want to get involved as it is. I'm definitely not diving in headfirst."

"We don't know what else to do," Sarah said.

Amy narrowed her eyes. "Of course *you* don't. You shouldn't know about this stuff to begin with."

"I *had* to recruit her," Luna spat. "Because you're too selfish to do your job."

"If you can find other people to step in, then you clearly don't need me," Amy pointed out. "After everyone abandoned me, I gotta do what's best for me this time around."

"But—"

"Nurse!" Amy screeched, leaving no time for Luna or Sarah to object.

The nurse swung the door open instantly, as if she'd been waiting outside. After Luna's previous visit, she'd likely been flagged.

"Would you escort them out, please?" Amy asked, turning her back to her two visitors. "And make sure they don't come back."

"Of course." The nurse ushered Luna and Sarah toward the door. "Come on."

"Please think about what we've said!" Sarah called over her shoulder, hoping Amy would come to her senses.

"There's nothing to think about," Amy countered before the door clanged shut behind them.

Sarah and Luna collected their belongings at the front desk and left the building. Luna didn't care for the disapproving glances the nurses gave them on the way out, as though they blamed the two of them for Amy's outburst.

"Amy's uh . . . different than I remember," Sarah admitted as they crossed the parking lot.

"She's traumatized," Luna said defensively. "Chance did a number on her."

"We're *all* traumatized by what happened, Luna," Sarah reminded, opening the door of her SUV. "It's no excuse to be selfish. At the very least, she could've heard us out. She should want Chance stopped as much as we do. I mean, what's to stop him, *them,* from going after her if they kill us?"

"I know," Luna agreed, "but she doesn't know what else to do. Come on, Sarah, she's scared."

"Yeah? Well, that makes three of us."

Chapter Thirty-Five

SARAH DROPPED LUNA off near the front gate of the apartment complex and drove away. She was determined to dig up dirt on Chance's background and see if she could find more information about the men he was working with. They exchanged numbers, and Sarah promised she'd call the second she learned anything. Luna didn't hang too much hope on that. After the high school fiasco, Luna had done plenty of her own digging, but there wasn't much to find. The men after Chance kept low profiles.

Maybe Sarah would have more luck.

Notebook tucked neatly under her arm, Luna walked through the complex. She froze in her tracks when she spotted Amanda and Chance sitting on the porch, locked out of the apartment. Amanda spotted her first and stood. Something akin to anger flickered in Chance's eyes.

"Luna, where have you been?" Amanda asked, drawing her eyebrows together. "I was hella worried! You disappeared from the funeral, and no one seemed to know where you went."

"Don't worry about me. I've been to so many funerals, I think I'm almost a pro," Luna retorted, throwing a quick glare in Chance's direction. "I went to talk to somebody, is all."

Amanda's eyes flicked to the thick book under Luna's

arm, and a flutter of uncertainty ran across her face. "Who'd you talk to?"

"One of Max's relatives," she lied, and this time, she felt no guilt. It was getting easier to dupe her roommate.

Amanda opened her mouth, but Luna stepped past her onto the porch, fidgeting with the key in the lock.

"Funerals are always tough," Chance said in a mock sweet tone.

Luna glared at him. Before she could make a smart-ass retort, he stood and pulled her into his arms. The strength of his grip scared her. The smell of his cologne, the very same from high school, filled her nostrils, bathing her in the familiarity of her nightmares. In her head, it was easy to imagine blood covering his skin.

"See? Friends," he said pointedly to Amanda.

Luna struggled to break away and caught the evil, crooked grin Chance cast her way when he let go. She whipped the door open hard enough for the edge to catch him on the arm.

"Oops, my bad," she said in her own mock sweet tone.

Luna went inside and tossed the key on the counter. She headed to her room, sat on her bed and set the book beside her, then peeled off her shoes and tossed them toward the closet. Chance appeared in the doorway.

"What do you want?" she asked through gritted teeth as she pried a silver bracelet off her wrist.

"Where did you go today?" he asked, leaning against the doorframe, arms folded across his chest.

"If I didn't tell Amanda, I'm certainly not going to tell

you." She set the bangle on her dresser. "Besides, it's none of your business. *Amanda* is your business. Where is she anyway?" Luna asked with a flair of irritation. For having such a strong infatuation with him, Amanda didn't seem too worried about keeping an eye on his activities.

"She ran to the store."

Luna gulped, hoping he wouldn't be able to see how uncomfortable the two of them being completely alone made her. She hid it beneath a seething glare. "Then you should be there with her."

"Fine, don't answer my question. I have ways of finding out the truth."

"Good luck," Luna murmured. "I have a life that is not going to be controlled by you."

He continued, stepping closer to her. "That's what you think. I did it once, and I can do it again."

Luna curled her hands into fists, watching the corner of his lip lift into the slightest smirk. An instant trigger. Her system pumped full of adrenaline, and she launched herself at him, punching him in the face, chest, and anywhere else she could reach. He had an easy time deflecting most of her blows until her weight knocked him to the carpet. Luna continued the assault, pummeling any part of him within reach. Bruises blossomed on the sides of her fists, but she didn't stop. She couldn't.

Chance grabbed her wrists and slung her sideways. Her skull hit the floor with a *thump*. Black spots dotted her vision. Chance crawled on top of her, pinning her to the ground with his dagger to her throat.

"Heh." He used his free hand to swipe his multicolored hair out of his eyes. "You caught me off guard."

"Kill me if you're going to do it, you bastard," she dared him. Her hand wrapped around the blade so tightly that it sliced into her skin. She used to fear death, but maybe it would be the only way to feel peace. She'd see Max again. Violet. Her father. Maybe it wouldn't be so bad.

Chance leaned closer. Lips brushing hers, he whispered, "I'll pass, kitten." When she thought he'd back away, he kissed her, sliding his blade from her clenched fist at the same time. She gasped into his mouth, and he smiled. "You really think I'm going to kill you because you tell me to?"

"Sure. You seem good at taking orders."

Chance shifted backward onto his knees and pointed the knife at her. Her blood dripped along the edge. "You never cease to surprise me."

Luna sat up, wiping her mouth with the back of her hand. "Get out of my room before I find something else to hit you with."

"No, no. This is far too enjoyable for me. Fighting like this? Really brings me back to better times."

"Good for you," she said stiffly, studying the new slice across her palm.

"You know all about that, though, don't you, Luna? Physically, you might've left high school behind, but mentally, you're still there. In the exact place I left you."

Luna balled her bloody hand into a fist, hissing at the stab of pain. She focused on it, using it to center herself. He wanted a reaction. That was the point of this. She would give him none.

"While we're reminiscing, whatever happened to that little freak you used to talk to in study hall? I think its name was Amy."

"You have no right to talk about her."

Chance leaned closer, eyes sparkling with delight. "You went to see her today. You know where she is."

"Doesn't mean I'll tell you."

Chance's eyes lingered on the ugly wound on her palm. "No matter. The next time you visit her, I'll follow you."

"I'm not going to see her again," Luna said. She'd done all she could do as far as Amy was concerned, and after being thrown out twice, Luna had likely been blacklisted. There was no reason for her to go back. This way Amy would stay guarded in her ward. She would stay alive. *If I had avoided Max, would he still be alive too?* she couldn't help but wonder.

"Don't do that," Chance said, grabbing her chin. "Don't think about him when I'm right here."

The intrusion startled her. "How did you—"

"There's a look on your face when he's on your mind."

Luna closed her eyes, not wanting to see him. She wanted to drift far, far away into another life. A tear ran down her cheek, and she waited for Chance to say his piece. Instead, he grasped the back of her head and bent down as if he was going to kiss her. She turned her face away.

"Come now, don't be like that," he whispered in her ear. "You act like you want nothing to do with me, and yet, you have an entire scrapbook about me. Why would you make that if you didn't miss me? Miss *this*?"

Luna paled, meeting his gaze. Had he read it or had Amanda told him it existed? "For a long time, it was impossible to go back to normal. I kept reliving that night again and again. That was the only way to make sense of it."

The gentle grip on the back of her neck roughened, and Luna squeaked in surprised pain. "For a long time, I couldn't remember my own name."

"You took lives, Chance."

"At least you had people to lose in the first place," he said and let go.

"Not anymore."

"You have Amanda."

"No, I don't. Like Violet, you got in her head. She's not Amanda anymore." He was a disease infecting everyone he came into contact with. "You won. Is that what you want to hear?"

"I didn't win yet," he said, narrowing his eyes.

The hair on the back of her neck stood up, caught in a strange mix of fear and anger. She understood the meaning too well. Chance thought he had the world in the palm of his hand, that everyone and everything was putty.

Not me. Never me.

"Until you've walked in my shoes, you'll never understand. I wouldn't expect you to." There was a downturned curve to his lips she wasn't used to seeing.

She scoffed. "Good because how could I possibly understand a Satan-worshipping murderer?"

Chance waved a dismissive hand. "The Satan thing was a phase to test something. And it failed so, no, I'm not a *Satan-*

worshipper."

Luna shrugged, not convinced.

"*My point,*" he said exasperated, "is that everyone expects something from me, and no one wants to give back. So I taught myself that people are disposable to make that fact easier to swallow, but it's not."

"If you had feelings, you wouldn't be able to do the things you've done," Luna said.

Chance scoffed. "You'd think, right? But no. Things have never been black and white to me. I've been in your shoes, but I figured out how to prosper from it."

Luna couldn't fathom a reply. Her worst enemy was pouring his heart out. It should be a moment of triumph, but she felt nothing. Chance waited for a response, and when he didn't get one, he tucked his dagger away and left the room. The *click* of the front door reminded her of Amanda's absence. Was she finally home or had Chance decided to leave? Luna hid her notebook under the mattress, then made her way down the hall to find out.

Amanda glanced at her from behind the kitchen counter, but Chance, seated by the window in the living room, kept his gaze trained on the television. Luna ignored them both as she rummaged through the fridge. While Luna poured herself a glass of orange juice, Amanda approached her, eyes on her hand.

"What's that?" she asked.

Most of the blood had dried to a thin crust on her palm and wrist, making the wound appear to be much worse than it actually was. Luna held it up, then let it drop back to her side. "I broke a cup."

Amanda cast a subtle glance over her shoulder at Chance. Did she connect the dots? The expression vanished, and she grabbed a dish towel, leading Luna to the sink. "Let's get this cleaned up."

Luna didn't have the energy to protest.

"So much blood," Amanda murmured. "You didn't . . . do this to yourself, right?"

Luna watched the water run red, too drained to be annoyed.

"You need to get out of the house for a bit," Amanda said as she dried Luna's hand. "Let's go. We can grab a bite or walk around the mall and talk."

"I don't know, Mandy. I'm tired," Luna protested, ripping her hand away as if Amanda's touch was poison.

"You're always tired or busy when I ask to hang out. Stop making excuses and spend some time with me, please? I think it'll do us some good. If anything, it will take your mind off things."

"Is now really the best time to do this? I'm still wearing my funeral clothes."

Amanda pursed her lips. "I know you're avoiding me, Luna, but I'm trying to be your friend. You need someone to lean on, and you're never going to get better by pushing everyone else away."

Luna puffed her cheeks in frustration. Couldn't Amanda take a hint? She was pushing *herself* away. Luna didn't give two shits about bonding with her at this point, but she was always up for a distraction from herself. "Okay, okay. We'll go, but no *Malcolm*, please."

At the sound of his fake name, Chance side-eyed her, but Luna ignored him. Amanda stuck out her hand, oblivious to their exchange. "Deal."

Luna returned the handshake, but in her head, she screamed. Emotionally, she was shot. She didn't want to be around other people, certainly not a bunch of strangers, but Amanda didn't sense the dread that clung to her. Amanda didn't sense any of that. She grinned and grabbed her keys off the counter, nearly giddy as she led the way to the front door. Luna couldn't understand the reaction as she followed with unsettling déjà vu.

"I'll be back in an hour or two, sweetheart," she said to Chance, giving him a peck on the cheek.

He hugged her. "Okay, I'll be here," he said, staring at Luna over Amanda's shoulder.

Luna walked out the door, not waiting for Amanda to catch up. Her friend was all too happy to yap the entire drive to the mall, catching Luna up on all three of her sisters. Luna mostly blocked it out, instantly overstimulated by the over-packed parking lot. The feeling of doom increased when they went into the first dress store they saw. Amanda thrust a pile of colorful fabrics into Luna's arms, then pointed her in the direction of the dressing room.

Luna closed her eyes and sat on the small bench as she composed herself. In her head, she was seventeen, Susan dressing her for prom. Luna glanced at the array of gowns Amanda had given her, intentionally avoiding the yellow one. With a sigh, she grabbed a purple sundress and threw it on, not bothering to glance at her reflection. She didn't care how she looked. The important parts of her, the places where the light used to be, were gone now anyway.

She went to find Amanda. Her blonde friend was admiring a blue gown and Luna felt sick, once again seeing Susan in her likeness. The next hour was a blur. Amanda tried on dresses and shirts and jeans and bought an armful of clothes for both of them. Luna kept her head down as she followed her friend to the car. The only part of the trip Luna enjoyed was the sensation of peace that settled between them. Once they were back inside the apartment, it vanished.

"Hey, honey," Chance called over his shoulder, eyes trained on the television. Luna wondered which of them his greeting was really intended for.

"I missed you," Amanda gushed.

Luna rolled her eyes as Amanda handed her a colorful armful of ridiculous clothes she'd never wear. Amanda went to sit beside Chance, and Luna disappeared into her room, tossing them atop a rainbow pile on her closet floor.

There was no place in her life for pretty things. If there was, it was only for them to be destroyed.

Chapter Thirty-Six

CHANCE SAT IN the dark living room, eyes on the television though his mind was everywhere else. Amanda was fast asleep in bed, and he was relieved. He should've felt bad, considering it was the cocktail of pills he'd slipped into her drink at dinner that had knocked her out. Rather, he was focused on his own exhaustion and tried hard not to give in to it.

He wasn't sure how long he had before Cody would come knocking for answers; he wasn't known for his patience. Chance had made quick work of getting rid of Max, but Amy was proving to be harder. He couldn't find her, and Luna wasn't going to help him.

Chance thought over his conversation with her again. Would there have been a better way to get the information he needed? He cringed every time he remembered the way he'd opened up and still got shut down.

Embarrassing, he chided himself. Then, in an attempt to rationalize his own behavior, *Someone deserves to know the whole story.*

Wearing his heart on his sleeve wasn't something he'd ever done, and he didn't like how it made him feel. Vulnerable. Small. *Human.*

This place was starting to make him feel like a caged animal. If the police didn't get him, Cody and his minions would.

Chance had been able to fool Luna about how much danger he was in, but it wasn't an act he'd be able to maintain forever. Sooner or later, he'd disappear from this life crafted on a fake foundation, and there was still so much unresolved between the two of them.

Scuffling in the kitchen made him jump. Luna had emerged from her room to scrounge up a bowl of cereal. "Wow, I barely ever see you eat," he said as he approached her from the darkness. "What's the occasion?"

Her hand quivered as she poured the milk, splashing some onto the table. "Damn it," she said to herself, then glanced up at him. "Are you always here?"

"Amanda lets me crash when I need to."

"Which is always because you don't have a place to go," she said, mopping up the mess with a nearby rag.

"I do. I just find it more comforting to stay here. In case you need me," he said, grinning.

"Yeah, okay," Luna replied, picking up her bowl, ready to disappear back into her room again.

"Wait," Chance said on instinct. He didn't have a real reason to say it other than the simple fact that he didn't want her to go.

Luna surprised them both by obeying. "What?"

"What did Max tell the cops about what happened in the woods?" he asked, hoping she couldn't tell how desperate he was to know.

"You could've asked him that yourself if you didn't kill him," Luna snapped.

Chance bit his lip. *I had that coming.* "Max never told you the truth, huh? That me and him have a bit of a *history.*"

"We *all* have history. We've been caught up in each other's lives since elementary school," she said, wrinkling her face as if the fact was sour candy.

She wasn't wrong, of course, but she had no idea how deep the rabbit hole went. Chance almost felt sorry for her.

"While we're here, asking each other ridiculous questions, I've got one for you," she said. "Why aren't you in jail?"

The smirk fell from his face.

"Cops suspect you over and over, but they never arrest you. Why is that?"

"DreamWorld is an amazing place," he said, spewing the first lie that came to mind. "I kill for it, and in exchange, I get protection." That was *almost* true except it wasn't DreamWorld that had his back.

It was Cody. Always had been.

"All the cops had to do was match Max's and Violet's bullets to your gun. Your fingerprints were all over it."

"Police never found the gun, apparently."

"It disappeared?"

"That's one way to put it."

"What? You think *I* took it?" she asked, gesturing to herself with a stunned raise of her eyebrows. "You have to be kidding me."

No, but I know someone who would. "I wasn't pointing fingers. I'm saying someone did."

"Maybe you have a friend after all," Luna said, "but it's

not me." With that, she disappeared down the dark hallway.

Chance watched her go. He had expected as much. In three years, plenty of people had the opportunity to move the gun, many of them on his behalf. Luna would be as clueless as he was. He listened for sounds of life somewhere deeper in the apartment. When he was sure she wouldn't come back, he ruffled his hair and gazed at the rumpled blanket on the couch.

The exhaustion was growing heavier. Desperate to fight it, he paced the living room, debating what to do. Should he bite the bullet and come clean to Cody about his lack of luck in getting his assignment done?

That's a terrible idea. He shut it down as he wandered into the kitchen.

A hint of Luna's perfume lingered in the air, and he took a deep breath, filling his lungs with it. He thought of the night he'd slept in her bed. The way her warm body had felt pressed against him.

She doesn't understand how much I need her and how much she needs me. If he failed, Cody wouldn't only come after him, he would send men after Luna as well. Likely Amanda, too, just to leave no loose ends.

Like it or not, Luna was *his.* He needed to cement that fact. Tiptoeing down the hall, he pushed open her door.

"What do you want?" she snapped from the darkness.

He didn't answer. *That* mind was taking over, the predator in him picking out her silhouette in the weak moonlight streaming through the cracks in her blinds. He took two steps into the room and closed the door behind him, submerging them both in darkness.

"Where did you go?" Luna asked in a quick breath of air.

Fear. He could hear it, and the predator in him stirred as he climbed onto the edge of her mattress.

She sat up and shrieked, "Get out!"

"No," he replied, calmly, gently, as if they were playing a game.

"Amanda!" Luna yelled.

"She's sleeping, kitten," Chance said, almost amused.

"Amanda!" Luna howled again.

Chance lunged forward, grabbing the back of her head with one hand and slapping his palm over her mouth with the other. "I promise she won't hear you," he whispered in her ear. "And why would you want her to? Didn't I warn you what would happen should she learn too much about you and me?"

Luna fell silent, and Chance was proud.

"Come here," he said, shifting his hands to her waist to pull her against himself. "I want to be close to you for a while."

"No, let go!" she demanded, and grabbed the edge of her mattress, trying to pull herself free.

"*Shh*," he said, grip tightening as he tried to pull her into his embrace, to hold her the way he had after her night terror fit.

"No!" she cried out.

Tension crept into his spine. Why wouldn't she relax? He was being as gentle as he could manage. He slapped his hand over her mouth to cut off the sound of her screams, already tired of the struggle. "Yes. You mean to say *yes.*"

"N-no."

He grasped her jaw so tightly her eyes began to water. "Say it."

She stayed quiet, so he nodded her head slightly with the hand pinched across her face.

"Yes," she then squeaked.

Chance's shoulders slumped with relief as the fight left her body. He tried again to pull her to him, and this time was greeted with success. She was rail thin, her nervous tremors almost violent. He pulled her closer, dipping his nose into her raven hair to breathe in the scent.

"I'm not going to hurt you," he whispered, running his fingers through her hair. He wanted *more* of her, *all* of her.

The second he finished speaking, she tried to bolt. He grabbed her, pinning her to the bed, and crawled on top of her. They were so close he could feel the heat radiating off her skin through her nightgown.

She met his eyes, and he pressed his lips to hers. She punched at him, screams muffled by his mouth over hers. The longer she screamed, the more violently he kissed her, biting down on her bottom lip until he tasted blood.

"*Shh*," he said again, fingers stroking the side of her face when he finally pulled back. "Just stop fighting."

Her pupils were blown, blood dotting her bottom lip, but she didn't waste the opportunity to aim another blow at his face. He'd been ready for it and caught both of her delicate wrists, pinning them to either side of her.

"Let me go," she insisted, glaring up at him through the shadows. "You have no right."

"I've *earned* the right," he growled.

Terror filled her eyes before he kissed her. She tried to scream. Paranoid Amanda would hear, he let go of one of her wrists, wrapping his hand around her throat. He pressed until she gagged, choking for breath. Using the moment of distraction, he sat up and slid his shirt off before he lightened the hold enough for her to take a breath. When their lips met again, she used her free hand to grab a handful of his hair, yanking as hard as she could. He pulled back and growled.

"This has been a long time coming," he said and recaptured her hand. "So you might as well stop fighting."

He adjusted his grip so both of her wrists were in one of his hands. His other hand trailed down her side to rest on her hip, using his knees to open her legs.

"Don't do this. Please," Luna begged, tears streaming down her face.

Chance clamped his palm to her face. She continued to struggle, but it was easy for him to pretend she wasn't, that she was writhing in pleasure. Luna tried to buck him off, the gesture only succeeding in bringing their bodies closer together, and he groaned. His free hand fumbled clumsily with his belt; the sound of clanking metal filled the room.

"Relax," he said as he snagged it out of his belt loops and snaked it around her wrists. "You'll enjoy it."

He sat back, admiring his work as he pulled his pants and boxers off. Being completely naked so close to the object of his obsession brought its own level of excitement. Luna kicked at him, and when she realized he was too far away to hit, she opened her mouth, ready for another scream. He pounced, clamping his hand down tight. The sound she made as the hope left her was a terrified whimper, muffled by the wad of bedsheet he managed to cram into her mouth.

Subdued, he sat back for a moment, taking the opportunity to look her over. He trailed his hand down her thigh, letting his nails dig in when she started to fight again, forcing her to still before he yanked her nightgown up to expose her stomach and panties. Arousal made it hard to focus as his fingers skirted across her skin, exploring every inch of her. He paused briefly to finger the scar on her stomach—his mark.

"Stop . . . please . . ." she whimpered against the makeshift gag.

"Not until I've had my fill," he said, voice emotionless as he dipped his hand lower, grasping the silky fabric of her panties.

With a quick flick of his wrist, he tore them off. Luna must've sensed her words would do no good because she said nothing, biting harder on the gag. The moonlight reflected off the copious tears running down her cheeks. He reached up to thumb the liquid away before he lined himself up with her entrance. Without so much as a warning, he pushed himself inside her. Both gasped—one in pleasure and one in pain. Chance's eyes rolled back in his head, and he barely heard Luna underneath him as he worked himself in and out of her. Once he caught her staring up at him, eyes haunted and glossed over with tears.

"Just remember . . ." he panted between thrusts, "that this . . . is your . . . fault."

Not too long after that, he brought himself to climax,

releasing his semen inside her. A second later, he collapsed onto the bed beside her, resting the side of his head on her chest. Sweat matted the hair to his forehead as he peered up, uncertain what expression he'd find on Luna's face. Her eyes were closed, and he sat up. Her eyes fluttered open when he pulled the gag from her mouth.

She didn't move beneath him, and he studied her warily, expecting her to scream for help. Her teary eyes stayed on the ceiling.

"I'm going to untie you now," he said, bringing his mouth close to the side of her face. "Nothing stupid, right?"

She didn't respond, and he tugged the belt loose. It slumped to the floor with a muffled *clang*, and Luna pulled her arms down to her sides. Chance was ready for her to try and hit him again, but she didn't seem to notice he was there anymore. She pulled her nightgown down to cover her intimate parts and turned onto her side, facing away from him.

"Hey, come here," he said, and reached for her, bringing her into the curve of his body.

She didn't resist. He held her tight, wishing he never had to let go.

Chapter Thirty-Seven

NIGHT BLED INTO morning. Pale rays of dawn spilled through Luna's window, casting a cruel light on the dark smears of blood staining her pink blanket. She didn't so much wake as *drift* back into herself. Her face was raw and swollen from silently crying, every inch of her aching with a deep heaviness, her lower body especially. She blinked slowly, eyes fluttering open to glance warily across the bed. Chance was gone.

Luna curled her hands into tight fists, but the tears refused to come. All that remained was emptiness. She folded herself into a tight embrace, a stranger trapped inside her own skin. Her wrists and thighs were marked with angry red gashes and bruises.

Every time she closed her eyes, she could see him looming over her, his rage a cage tightening around her. A shiver of disgust crawled through her, though not at herself for not escaping or at him for the horrors he'd inflicted, but for what he'd forced her to endure during the night.

When she finally stood, the slickness between her legs became apparent. Horror crashed over her in a tidal wave of shame and despair. She nearly screamed but swallowed it down, terrified he might return, or worse, that Amanda might walk in and see her like this at her absolute lowest.

Where did *he go?*

She scanned the room, expecting him to emerge from the shadows. When she concluded that she was indeed alone, she bolted to the bathroom and slammed the door behind her, locking it. On autopilot, she turned on the tap and stripped off her nightgown. She didn't want to face herself in the mirror but couldn't help a glance as she passed it on the way to the shower. A dark bruise bloomed across her left cheek. Her lips were swollen, scratched raw from his bites.

She forced herself under the scalding water, letting it wash away the grime and filth he'd left on her skin, taking the smell of him with it. When the water finally cooled, she climbed out, trembling, and dressed quickly before fleeing back to her room.

From the doorway, the bloodstains on her sheets were impossible to ignore. A low, trembling whimper escaped her throat as she gathered every item he had touched—blankets, sheets, even the pillowcase—torn between burning them and washing them. She wanted to take it all to the police, but the memory of that cold interrogation room, the officer's pity and disbelief, stopped her. What if no one believed her *again?*

Mechanically, she threw everything into the washing machine, her mind shutting down as it whirred to life. She didn't dwell on what it meant to wash away the evidence. She sank to the cold stone floor of the laundry room, staring blankly at nothing.

Sex wasn't something she thought about often, but she hadn't imagined this to be how her first time would go. She had pictured it with Max, in a world filled with trust and warmth, not fear and violence.

Time slipped away from her, unmeasured and cruel, lost in the void of her thoughts. The hum of the dryer was the only sound anchoring her to reality. The sharp *beep* at the end of the cycle jolted her back to the present. It took every ounce of strength just to stand, gather the linens, and drag herself away.

Steeling her face, she entered the apartment. There was no one present as she went down the hall to her room. Autopilot stayed as she went through the process of redressing her bed. Her hands worked with quiet precision, but her mind was trapped elsewhere. When she stepped back and looked, it wasn't the crisp, clean surface she saw. In her mind's eye, the stains lingered. The ghost of last night clung to every thread, haunting her with what had been done, and what she had survived.

After that, Luna found herself shaking so hard she was barely able to down a glass of orange juice without dropping it.

Amanda was the first person Luna saw that morning. She wanted so badly to run to her, to hug her, to let out what had happened, but this Amanda wasn't the friend she remembered. She was a stranger. So Luna sat quietly at the kitchen table, eyes fixed on her empty glass, mind racing to devise a way to retreat into her room now that she'd been seen.

"Morning," Amanda greeted cheerfully, brewing herself a pot of coffee. "You're up early."

"Yeah, I uh . . ." She didn't know how to finish the sentence. She stood abruptly, placing the glass in the sink with a *clink*. "I couldn't sleep."

"Insomnia's a bitch."

Luna nodded silently, biting her nails, each tiny crunch a

desperate attempt to ground herself. "Is uh . . . is Malcolm—"

A low voice cut in from behind Amanda. "I'm here."

Luna squeezed her eyes shut, willing her panic, her pain, to stay hidden beneath a calm façade. Chance breezed past her on his way to Amanda and gave her a quick kiss. Luna recoiled, unable to take her eyes off him. He was shirtless, and in the bright fluorescent lights, she swore she could make out the purple-blue hue of a few bruises across his chest.

Amanda glanced at Luna, confusion knitting her brow. "He's here. Why do you ask?"

"I— I—" Luna stammered, words failing her.

A cruel smile twisted Chance's lips as he watched her struggle. Then, with a slow, deliberate motion, he pointed to the back of Amanda's head and drew his finger across his throat. A silent, chilling threat.

"It was . . . quiet, is all. I didn't think you guys were home," Luna said, her voice barely steady. "Well, if it's all right with you, I think I'm gonna try to get some sleep."

"But—" Amanda started, but Luna was already turning away.

Jogging down the hall, Luna's heartbeat echoed in her ears. She slammed her bedroom door, a small victory. There was no lock on it, and she wished there was. It would've solved so many problems. Part of her braced for Amanda to come after her, to demand answers or drag her back out. But the silence stayed and relief washed over her. She sank to the floor, her eyes fixed on the bed she wanted to burn to ashes.

For everything Chance had ever done, everything he'd

promised, she didn't know why she thought it would end with a quick death. Chance hadn't just wanted to break her body. He wanted to break her *soul*.

I'm not going to be a victim, she vowed. The words burned inside her, fierce and unyielding. A mantra. *He will not break me.*

She picked herself up, every movement trembling but determined, and dressed quickly. The weight of the day ahead pressed down on her as she left the apartment, resolved to find strength in the only place she still trusted: her mother's arms.

***

AFTER EATING DINNER and spending some quality time with Rose, Luna fell asleep in her old room. When she woke, panic blurred her memories. It was like the past three years had never happened, and she was a teenager again. Wide-eyed, she hurried out to the hall, nearly bumping into her mother. Half of Rose's coffee splashed over the side of her mug and onto the floor.

"Whoa, careful," she chided, wiping at a dark splotch of coffee on her robe. "Everything all right?"

Luna calmed as the dream faded and reality set in. She was an adult. She was with her mother. She was, for the time being, safe. "Yeah, I . . . had a nightmare, is all."

"*Ya asal*," Rose said, wrapping Luna into a hug with the hand not holding the mug. "I can make you some breakfast if you're hungry."

Luna stepped out of the embrace and shook her head, grateful her mother didn't ask for details. "I think I should be getting back. I've got work in a few hours, and Amanda will probably be mad that I've kept her car this long." She didn't add how she'd taken it without permission. She'd been so desperate to get away, she decided it was one of those times to do the thing and ask for forgiveness later.

"Of course," Rose said, resuming her trip down the hall.

Luna stepped outside, the cool morning air brushing against her skin as she walked to Amanda's car. The drive back to Bowling Green seemed longer than usual. Shadows from the passing trees danced across the windshield, mirroring the weight settling deep in her chest. She had planned to drop the car off first, but the thought of returning to the apartment churned her stomach. Bypassing it altogether, the familiar hum of the road carried her straight to work.

Keeping busy was good for her mind, and she was okay until break time came. Then she was left to face her thoughts on her own. Sarah sat down at the table, startling her back to reality.

"Are you okay? You've been quiet today," she said.

Luna stared down at the dark liquid in her cup. It was either cola or root beer, she wasn't sure. In her daze, she couldn't remember which button she'd pressed. "I'm fine."

Sarah wasn't convinced. Her eyes searched Luna's face, gentle but unwavering. "You're clearly not."

Luna bit her tongue, tasting the bitter edge of tears she refused to let fall. "Have you . . . found anything out?"

Sarah sighed. "No, nothing yet. I've narrowed down a few possible connections but nothing concrete."

Luna nodded. That was the answer she expected.

"Did Chance do something?"

Sarah's question landed softly, but it cracked something open inside her. She clenched her fists under the table, knuckles white, struggling to hold herself together. "It's been tough the past few days," Luna admitted.

A flicker of sympathy crossed Sarah's face. "If you want a friend, you can always crash at my place."

Luna's eyebrows shot up. Why would Sarah make such a generous offer? Would she be expected to do something to pay her back? "Really? You wouldn't mind?"

Sarah's brow furrowed in confusion, as if Luna's hesitation was foreign to her. "Why would I? I wouldn't want to stay somewhere Chance visits either." Her hand reached across the table, warm and steady, capturing Luna's. "As long as I'm around, consider me your escape."

Chapter Thirty-Eight

WHEN THEIR SHIFTS ended, Luna followed Sarah home. She could've felt bad that she'd held her roommate's car hostage for a full day now, but Amanda had only tried to call once so it seemed she wasn't that worried about it. Luna pushed away her concerns and parked beside Sarah in a crammed lot.

She lived in a tiny studio apartment, which meant Luna would either have to sleep on the couch or the floor. She was content either way. Both options were better than her own bed. She and Sarah stayed up until midnight, talking.

Then Luna's pager beeped. Amanda's number popped up on the screen, and Luna curled her lip at it. She'd anticipated this but thought Amanda would've waited until the morning to try calling again.

"Who is it?" Sarah asked.

"Amanda."

"Ignore it. If she asks tomorrow, tell her you were asleep and didn't hear it go off."

Those were reasonable words that Luna was tempted to go along with. But her shoulders slumped with guilt. "I've had her car for so long, she's probably furious. I took it without asking."

Understanding washed over Sarah's face. Hesitantly, she

said, "I have a phone in the kitchen you can use."

"Thanks," Luna murmured and wandered into the tiny, boxlike space that was little more than a counter and a fridge to dial Amanda's number.

The line clicked as someone answered, and she launched into apologies. "Hey, Mandy, I—"

"Not Amanda, darling," Chance's silky purr poured through the earpiece.

Luna's mouth went dry. Sarah's eyes doubled in size as she leaned closer, listening in. "Where's Amanda?"

"She's here. Perfectly fine . . . for now," he said casually.

"You better not hurt her," Luna said, grip tightening around the phone.

"I won't," he started, "if you come home. I miss you."

"Don't do it," Sarah whispered.

Immediately after Chance said, "The decision is yours," he hung up.

Luna stared at the dead phone.

"Obviously, you can't go," Sarah insisted.

Luna put the phone back on the base. "Amanda is in danger. I can't just do nothing."

Sarah grabbed Luna's wrist. "She's in danger even if you do go. You can't listen to him."

Luna blinked her wet eyes. "What's the alternative? Stand by and watch him hurt someone else I love?"

Sarah's face fell. "I don't know, but I don't like this."

"Trust me, neither do I."

Sarah huffed. "If you're determined to go, then I'm

coming with you."

Luna opened her mouth to protest, but Sarah said, "I can't leave you in that situation with him. I didn't see the signs with Susan, and that cost her her life. What kind of person would I be to blatantly let something like that happen again?"

Normally, Luna wasn't a hugger—she despised any kind of physical contact—but she couldn't stop herself from wrapping Sarah in a tight hug. "Thank you," she said into her bright blonde hair.

"Of course." Sarah snagged her keys off the counter. "Let's do this."

As Luna climbed into Amanda's car, the hair stood up on the back of her neck, sensing danger. She felt a bit better not being alone, but if Chance was going to snap, Sarah wouldn't be able to stop him any better than Luna could. They were both small women, thin and dainty.

Still, two is better than one. She held onto that thought as she made her way to the complex.

Sarah parked beside Amanda's car and met Luna on the sidewalk. When she hesitated to walk the path to the door, Sarah stood quietly beside her, giving her time to gather herself.

"You've got this," she encouraged when Luna finally started to lead the way.

Luna devoured the words, hoping they would give her strength, but the closer she got to the front door, the more her legs began to shake. What was she *doing* here? Why had she thought this was a good idea?

She turned to Sarah. Her ice-blue eyes were wide with

understanding. *She believes in me*, Luna told herself. *I need to believe in myself.*

When Luna opened the door, she expected to see Chance and Amanda curled up on the couch, but her roommate was nowhere in sight. Chance was. He'd been in the middle of pacing the living room when the door opened, his blue eyes wide and wild.

He shoved away the bewilderment and smiled politely at Sarah as if she were an old friend of his. She was not. "Well, isn't this a pleasant surprise, Sarah. It's been a long time."

An animalistic expression washed over her face. The patient kindness that had been there only thirty seconds before disappeared behind a dark, black hatred. "Not long enough."

"Well, I'd ask where you've been, but I see now," he said to Luna.

Luna tried to shoulder her way past him. "Where's Amanda?"

He held his hand out, blocking her path. "What have you two been up to?"

"None of your business," Sarah snarked, giving him the bitchiest grin she could muster as she smacked his hand away.

Luna took the opportunity to dart down the hall. Chance followed closely behind as Luna approached Amanda's room and eased the door open.

"Stop looking at me like that. Amanda's fine," Chance said, rolling his eyes when Sarah glowered at him.

Luna peeked inside, making out the familiar shape of her friend on the bed. A loud snore announced that she was still breathing.

Chance raised an eyebrow. "Satisfied?"

She was. For now, Amanda was accounted for, and the world seemed a little easier to manage. Luna exchanged a glance with Sarah. "My room's this way."

Chance stayed by the entrance of Amanda's room, watching the girls enter Luna's room.

Sarah took satisfaction in slamming the door. "I can see why you don't want to stay here. He's such a creep."

"That's one word for it."

With a sigh, Sarah plopped down in the chair in front of Luna's desk. Then she stared at the bed. Luna followed her line of sight. She'd honed in on a ruddy splotch on her pink blanket— the remnant of a stubborn bloodstain that hadn't washed out completely.

"What happened?" she asked. But judging by the look in her eyes, Luna sensed that she already knew.

"I . . . don't want to talk about it."

"Ah," Sarah said, eyeing the stain again.

"Can you . . . stay here tonight?"

"I already planned on it." Sarah tossed her coat onto the desk. "I don't mind sleeping on the floor."

"You don't have to do that," Luna said. "The bed is big enough for both of us." She didn't mention that Sarah's presence there would provide a safeguard in case Chance decided to creep into her room anyway.

"If you insist," Sarah said, pulling off her shoes. She climbed into bed, and Luna did the same.

They were both such small women that with both of them under the covers, there was still plenty of room. When Luna was about to fall asleep, Sarah inched closer, snuggling against her. A sheen came over Luna's eyes. Not from sadness. But from gratitude. For the first time in her life, someone had stood up for her. And she had no idea how she would ever pay Sarah back for all she'd done.

Chapter Thirty-Nine

IN THE MORNING, the two friends left the apartment together and went back to Sarah's until it was time for work. Sarah gave Luna a ride, hanging around the restaurant prior to the time to clock in, and Luna did the same until it was time for her to clock out. At the end of the day, they went back to Sarah's to start the process again. They spent the next few days like that, and Luna started to relax a bit, finding comfort in the new routine. Amanda called a few times, but Luna ignored them all. She had returned Amanda's car, so there was no reason to answer. With Sarah, Luna felt protected from everything: from Chance, from the men he worked with, from Amanda's coldness. *Everything*.

Then the day came that Sarah wasn't scheduled to work when Luna was. It was the first time she'd had to go out solo in nearly three weeks, and she barely thought herself capable of it.

Despite being surrounded by people, Luna felt alone. After the lunch rush died, she decided to sweep around the counter, hoping the mindless labor would be enough of a distraction for a while. And it was, until she spotted the man by the window. A man with blond hair tinged with a blackness that rivaled her own. He wore a simple white tank top and heavy blue jeans instead of his usual all-black attire. Everything Chance wore tended to have a classic goth vibe to it, and although she'd never seen him in normal clothes, there was no mistaking him.

He sipped on a cup without a lid, staring out the window. How had he slipped in without her noticing? Feeling someone looking at him, he glanced at her. When their eyes met, he dropped his cup, everything moving in slow motion as dark pop seeped across the floor.

"Luna! What are you waiting for? Clean up that spill!" her boss yelled, tossing a mop to her.

Swallowing hard, Luna moved from behind the counter. As she neared the mess, everything in her peripheral vision went fuzzy, her vision narrowing to the spill and the man she'd tried so hard to avoid. She kept her gaze fixed on the floor as she pressed the mophead down.

"Working hard, Luna?" he asked as she smeared the liquid around.

It didn't occur to her that she was having a panic attack until she found it difficult to draw in a breath. The mop slid from her hands, and her vision blurred. Was she going to faint? She kept her focus on the discarded tool at her feet, breathing through her nose.

"Aren't you afraid Amanda will see you here? She bent down to grab the mop.

"I honestly don't care. I'm not trying to hide." His black boots thudded on the floor as he slipped from the chair to crouch beside her. "You've been doing a good job of that, though." His voice was soothing, as if he were trying to be gentle, and that left her feeling worse.

"Why are you bothering me at work?" she asked, clutching

the mop handle tight. If she had to, she would use it to put distance between them.

"It's been hard to see you at home," he said, reaching out to tuck a strand of hair behind her ear. "You're always with that bitch now. What is she to you?"

"The only friend I've got."

"Oh, come now. You enjoy my company."

"Life was good without you in it," she said, rising to her feet. If there weren't so many witnesses, she would've kicked him in the face.

Chance smiled, a boyish grin that didn't match the tone of their serious conversation, as he rose to his full height. "You've missed me too. I know you have. Even if you hate me, I'll live in your mind forever."

"Shove off already."

His smile gave way to a grimace. "I've done everything to gain your affection, but none of it is good enough. Tell me what is!" he demanded, looming above her.

A man at the next table eyed him, chewing a bite of his burger slowly as if he debated whether or not to come to Luna's defense.

"Are you kidding?" Luna scoffed.

"Aren't you curious about the DreamWorld stuff at all? What it can do? What *we* can do?" he asked, ignoring her question. She huffed and started to walk away. Chance grabbed her elbow, fingers digging into her skin as he stopped her. "Don't ignore me, Luna. You remember what happened the last time you did."

There it was: he was jeering about Max's death. She'd

wondered how long it would take for him to rip at that wound.

"How dare you! He was my best friend, and you took him from me."

"Yeah, you two had a real *special* bond, huh?" Chance seethed.

"It's none of your business what we were. He's gone because of you."

"Apparently, the only way I can get your attention is by doing the extreme."

"You don't want to do this here," Luna said, jabbing him in the ribs with the mop to put space between them. "There are witnesses."

Chance smirked. "Trust me, doll, I know."

If she had any hint of luck, Amanda would walk through the door and see her "boyfriend" manhandling her roommate, then break up with him on the spot.

Luna had no such luck.

Chance rested his hands on the tops of her arms. She glared into his eyes, fantasizing about slapping him across the face. If she had been anywhere else, she would've done it. He smirked in that predatory way, as if reading her thoughts. Luna struggled against his viselike grip, and when she couldn't free herself, hot, humiliated tears threatened to drip from her eyes. She didn't want Chance to see her cry. Not again anyway.

"Let go of me, or I swear I'll scream," she whispered, words burning as she forced them through her tight throat.

Dramatically, he released one finger at a time. "As you wish."

She hurried to the counter, covering her face with her hand to hide from her coworkers. The girl working the register watched her curiously, but Luna didn't have it in her to field any questions. The thought of being around people seemed suddenly too much. What would it take to get her boss to send her home for the day?

She considered calling Amanda so she could come and catch Chance in the act, but stopped herself. It would change nothing. If Amanda *did* come, he'd make up an excuse and she'd believe him.

No matter what Chance did, he would always get away with it.

Chapter Forty

THOUGH THE LAST thing Chance felt was cheer after the encounter with Luna in the restaurant, he kept it on his face when he got back to the apartment. When Amanda finally fell asleep that night, he let the expression drop. How much longer would he have to keep up this act?

Things weren't exactly working in his favor. He wandered down the hall and pushed open the door to Luna's room, staring at the empty bed. He'd put himself in this situation to be closer to her, and now she was gone again.

Cornering her at work had been his last resort. He needed her to understand that being safe from him didn't necessarily mean she was out of danger. Three weeks, and he'd made no progress with Amy. Until she was dealt with, Luna was in danger no matter where they both were.

Chance didn't want to play this game anymore. He wanted to take Luna and move far away. Somewhere Cody would never be able to find them. Except that place didn't exist. He had eyes everywhere. Chance reached up to run his fingers through his hair, hating that he'd been reduced to this person. This freeloader who had nothing to offer and no one to lean on.

I need a new plan, he thought.

He'd work on that tomorrow. In the meantime, he needed

to get some real sleep. He couldn't remember the last time he'd gotten a full eight hours, and it was taking a toll on him. For one night, he'd have to accept the risk of encountering Cody's men on the Other Side. He lay in bed beside Amanda and fell asleep. When he woke to see familiar forest-green eyes, the first word out of his mouth was "Fuck." Cody had given him time, as promised, and he would want results. Nothing else would pacify him.

"What's the matter? Not happy to see me?" Cody asked, raising his eyebrows tauntingly.

Chance scowled.

"You're not adjusting back into the world too well, it seems."

Chance quirked an eyebrow, trying, and failing, not to let Cody see how much he got under his skin. "That'll take *time*, remember?"

"You've had that. Nearly an entire month. What have you been doing with the gift I've given you?"

"I've managed one Keeper so far," Chance reminded him, putting his best foot forward.

"So you've said. What's kept you from getting the second one?" Cody asked, irritated.

The last thing Chance wanted to do was admit that he didn't know where Amy was. He'd been able to find traces of her in DreamWorld, but with limited magic, it didn't help him much.

Cody continued. "It seems to me that you have too many *distractions* keeping you from your mission." He tilted his head to the side, eyes narrowed to peer into the depths of Chance's soul . . . whatever was left of one anyway. That was probably why the others listened to him so well. Though he was young and wasn't *technically* in charge yet, there was something deeply unsettling in his eyes. An unhinged type of evil waiting for the smallest excuse to be set free. "But not to worry. We have a way of handling those."

The slight smirk on Cody's face told Chance everything he needed to know. It was a threat. But to him or to Luna, he couldn't be sure.

"That's not necessary," Chance said, trying not to let his panic show. If Cody picked up on any of it, things would only get worse. "I'll do what you asked me to do. I just need more time."

"For your sake, that better be true."

Chapter Forty-One

WHEN LUNA'S SHIFT ended, she called Sarah to pick her up. Sarah's voice came through, distant, distracted. She was on the other side of town running errands and wouldn't be there for at least an hour. For as much as Luna wanted to mention Chance's visit, she bit it back and muttered, "Okay" before she hung up. Anxiously, she ordered a side of fries and chewed on them mindlessly, the greasy comfort doing little to soothe the tight knot in her stomach.

The walls felt too small, too confining. What if Chance knew what time she got off? What if he came back before Sarah pulled up? She couldn't shake the fear that any second now, he'd walk through that door, his presence looming over her again.

By the time Sarah eased into the lot, Luna was nearly on the brink of a panic attack. She rushed to the car, the cool air outside a sharp contrast to the stifling fear inside the restaurant. Sliding into the passenger seat, Luna exhaled deeply, her muscles finally beginning to relax though her mind still raced with the what-ifs.

As Sarah made her way out of the parking lot, she side-eyed her. "What happened?"

Luna blinked, trying to clear her vision. She didn't want to tell her about the encounter with Chance, even though it was all she could think about. It was embarrassing, but if she didn't say something, she was sure one of her coworkers would fill Sarah in the next time she worked. Luna clicked through the stations on the radio, trying to decide the best way to explain everything. When she lifted her puffy eyes back to the road, it was just in time to see a silver van slam into the driver's side of the SUV.

Metal crunched and screeched as the vehicles warped together, the sharp sound hurting her ears. The force of the impact jarred every bone in Luna's body as the mass was forced sideways. Tiny orange-yellow flickers marred the asphalt as the pile of cars scraped across the road. Sarah's SUV flipped away from the van, landing upside down a few feet from the site of impact. Smoke filtered from the engine.

Luna's head slammed into the dashboard so hard she saw stars. Her seat belt held her upside down, blood rushing to her head. A piece of broken glass from the shattered windshield had embedded itself in her forehead, barely missing her eyes. Crimson rivers poured from both nostrils.

Beside her, Sarah's eyes were wide, a stream of blood running from her nose and her mouth. A jagged shard of glass was firmly lodged in one cheek.

Luna tried to drag herself out of the seat belt and gasped in pain. It held tight, cutting into her skin in a perfect line across her abdomen. Blood trickled from the laceration on her forehead, and a deeper, more worrisome series of cuts marked her arm and leg. Her eyelids grew heavy, and she fought to keep them open. On the verge of passing out, she struggled to free herself. She needed to get out of what was left of the vehicle before the engine caught on fire, but the seat belt wouldn't loosen. The buckle had broken, locking it in place. She glanced over at Sarah, but she was limp, eyes closed. Luna gave one last attempt at freeing herself before the blackness pulled her under.

Chapter Forty-Two

WHEN LUNA OPENED her eyes, she could make out the blurred outlines of a white hallway. The walls rushed by. She was moving, but not of her own accord. She tried to sit up, jostling the oxygen mask over her face. Steady hands eased her back down on the gurney. Figures cloaked in light-blue scrubs with masked faces wheeled her through the building.

"Twenty-year-old female, head and neck trauma," one of them said.

Groaning, she tried to figure out which one was talking. A white cap hid all but a few wisps of blond hair and a surgical mask covered the lower half of a pale face. Sapphire-blue eyes stared at her from above the white line.

"Vitals are stable," he said to one of the other figures.

She tried to cry out but no sound emerged. Gasping, she met Chance's gaze one last time before the darkness took her back under.

***

WHEN LUNA CAME to, there was an awful pain in her abdomen. A mean bruise lined a chunk of her ribs, making each inhalation difficult and painful. It was like she'd been in the worst fight of her life and lost. Her eyelids fluttered open, revealing a white ceiling above her. Her vision was fuzzy, so she blinked a few times trying to clear it. She wanted to move and see where she was, but the pain made her hesitate.

"You're awake!" Rose screeched.

Luna groaned as she tried to sit up. Her mother stood beside her bed, tissue clutched between her hands and Luna's—the same way she'd held Abrahim's hand. A few feet away stood Amanda.

Diverting her eyes back to her distraught parent, Luna croaked, "I'm okay, Mom."

Dabbing at the corners of her eyes, Rose continued. "Oh, first Abrahim, and then I heard you were in the hospital for a grisly car accident. I was so worried I had lost you too!"

"I'm okay, really," Luna said, wondering how loud she was talking and if Rose could hear her.

"What happened today, Luna?" Amanda asked, taking a small step toward her and placing a comforting hand on her knee.

"I-I don't really remember. Sarah picked me up from work and . . ." Luna struggled to recall the accident. She stared at the empty half of the room, expecting her to be there too. "Wait. Where's Sarah?"

Amanda and Rose exchanged a glance. Something about it gave Luna a horrible feeling of dread.

Eyes volleying between them, she asked, "What is it?"

Amanda sighed. "She's alive, but she's in surgery right now."

Luna relaxed against the pillow, staring up at the white ceiling. Surgery. That could be good or bad. For the moment at least, it meant she was alive, and there was the expectation she would stay that way.

Rose cut in, rubbing the bandage covering her daughter's forehead. "Luna, you need to be more careful from now on!"

"It was an accident, Mom," Luna said. The situation had been out of her hands. A random twist of fate smack-dab in the middle of everything else.

Rose didn't seem convinced, but Amanda tried to be upbeat. "The doctors said you're a little banged up but otherwise okay. You'll be here for the night, but there's a chance you could come home tomorrow."

A horrible thought dawned on Luna. Until Sarah healed, she wouldn't be able to go back to her place. If Luna was released first, she would have to return to Amanda's. To *Chance*.

"We'll come get you whenever. I mean it when I say call *anytime*. Don't hesitate, don't be stubborn. Let me know when to come get you," Amanda said.

Luna was about to ask Rose if she could pick her up instead when someone called into the room, "Visiting hours are up."

Luna's blood ran cold. That was the last person she wanted to face.

On her way into the hallway, Amanda said, "Keep an eye on her, please."

"We'll see you tomorrow," Rose said, hugging her daughter gently.

"Bye," Luna uttered and watched her mother go. She strained to hear Chance's reply to Amanda but couldn't make out more than a faint murmur.

Alone, Luna tried to get comfortable against the stiff bed. It was going to be a long, restless night, for sure, and she wished Amanda had snuck in something to help her sleep. She closed her eyes, trying to relax. Footsteps approached. Chance appeared at the foot of her bed. He wore light-blue scrubs, and a surgical mask hung loose around his neck. The white cap she'd seen in her hallucination upon arrival was gone, revealing messy multicolored hair hanging in his sapphire eyes.

This was the first time they'd been alone together since he had snuck into her bed, and she didn't want to imagine what he was thinking. She'd survived a car crash only to die by more painful means.

Of course.

"Come to finish me off?"

"No . . ." he said, trailing off as if there was more to the sentence. But he didn't say it.

"Why are you here?" she demanded, trying to sit up, to not seem as vulnerable as she actually was, only to be rewarded with a stabbing pain in her ribs.

"Part of my job is to tell you what's wrong with you," Chance said, swiping his hair out of his eyes with an irritated flick of his wrist. "You have a concussion, whiplash, and some bruising. There's a minor crack on one of your ribs, but you're going to be all right." He opened his mouth once more, then closed it again, chewing on his bottom lip.

"Great," Luna scoffed. "More fun for you, then." She wished she could flip away from him, but the IV in the crook of her arm prevented her from moving. It reminded her a bit of her dog-chain prison in the cabin. She didn't like it.

"What happened today?" he asked quietly, scrunching his pale face.

"I think it's pretty obvious. Car crash? Hello?"

"Did you hit someone or did they hit you?"

The question threw her off. Why did he care?

"Don't look at me like that. It's a pretty straightforward question."

She huffed. "We were hit."

He scratched the stubble on his chin and said, "It was because of me."

Luna didn't know what to make of his words or the tone with which he said them. "*You* hit us?"

"No," he answered, then stared past Luna. "But I know who did."

"Your friends?" she asked. Of course. It made perfect sense.

Chance was silent. "Doctors want you to stay overnight for observation."

"No. I want to go home."

"Luna, be reasonable. You're p—" He stopped, drawing his face tight as if he'd bitten into something sour, then said, "You were in a car accident."

"I don't care. I'm refusing treatment." She forced herself to sit fully upright, earning a much sharper jab of pain in her ribs.

"Legally, I'm allowed to."

Chance flared his nostrils but seemed too tired to argue. "If you're sure, I'll get someone to start the discharge papers. Be back in a few."

Luna watched him go, relieved. As soon as he was gone, her gaze landed on the phone. She reached for it, wincing when a stab of pain shot through her. In a hurry, she dialed her mother's number, but there was no answer. Most likely, she was only halfway home and wouldn't know Luna had called for a good thirty minutes or so. She hung up, disappointed, and considered her options. She didn't have the number to the car phone memorized, and if she stayed in the hospital, she wasn't guaranteed safety. Chance killed her father; he could easily do the same to her. But the only other place she had to go was back to the apartment with Amanda, and she already knew how easy it would be for Chance to get them alone.

Either option is Russian roulette, she thought, dismayed.

When Chance came back, he held a stack of papers for her to sign. She wasn't sure she was making the right move, but she didn't want him to sense any doubt or fear in her, so she forcefully scrawled her signature on each page.

As Chance bundled the paperwork, he said, "Since you're dead set on leaving, I'll drive you home. I get off in ten minutes anyway."

That caught Luna's attention. "Wait. If you're leaving, I'll stay."

Chance waved the signed papers in the air. "Too late for that."

"I'm not going with you."

"You don't have a choice."

"Fine," Luna snapped. All she wanted was to get a good night's sleep, and now doubted that would happen.

Chance approached the bed, and instinctively she searched his hands for weapons, her mind a storm of possibilities.

"What are you doing?" she demanded, wishing she could move away from him.

Exasperated, he said, "My job." He ripped the tape off her arm and gently slid the IV needle out. He pressed a cotton ball against the wound, then raised her wrist to trap it in the crook of her arm.

Her eyes drifted to the name tag pinned hastily to his shirt, studying every letter of the fake name. "How do you live with yourself?" she scoffed, flicking it once.

"Quite easily, actually," he answered with the slightest hint of irritation while he taped the cotton ball in place. "Get dressed. I'll be back in a minute to take you home."

Luna searched around her bed. She didn't have any clothes. What she'd been wearing had been cut off when she was brought in. "They took my clothes."

"I think Amanda left some in my truck," Chance said as he left the room.

Luna stood up cautiously, worried her legs might not support her weight. She had a very limited window to figure out her next steps. The gown left her uncomfortably exposed, but she still considered leaving the room to hail a cab, leaving Chance none the wiser. Problem was, along with her clothes, her wallet was also gone, eliminating that possibility.

She racked her brain for an escape. She didn't want to ride with Chance. He might drive her somewhere to kill her, or worse. She thought of their conversation in the restaurant and worried he might have another kidnapping up his sleeve. His nice act could be a façade to get her to let her guard down. Desperate, she scanned the room for something she could use to defend herself, but ended up staring at the phone again.

She dialed Amanda's number, relieved when her roommate picked up on the second ring. "Hello?"

"Mandy, it's Luna." Footsteps announced Chance's return. "Malcolm is bringing me home so please make sure the door is unlocked. We should be there in about twenty minutes."

"Oh, but what—" Amanda started to ask, but Luna hung up before she could finish the question.

Chance smirked when she met his eye. His work scrubs were gone, and he had donned his white muscle shirt and blue jeans from earlier. His hair was slightly tidier, though his eyes were dull with exhaustion. A series of purple scars ran up and down the muscles in his arms. They were faded, and Luna shivered, wondering how old they were.

"Insurance," she said, pushing the phone away from her.

"Whatever you gotta do." He tossed a bundle of clothes on the bed.

She grabbed them, shuffled into the bathroom, and locked the door behind her. The sickly smell of antiseptics filled her nose as she stripped off the paper gown and put on the clothing Chance had provided. They were Amanda's spare gym clothes—the shorts smaller than she was comfortable with and the tank top a bit too tight, but they would have to suffice. Luna splashed her face with cold water from the sink and left the bathroom. Chance looked up at the sound of the door opening, and Luna avoided his gaze, uncomfortable in the tight clothes.

"Come on," Chance said, rising from the bed.

"Amanda is expecting me home, so if you make any wrong turns, go a way that takes so much as a fraction of a second longer than it should, you'll regret it," Luna warned as she passed him.

He grabbed her elbow, forcing her to stop. His gaze swept over her, inspecting every inch as if searching for signs of injury. Luna yanked her arm free, shaking off his touch. "Are you really okay?" he asked.

Luna pretended not to hear him as she sulked out of the hospital. Each step toward the parking lot felt heavier. Near the door, Chance's truck loomed, an omen of death. When she finally slid into the passenger seat, the familiar *click* of the door locking behind her sent a chill down her spine.

Chance settled into the driver's seat, and Luna couldn't help but remember every other time she'd been in this exact position, the air thick with uncertainty. What were his intentions?

Where is he going to take me?

The car hummed as they pulled out of the lot, but the silence between them was suffocating. Luna's mind raced, waiting for the first sign that something was wrong—an abrupt turn, a sharp detour, a threat she couldn't escape—but Chance didn't give her any clues as to what he was thinking. His hands gripped the wheel, his gaze fixed on the road ahead, his lips pressed into a thin, unreadable line.

"Hungry Like the Wolf" by Duran Duran blared from the speakers, and Luna rested her cheek on the window. At last, he turned into the apartment complex and killed the engine.

"You really did just want to drive me home?" she asked, unable to contain her surprise.

Chance was silent, reaching up to scratch a spot below his eye. Getting out of the vehicle, he circled around and opened her door, staring at her with determination. "I have to help you."

"I can handle myself," she protested.

"I don't care if you can. You refused treatment at the hospital, and you'll be in agony once those pain meds wear off."

"You're not even a real nurse's aide."

"Never said I was."

"I thought the goal was to make me suffer," she stated as she stepped out of the vehicle. A head rush made her woozy, and she leaned against the side of the truck, waiting for it to pass.

"You've done plenty today," Chance said, snaking an arm around her waist to hold her up.

Luna pushed against his chest, but she was too weak to free herself. "Don't touch me. I don't want your help."

"Too bad," he said, dragging her to the apartment as if she were a rag doll he could move however he saw fit.

Chapter Forty-Three

CHANCE KNOCKED THREE times on the door. When Amanda opened it, her eyes went wide, but she stepped aside to allow them to enter.

"Finally!" Amanda exclaimed. "I was starting to worry that something happened."

Chance gave a short grunt, shifting his weight as he helped Luna across the threshold. "Your friend is stubborn."

"Preaching to the choir," Amanda murmured as she shut the door. Her gaze lingered on Luna's bruises and the stiffness in her movements. "What happened? I thought they weren't supposed to release you until tomorrow."

"I refused treatment."

"She doesn't seem to understand that a cracked rib will *hurt*," Chance added, frustration barely concealed.

"Why do this to yourself?" Amanda asked.

"Why stay? There's not much the doctors can do for me anyway. All they're doing is running up a bill," Luna said, swatting at Chance who still had his arm wrapped around her waist, much to her annoyance.

"Fine," Amanda relented, "but you at least need to lie down."

"I'm going to," Luna snapped, shooting a glare at Chance

as she finally shrugged him off. "You've done enough. Please leave."

"He's only trying to help," Amanda said.

Luna wanted to rip her hair out. It was so obvious what was going on. How could she not see it? "Don't you see what's actually going on here?"

For a moment, the room stilled. A shadow passed over Chance's face, and his eyes hardened. Luna felt herself recoil beneath his glare.

"Yeah. I see my injured friend being stubborn to her own detriment," Amanda said.

Chance visibly relaxed.

Luna sighed, lifting a hand to the bandages covering her forehead, wincing as her fingers brushed a tender spot. The pain meds were wearing off. Her limbs were heavy. Everything ached. The edges of her vision blurred, and the nausea she'd been keeping at bay all day suddenly churned in her stomach. The world was starting to spin, and she needed to get some rest. She didn't have the strength to deal with any of this and had made it this far on adrenaline alone.

"I really don't wanna talk about this, okay?" Her voice cracked. "I'm tired."

Amanda's face softened as she glanced at the bandages. "I understand."

"I'll help her get settled in bed," Chance said, leaning over to press a kiss to Amanda's lips.

Luna's eyes narrowed. "I don't think so."

"You're in no state to refuse help," Amanda insisted.

"Malcolm knows what he's doing. He does this stuff at the hospital all the time."

Luna opened her mouth to argue, but the words caught in her throat. Nothing she said would change Amanda's mind.

She doesn't care, Luna thought bitterly, shoulders sagging. It was a terrible explanation, but it was the only one she had.

Luna made her way down the hall, each step dragging with defeat. Chance followed close behind. As soon as they crossed the threshold into her room, the door shut with a soft *click*.

Luna lowered herself onto the bed, arms crossed tight over her chest. "I don't know what you've done to Amanda to make her so blind to what's going on here, but I need you to undo it."

Chance paced a few steps toward her window, then stopped. "Do you . . . need anything? Some tea or crackers? You feel okay?"

Luna raised an eyebrow. "Do *you*?"

"You don't get it, do you?"

"I don't understand anything," Luna said with a frustrated sniffle. "You know, I was so close to telling Amanda the truth out there, and I'm not sorry."

Chance puffed out his cheeks and let the air out slowly, like he was trying to release more than just air. "If you were really going to risk it, you'd have done it by now instead of running off with Sarah. But look . . ."—he shifted his weight, glancing away for a second before locking eyes with her again—"it was my fault you almost died. The least I can do now is nurse you back to health."

Luna chuckled darkly. "Did you hit your head or something? First you want to kill me, now you're trying to help me?"

Chance's face was unreadable, as if he'd already rehearsed this moment a hundred times in his head. "I never said I wanted to kill you," he said flatly.

The silence that followed was sharp enough to cut, but Luna couldn't fathom a reply. He went to her closet, rummaging. When he emerged, it was with the nightgown she'd worn from *that* night. He tossed it at her. With shaking fingers, she felt the soft material, remembering his hands and how they'd been anything but soft.

"I'm never wearing this again," she said, digging her fingers into the fabric to stop herself from shaking.

"Just put it on," Chance ordered, turning his back to her. "I won't look.

A fresh stab of pain reminded her how hard it would be to sleep with clothes that were even slightly restricting. Her nightgown was the best choice, but she'd rather be in pain than leave herself vulnerable again.

Chance faced her, eyebrow raised. "You obviously can't do it on your own," he stated, striding back to her.

"I don't need your help," she hissed, balling her hands into fists.

"Relax. I'm not trying to hurt you. Part of what I do every day involves dressing people. Stop acting so damn proud and let me help." Ignoring her protests, he yanked her shirt off, wincing at the bandages and bruises dotting her abdomen.

She hurried to pull the flimsy fabric into place, no longer in the present but in the memory of him in her bed. A sob left her lips.

Chance froze. "Stop it."

Distant, she asked, "What else am I supposed to do? You've made me into this . . . this ghost of myself."

"I'm not proud," he admitted, narrowing his eyes to slits. "But you chose to be a hero. I gave you a choice. You could've stayed away. Saved yourself."

"Am I supposed to be grateful? The choice you gave me wasn't much of a choice at all. This is wrong." She meant for the words to be strong, but they came out as a shaky whisper.

"You think that word means something to me? *Wrong.* Am I supposed to feel guilty now? Because I don't. I've made mistakes, I admit that, but I always tried to do what I thought was best for you. The irony of this whole thing is that you were the first fucking thought on my mind when I came out of my coma. Imagine that. Three years of not knowing who I was, but I somehow remembered you. I lay in that bed, thinking of everything that happened in the cabin. Everything that went wrong. And I decided it started with me showing *mercy.*"

"So, what, you think this is justified? That it's okay to do whatever you want with me? I'm a human being."

"This isn't much fun for me either, if we're being honest with each other."

"Then *leave,*" she said, nearly pleading.

"Not yet."

"Get out of my room!" Luna shouted, shakily standing.

Curling her hands into fists, she screamed, "Ama—"

Chance smacked a hand over her mouth. "Amanda's life must not be worth very much to you."

Slowly, he removed his hand, and Luna snarled. "You're going to hurt her in the end regardless of what I decide, right?"

Chance scoffed and pushed her onto the bed. Luna's mouth went uncomfortably dry. Chance's face lingered close to hers, then moved past it to prop up her pillows. "Let me ask you a question, kitten. What do you think Amanda can do for you? Call the police? Then what? I go to prison? You really think that would end this?" he asked, calmly, coolly, in a tone Luna was beginning to recognize signaled danger. He brought his face back to hers and said, "It won't. I can continue all of this from there without a problem. There will always be more of me. Plus, you know Amanda can die in her sleep at any time. And guess who the police would suspect should she happen to get her throat cut with only her roommate around? Good luck trying to explain your way out of that one."

Luna wanted so badly to argue, but how could she? He was right. There was no way out of this except her death or his.

"Go to sleep before you do something stupid," Chance ordered.

Luna couldn't think of anything else.

Chance hovered over her, bending down to plant a soft kiss on the bandages on her forehead. "I'll try to get you some pain meds first thing in the morning. If you need anything during the night, let me know."

"I will never call for you." There weren't a lot of things

she could guarantee in her life anymore, but that was one sure thing.

Chance pointed a bony finger in her direction. "I mean it. Don't do anything stupid or you'll regret it."

As if every day wrapped in survivor's guilt wasn't one big regret.

Chapter Forty-Four

*P*REGNANT.

Chance couldn't get the word out of his brain. Time passed as he sat at the kitchen table, more solemn than he'd been in a long time. He had lain with Amanda until she'd fallen asleep, then eventually worked up the nerve to get out of bed and pace the apartment. There would be no sleeping tonight.

Every time he closed his eyes, he saw that word in Luna's patient chart, followed by her expression as she lay in the hospital bed, eyes glazed with medication and pain. It haunted him. Made worse by the fact that he'd been unable to tell her everything. He should have, it was *technically* his job, but he couldn't go through with it. Every time he'd tried to force the words out, they lodged in his throat and choked him. Then the moment had passed.

What will she do when she finds out?

He scoffed to himself because that was easy to answer. She'd run. It was her solution to everything.

I can't let her do that again.

No doubt the car accident had been Cody's doing. He'd given Chance the warning that he would get rid of all distractions. Then this had happened. Chance didn't believe in coincidences.

Fuck, he thought, raking his hands through his multicolored hair for the hundredth time.

He'd known since Cody's reappearance that he would have to disappear again, but he thought he would have more time to create a plan. And he thought playing by the rules would buy him that time. Now, he didn't know what to do. If he left now, Cody would go after Luna. But she wouldn't willingly leave with him either.

I need to tell her the truth, he thought, firm in his decision.

That she would believe him was a long shot, but he had to try, didn't he?

"Malcolm, are you coming to bed?" Amanda called from the edge of the hallway.

"In a bit," he said, refusing to meet her eyes. He couldn't let her see him like this. He had no way to answer her if she dared to ask him what was wrong.

"Okay." The sound of her footsteps announced her departure.

Thank you, God, Chance thought, tilting his head back to stare up at the ceiling.

He needed to silence his thoughts, if only for a little while. Standing up so fast the chair screeched, he gathered his keys and headed outside. The bar was calling his name.

***

AN HOUR PASSED, and Luna was still awake. She stared at the door wondering when Chance would come back. It wasn't a matter of *if* but *when*. In this state, she was in no shape to fight, and she was sure he'd already come to the same realization.

Groaning at the stiffness in her lower back, she sat up. With the pain meds wearing off, every movement hurt, but she forced herself to stand, wobbling into the kitchen.

She tried her best to stay silent, fearing any noise might attract Chance's attention. Her hands shook as she held a glass under the faucet, filling it. Slowly, she lifted the water to her mouth, eliciting a flare of pain from her ribs. The glass slipped from her fingers, crashing onto the floor.

"What are you doing up, Luna?" a voice asked from behind her.

Heart hammering, Luna leaned on the counter for support, watching Amanda drift from the shadows at the end of the hall. She could've melted with relief. "I wanted a glass of water."

"You should've called for me. I would have gotten it for you," Amanda said, then sighed at the mess. She bent down to start picking up the pieces. "Well, it's good to have you home again. I missed having you here, girl."

Luna missed her, too, but she wouldn't admit it because it felt like the version of her roommate she missed was long gone. Luna tried to start the walk back to her room, but she miscalculated, sending a fresh stab of pain straight to her ribs that halted her. She grabbed the wall trim, steadying herself.

Amanda stood with a handful of glass shards in her palm. "Are you okay?"

"I'm fine," Luna muttered through gritted teeth.

"So . . ." Amanda made a face. She didn't believe a word Luna said but didn't seem to have it in her to argue either.

Swallowing down whatever she'd originally been about to say, she tossed the glass shards into the trash. "Look . . . I'm sorry about the whole Malcolm thing, okay? I want you both in my life."

"That's the problem: You see what you want to see. You choose to believe the story that keeps you comfortable."

Amanda's lips pressed into a thin line. "That's not fair."

"You're telling me," Luna said. "But I'm not trying to fight about it. If that's what you want to do, then fine, but I'm not going to live here anymore. I don't feel safe. Believe me or don't, but he's not the guy you think he is."

"What has Malcolm done that could possibly be so bad that you have to use all these dramatics?"

Temptation to spill everything bubbled to the front of Luna's mind, but the words stuck in her throat as she remembered that shadow over Chance's eyes. That certainty that he would deliver on his promise.

Amanda, interpreting her silence as an answer, waved a dismissive hand. "See? It'll be okay, you'll see. He works so much, you'll barely see him around anyway."

"It's your place, your decision," Luna said, each word measured. "But I won't do it." She swallowed hard, then added quietly, "I think I'm going to move back home. Mom could use the company."

Amanda placed her hand on Luna's arm. "I don't want that."

The corner of Luna's lip twitched into a bitter, almost sad smile. How could Amanda not see the pain she was causing?

A silence settled between them, heavy and thick.

Amanda's hand lingered for a moment longer, then dropped. "If that's what you need to do . . . I understand. But don't forget, I'm here. Always."

Luna wished those words meant something.

Chapter Forty-Five

LUNA MANAGED TO drift off into a dreamless sleep, and when she woke a few hours later, her stomach was a tangled mess. She rushed to the bathroom and stayed there, vomiting until she thought she would see her organs floating in the toilet bowl. Groaning, she sprawled on the floor, enjoying the feeling of the cold tiles against her skin. Then her stomach roiled again, and she forced herself up, leaning over the toilet in preparation for another round. She didn't know what was wrong with her but feared her anxieties had finally manifested into a physical illness, or perhaps the doctors missed something important from the accident.

Amanda knocked twice on the door, then cracked it open to peer at Luna, watching her slink back to her spot on the floor. "Are you okay?" she asked. "I'm really worried about you."

Luna lifted her head. All thoughts of their fight a few hours before were forgotten as she struggled to regain control of her churning stomach. "I'm fine, Mandy," she lied. "Don't worry about it."

"You're not," she countered. "I know you were trying to wait until the morning to go back to the hospital for Sarah, but I think we should go now."

"I told you I'm—" Luna tried to argue when a surge of

nausea caused her to bend over the toilet and vomit again.

"That proves my point," Amanda said, face scrunched in disgust.

Luna's resolve gave out as her stomach twisted again, sending another wave of queasy pressure through her core. She clutched her side.

"Okay," she murmured. "We can go. Just . . . please don't have Malcolm take us."

"He's not here."

Relief washed over Luna. She exhaled and pushed herself upright, legs unsteady beneath her. The room tilted slightly. Her body swayed, weightless and weak, like she'd been hollowed out. Dizziness surged, and she nearly toppled over.

Amanda caught her before she could fall, wrapping an arm around her. Luna leaned on her, head spinning. She didn't know where the sickness had come from, but she couldn't afford the time it would cost her. Not with everything that was going on with Sarah. She needed to be there, to check on her, to know how the surgery had gone. But how could she help anyone if she couldn't even stay on her feet?

"I feel horrible, Mandy," Luna whimpered.

Amanda gave her a sympathetic pout as she wrapped her arm around her shoulders and said, "Come on." It was slow progress helping Luna to the car, but they made it, and Amanda eased her into the back so she could lie slumped across the seat.

The drive was quiet. Luna fought off the urge to vomit, her body dry heaving more than once. There was nothing left in her stomach, but the sensation wouldn't go away. Her hands gripped the edge of the back seat until her knuckles turned white.

When they finally made it to the hospital, Amanda helped her out. "Sorry!" she said quickly, catching her as Luna nearly collapsed against the car door.

Inside, the lobby was cold and too bright. The smell of antiseptics hung heavy in the air, mixed with the faint bitterness of burnt coffee from a vending machine in the corner. A receptionist behind a thick pane of glass slid over a clipboard, and Amanda filled out the intake forms while Luna sank into one of the plastic chairs.

Luna shifted, fidgeting, never able to get comfortable in the stiff seat. Every few minutes she made a beeline for the bathroom, each trip more draining than the last. Her skin had gone pale, her limbs heavy. She barely registered the people around her. They were just faces that blurred together in the haze of her nausea and the pounding in her head.

When her name was finally called, Amanda helped her down the hall and onto the narrow bed in the examination room. Luna curled up on her side, arms wrapped tightly around her abdomen, teeth clenched in response to the pain in her ribs.

The doctor examined her, running all kinds of tests. When they left to check the results, Luna pushed herself upright carefully. She swayed slightly but forced her feet onto the ground. Now that she was here, she needed to find Sarah's room and see how she was recovering.

Amanda put an arm in her way, stopping her from going far. "What are you doing?"

"I need to see Sarah," Luna grunted. "I need to know . . .

she's okay."

Amanda jutted out her lip. "You're in no shape to go wandering around the hospital. You need to stay here and wait for the doctor. I'll find out what's going on with Sarah."

Reluctantly, Luna nodded. "Thank you."

"Be back in a flash," Amanda said and left with a swish of the curtain.

Luna considered following her anyway. If the doctor wasn't going to show up anytime soon, why did she have to stay put? She couldn't dislodge the last glimpse of Sarah she'd gotten in the SUV: her bloody and broken body pressed against the steering wheel. Squeezing her eyes shut, Luna tried to banish it from her mind, but it wouldn't go. The only way to truly forget about it would be to see Sarah okay.

The minutes dragged, each second stretching longer than the last. The faint buzz of voices from the hallway filtered through the thin curtain, but no one entered. The ache in Luna's stomach dulled to a constant throb, but it was nothing compared to the twisting knot of fear in her chest.

When Amanda finally returned, her gaze stayed on the floor. Her face was ashen, and she wrung her hands together nervously.

A tight coil bunched in Luna's stomach. "What is it? Is Sarah okay?"

Amanda opened her mouth to speak, but the blue curtain swished open before she could get a word out. A doctor stepped into the space, clipboard in hand, his white coat rustling as he flipped through a few pages.

"Good morning, Miss Ketz," he said with polite detachment, eyes still scanning the chart.

Luna made a noncommittal sound in her throat.

The doctor glanced up, offering a brief smile. "It seems unfortunate to be at the hospital on your birthday."

Luna stared blankly, the words barely registering. *Happy fucking birthday to me.* In the whirlwind of everything that had happened, her birthday was the last thing on her mind.

"Looks like you've been experiencing some nausea and vomiting?"

Vomiting sounded easy. What she'd experienced felt as if she had been on the verge of expelling her organs. "Yeah. Something like that."

He nodded. "Well, the good news is, your injuries don't appear to be causing the symptoms."

Luna shifted uncomfortably on the bed, curling an arm around her aching stomach. "Then what is?"

The doctor hesitated, just for a beat. "I'm actually a little surprised no one told you last night." He glanced between the chart and her face. "You're pregnant."

The world tilted. Luna blinked at him, her brain slow to register the words. *Pregnant?* This had to be a mistake. A lie. A cruel, twisted joke.

"Wh-what?" she stuttered, sitting up too quickly. Her stomach roiled in protest, but she barely noticed.

"It's early, a few weeks along now at most," the doctor said, glancing back at his clipboard again. "That seems to be causing your symptoms."

Luna glanced at Amanda, struggling for words. She saw her surprise reflected back at her. "H-how is that possible?"

"You're a twenty-year-old woman, Luna. Surely, I don't need to explain the mechanics of it."

Luna's mind flashed back to Chance hovering over her, his rough kisses, the pain, the humiliation. The baby growing inside her belonged to him. *Does he know?* Was that why he'd dedicated himself to taking care of her a few hours earlier?

"Doctor, are you sure she's pregnant?" Amanda asked, still visibly confused. "The test could've been a false positive, right?"

"We ran it last night and again today. It's positive."

"But this is impossible," Amanda muttered, holding a hand to her forehead as if she was the one who'd received this news. "She must have some trauma from yesterday."

Luna held up a hand. There was no point arguing, not when she knew the truth. "It's all right, Mandy."

Amanda's eyes were wide, mouth hanging open.

Luna was too mortified to hear what she had to ask. Awkwardly standing, she said, "Thank you for your time, Doctor." She left the tiny ER cubicle, and a confused Amanda, in her wake.

"Luna?" Behind her, Amanda's voice rose in a mixture of disbelief and urgency. "Luna, wait!"

But Luna didn't slow. The sterile hallway stretched ahead of her like a tunnel, her footsteps echoing louder than they should have. Amanda caught up a moment later, grabbing one shoulder and spinning her around with more force than Luna expected.

"What happened in there?" Amanda demanded.

Luna turned away. "Drop it," she muttered, then started walking again, faster now.

Amanda chased after her. "But . . . but . . ." She struggled for words. "Where are you going?"

"I have to see Sarah," she said flatly. It was the only clear thought in her mind, the one thing anchoring her in the storm that had become her life. *Sarah. Just get to Sarah.*

"Luna, STOP!" Amanda shouted with rising desperation. There was a tremble in her voice that Luna couldn't ignore.

So she stopped.

"I'm sorry," Amanda whispered, eyes huge and shining with sorrow as she continued. "But Sarah . . . she didn't make it."

The words didn't make sense. Amanda's mouth was still moving, but all Luna could hear was a dull ringing in her ears.

"She died last night," Amanda said, barely audible. "I'm so sorry."

LUNA HAD NO recollection of climbing into the car or getting home. Amanda convinced her to do all those things, but given the fog in her brain, Luna couldn't figure out how. When she came back to herself she was lying in bed, rubbing her stomach. Within it was life. Luna thought of the irony of it all. She'd never wanted to have children, and now, she didn't have a choice.

There was no getting around the ugly fact that she was going to have Chance's baby. Sarah's sacrifice had been for nothing. Luna's eyes burned. She was so grateful for Sarah, for everything she'd done. For everything she'd tried to do. Could Luna have done something to prevent things from ending like this? Maybe if she hadn't been moping, Sarah would've been watching the road and not her.

If Sarah hadn't been so kind, she would still be alive right now.

Luna grabbed her pillow and held it over her face, screaming into it. When she was breathless, she dropped it, but she didn't feel better.

Amanda knocked on her door. "Hey," she said, scratching at her arm. "How are you holding up?"

Luna studied the smears of makeup on her pillow, not able to meet her friend's gaze directly.

"Want to talk about it?" Amanda asked. Luna wasn't sure which news she was referring to. "Being pregnant, I mean. This is huge. Very . . . unexpected."

"Oh." Luna did *not* want to talk about it, especially not while she was lying in the place where it had happened.

"How did it happen, Luna?" Amanda pressed, oblivious to her thoughts as she sat on the edge of the bed.

"I really don't know," Luna murmured, barely holding it together. She bit down hard on her lower lip, the sharp sting grounding her long enough to keep from unraveling.

Amanda leaned in, brimming with curiosity. "Was it a one-night stand or something?" Her eyes suddenly widened as the pieces clicked together. "Wait . . . is it *Max's?*"

Luna's stomach twisted. It would be easier to say it was than admit the ugly truth. She nodded slowly, swallowing back the burn in her chest. "Yeah," she said, the words tasting like poison.

"It-it's Max's."

Amanda gasped and grabbed Luna's hand. "You must be overjoyed! I mean, at least you have a part of him to hang on to, right? Raising his child is a tribute to him."

Luna's jaw tightened, desperate to keep the ache from spilling out. Her child was an affront to Max, an abomination who would bear a likeness to the monster who had torn their lives apart.

Luna stared down at their hands, trembling, as if holding on could somehow steady her.

"You don't have to talk right now," Amanda said. "I know you're going through a lot, but I want you to know I'm here for you whether or not you decide to have the baby." She withdrew her hand from Luna's and stood up. "Just remember that."

"Thank you," Luna said, but she didn't want to think about any of it. It was a big decision. Too big. Either way she chose, her life would be filled with hardships she wasn't sure she could handle.

Chapter Forty-Six

CHANCE COULDN'T WAIT until the end of his shift. It wasn't often that he truly had a *bad day,* but this one knocked everything out of the park. It was one thing to see a dead body he was responsible for, but it was an out-of-body experience encountering one he wasn't.

Seeing Sarah on the operating table surrounded by bloody surgical instruments stirred something in him. No, they'd never been friends, but it was a visceral feeling watching her body being carted away. In an instant, it could be him on the operating table fighting for his life. If he couldn't finish the job for Cody, it would be.

As he went to work sterilizing everything, he couldn't believe how close Luna had been to sharing the same fate.

Luck had spared her this time.

Chance clocked out a few minutes early and dressed, crossing town as quickly as he could. He didn't know how long it would take for word to get back to Cody that Luna had survived the attempt on her life, but once he knew, he would send others to finish the job. When Chance got to the apartment, he was relieved to see Amanda and Luna there, and that they were safe.

For now, he reminded himself as he went to the bathroom. "Safe" was a relative term.

Across the apartment, he heard the front door open and Amanda's shrill voice. She was yelling at someone. Luna? He tilted his head, trying to hear better.

A man. "Please, Amanda!"

No other fucking guys come here, Chance thought, and a flare of anger rushed through him. Cody wouldn't send assassins to his *doorstep*, would he?

He flew down the hall, desperate to protect his new home and the women in it, like a lion defending its pride. In the living room, he zeroed in on the culprit. A skinny punk with flipped brown hair and a triangular face. Chance didn't recognize him. He had Amanda's left wrist in his grip and wouldn't let go, even when Chance made direct eye contact with him.

"Who the hell are you?" he demanded. "Get your hands off my girlfriend or I'll make you regret walking through that door."

"I'm Reese," he said, letting go of Amanda.

"My *ex*." She tacked on, rubbing her sore wrist as she put space between them.

"I don't give a fuck who you are!" Chance told him. "All I care about is that you get out of here before I *make* you."

Reese sneered. "You think you're better than me because she's decided to give you the time of day? Well, guess what? It won't last. She'll dump you too."

"Man, get out of here," Chance said, lip quirking in amusement. He was *itching* to take his frustration out on someone, and if this lasted much longer, Amanda would see the side of him he kept hidden from her.

"She makes you feel powerful, doesn't she?" Reese sneered. "Well, she'll take that away too."

Chance had to resist the urge to say he didn't care if she did. "I'm not worried about it." He meant it too. The time was coming for a change. If Amanda decided to throw him out, it would give him the motivation he needed to come up with a new plan. Maybe Reese sensed that about him because the vicious sneer faded. He glanced at Amanda, then back to Chance.

"Whatever," he said and left.

"Thank you." Amanda buried her face in Chance's chest. "Maybe now he'll leave me alone."

He hugged her back but didn't say anything, waiting for her to break away, and forced himself to smile. Amanda waltzed to her room. Chance watched her go, but didn't follow. Instead, he stood in the middle of the living room as if he were another piece of furniture. A buzz of nervous energy moved inside him that he wasn't quite sure how to still. He wanted to peek in on Luna but would have to wait for the sleeping pills he'd put into Amanda's drink to work their magic first.

Chance checked on Amanda a few minutes later. She was asleep, sprawled out across her bed as though she'd come home in a drunken stupor.

Chance smirked. That was a green light. He closed her door, avoiding the squeal it made when pushed too fast, and crept down the hall to Luna's room.

****

THE *CREAK* OF the door didn't wake Luna so much as the dip of her mattress when someone lay down on the other side of the bed. She peeked over her shoulder. "It's okay, baby, it's just me," Chance said, his hand running down her side soothingly as if it was something he did regularly. She supposed that now, it was.

His hand came to rest on her stomach, and she froze, waiting for it to go lower, for him to touch her again. In her state of vulnerability, she couldn't fight. His hand stayed on her stomach, and that horrifying question came back to her. *Did he know?*

"Luna?"

"Yes?" she replied, staring at the shadows on the other side of the room.

"I . . . um . . ." He paused to clear his throat.

"What?"

"Never mind," he said, then pulled her small back against his chest. "Sweet dreams, kitten."

He may as well have said, "Sweet nightmares," it was all the same to her.

A thousand feelings washed over Luna. She was wary of what he wanted to ask, scared of what would happen next, and confused. She was also desperate to get away, but with Chance's arms locked around her, she couldn't go anywhere. The natural smell of his body overwhelmed all her senses, invading her. She listened to his snores as he easily fell asleep. Subtly, she tried again to break free, but his grip held. Resigned, she put her head back on the pillow.

What had he been about to say? And why had he been so

quick to abandon it? He'd never been afraid to speak his mind. So what changed? One more time, she tried to wiggle free and failed. Angrily, she turned around, facing him. She thought about grabbing the alarm clock off her nightstand and smacking his face with it, but it was just out of reach. His pale face without anger or menace was foreign. He looked almost . . . human. For that fleeting second, she saw him as Amanda must. The human veneer. Not for the first time, she wondered why out of all the people in the world he could've latched onto, he had chosen her.

Max knew why. She shivered as snippets of their last conversation came back to her. *And he'd taken it to his grave.*

She pushed against Chance, but the effort was so weak that he didn't stir from his slumber. She gave up. Whatever strength she had left, she was wasting. Her vessel wasn't in good enough shape to do anything, but that didn't mean she was out of options. In DreamWorld, the ability she supposedly had was rare and powerful. The only drawback was that she'd never been taught how to properly wield it. Her only experience was the prison Chance had created.

According to him, I brought him back.

I've bonded us, he'd said in the cabin.

Luna had never really thought about what that meant until now. She desperately wanted to make him disappear, whether that meant to kill him or put him back into the coma he had escaped. If he was telling the truth, then none of it would hold. As long as their bond was there, he would always come back.

Amy would know how to break the bond, she thought.

As a Keeper, she was Luna's best bet at getting answers,

but that came with its own set of challenges. Amy would never help. At least not until she got past her own hang-ups first.

Luna couldn't change what Chance had already done, but she could stop whatever he planned to do next. Content that she wouldn't be disturbed, she finally let herself drift away.

When she opened her eyes, she recognized her surroundings—the parking lot outside Brentwood. Luna tensed and glanced around as though searching for a wild animal. On this side of the Realm, she couldn't guarantee that Amy would be limited to the cell that held her Topside. Luna entered the building and went down the hall, barreling into Amy's room. The girl lay across her bed, eyes closed and a peaceful, dreamy expression on her face, logged out of both realms.

Luna's shoulders slumped. She didn't know why she'd thought her mission would be easy when Amy had already made her feelings on the subject clear. All it took to regenerate her anger was remembering her situation in the Real World. Amy may have given up fighting, but Luna was far from done.

She stormed up to Amy's bed, placing her hand on the girl's shoulder. "Wake up!" she hissed, shaking her unceremoniously.

Amy groaned deep in her throat. Luna continued to shake her until Amy's eyes popped open. "Huh? What?" She wiped away a bit of drool from the corner of her mouth. Her eyes cleared. "Luna?"

"Yes, Amy. I'm back, and this time you can't throw me out."

Amy drew her eyebrows together and sat up. "Didn't I

already tell you I wasn't going to be part of this place anymore?"

"Yes, but I can't accept that," Luna said. "Too much has happened, and I need your help."

Exasperated, Amy held her raised hands out to either side of her. "We've been through this."

"Well, there's an update. Apparently, Chance is working with these people who have been hunting down other Keepers. They were targeting Max, and now, they're targeting you too."

Unbothered, Amy said, "This isn't new information to me, Luna."

"Well, I bet you don't know the only reason Chance hasn't found you yet is because of me."

Amy's eyes narrowed in disbelief.

"Doubt me if you want, but I can send him to you and maybe then he'll leave me alone," Luna said. She didn't mean it, of course, but she was counting on Amy not knowing that fact.

Amy recoiled as if Luna had physically slapped her. The smallest smirk broke across her face that Luna couldn't quite decipher. "Is that right?"

Luna continued. "Help me. And I can help you. We can beat him."

Amy let out a long sigh that came from deep in her chest. "Fine. *Fine.* Tell me what you want me to do."

"Chance told me the reason he was able to remember everything was because of the spell he did to me. If we break it, he's vulnerable. How do I do it, Amy? As a Keeper, you have to know!"

Amy flared her nostrils and reached out, hesitating only a

second before clasping Luna's hand. The moment their skin met, Luna sucked in a sharp breath. A jolt, cold and electric, shot through her, locking her joints and scrambling her thoughts. Her pulse pounded in her ears.

She could *feel* Amy in her head.

Amy's brow furrowed, her grip tightening. Her body tensed as if fighting a current too strong to resist. For a long moment, neither of them moved. Then Amy inhaled sharply, stumbling back a step. Her hand slipped from Luna's, fingers trembling. Her gaze was unfocused, distant. "T-that bond . . ." she murmured. "It's some dark magic. Magic I've never dabbled in."

Luna tried to swallow down her panic and asked, "You can break it, right?"

Amy didn't answer immediately. She blinked slowly, as though coming out of a trance, then shook her head. "That's above my skill set."

"But you're a *Keeper*."

"So you've said," she shot back, folding her arms across her chest. "But there are forces far more powerful than me in this place. The only one who could interfere with that kind of magic would be the one who put it in place to begin with."

Luna recoiled. "Chance? You're saying I'd have to ask Chance?"

Amy shook her head. "No. Whatever's responsible for this is more powerful than him. You said he's working with a group of men?"

"Yeah. I don't know how many of them there are, or *who* they are, but Chance seems scared of them."

"There's a reason for that. I hate to tell you this, but they are the only ones who could help you."

Chapter Forty-Seven

CHANCE FELL ASLEEP with Luna still cradled in his arms, expecting to wake in the familiar sanctuary of his cabin on the Other Side. But an unearthly blackness tugged at the edges of his consciousness, pulling him away like a tide dragging him under. When his eyes finally fluttered open, he found himself on a desolate beach. Luna was nowhere in sight. He scanned the endless stretch of sand, eyes narrowing as the horizon curved endlessly in both directions.

It was a dream cycle in a place he didn't recognize.

He took a cautious step backward, muscles coiling, suspicion rising. He immediately thought Cody had trapped him somewhere. Before he could dive too deeply into his theory, a voice sliced through the silence.

"I thought it would be best if we talked here."

Chance whipped around. Reese stood there, hands casually tucked in his pockets, a sly smile playing at his lips.

Chance's jaw dropped, stunned. Words tumbled out before he could stop them. "What?"

Reese chuckled softly, a gleam in his eye. "Surprised?"

"Yeah, to say the least. Why are you here? Why am *I* here? Why am I seeing you right now?"

"Let me start at the beginning," Reese said, taking one of

his hands from his pocket to wipe his mouth. "I know you. Whatever, or whoever, Amanda thinks you are isn't the truth. Your name isn't Malcolm."

Chance crinkled his forehead, trying to figure out if Reese was one of Cody's men. He couldn't remember seeing him in the compound and doubted he was connected. There was a softness to him, a naïvety that had disappeared from Cody's men long ago. That only made Chance more confused, and he was unsure how to proceed. At the end of the day, it didn't matter how Reese knew, only that he could ruin everything if he told Amanda.

Should I murder him now or wait to see what else he has to say? Chance mused. "How do you know about that?"

"I'm a Walker, like you. When you confronted me, I thought you looked familiar, but I couldn't quite place where I'd seen you before. When I got home, I did some research and sure enough, it *was* you. You're my fucking role model, man."

Each sentence Reese spoke only made Chance more uneasy, and he was losing his ability to hide it. "Research? I'm sorry, but I don't recall you telling me what the fuck it is I'm doing here or who you are."

Reese raised his hands, palms forward, as if warding off an attack. "Okay. Here's the deal. I trained to be a Keeper once," he admitted. "My mentor taught me about some extreme cases to study, to learn consequences and procedures, and your story always stuck with me."

"You're a Keeper?" Chance asked. Nothing else Reese said had landed. If this strange man had Keeper powers, would Cody accept his sacrifice in Amy's place?

The words had barely landed before Reese shook his head. "Not anymore." He glanced down sheepishly. "I stole a memory amulet. Mentor found out and that was that. Rules are life or death for those people, and I'm not one of the good guys."

Chance laughed out loud at that. "That's okay. Neither am I."

"What you did . . . that was extreme," Reese said in wide-eyed wonder. "It's a shame you failed."

Chance pursed his lips. He couldn't agree more. He didn't want to think about how different life would be right now if Luna hadn't beaten him.

I'd be free, he thought. The word rang hollow. He was hardly able to wrap his mind around what it meant anymore.

"What's the plan now that you're back?" Reese asked, leaning forward to eagerly devour Chance's every word.

He didn't know how to answer. He hadn't made it this far on a plan, only a desperate need to stay alive.

Reese must've sensed the negative dip in Chance's energy because he made a face and asked, "Okay, well, what's the endgame to it all?"

That question he *could* answer. He wanted freedom. Freedom to use his magic as he saw fit without anyone trying to take it away. Freedom to live without the threat of his imminent death hanging over his head. Freedom to have his life be his own.

Chapter Forty-Eight

A WEEK CREPT by, one day blending into the next. Unable to work until her injuries healed, Luna stayed with her mom during the days. At night, she escaped into DreamWorld as often as possible, both to recover from her accident and to mull over Amy's words: *Whatever's responsible for this is more powerful than him.*

A horrifying thought. Luna had been under the assumption that the others were lesser than Chance. But what if that wasn't the case? What if they could do more, worse things? In a way, she supposed it made sense. Whoever they are, they had bonded with Chance as well, at least enough to give him the magic he needed. Having done that for him, there was no telling what else they would do to keep him protected.

If they'd been responsible for trying to kill her, she expected to find them hunting for her in DreamWorld, but they never came. No one did. Not a Keeper, not any of Chance's people, not Chance himself. The world folded out around her as if she were the only one in it, quiet and eerie.

Once again, she woke up unsatisfied with her experience. On any other day, she would've gone back to sleep, but today wasn't an ordinary day. It was her first scheduled day back to work since the accident. She wanted to quit, but if she did, her box would only get smaller and harder to escape from.

Cursing, she sprang out of bed and got dressed. Rose was in the kitchen nursing a cup of tea when Luna emerged from her room. She bid her goodbye and boarded the bus heading to Bowling Green. She wasn't excited to be back in the apartment again, but thankfully, she didn't see Chance on the way to her room. While rifling through her closet for her work hat, she heard Amanda enter the room.

"Hey, how are you holding up?" she asked, sounding too cheery for a situation that didn't call for it.

"I'm fine," Luna said. *Go, go, automatic lying machine.*

Amanda gave her a once-over. "You're going back to work already? Do you feel up to it?"

"Yeah. It's been long enough."

"They'll understand if you take a little more time off . . . considering."

"I'm good, really," Luna reiterated, adjusting her hat.

Amanda's face fell. "Well, take it easy, okay? You shouldn't be straining yourself so soon."

Luna didn't bother to mention that waking up in the morning counted as *strain* at this point. Out loud, she said, "Sure."

***

WORK WITHOUT SARAH was a sad affair. The restaurant was filled with customers and coworkers, but to Luna, it might as well have been empty. One of the tables had been layered with pictures and teddy bears, a little makeshift memorial for Sarah. Every time

Luna had to sweep the lobby, she was forced to see it, to remember another friend she hadn't been able to save. This one hurt a little bit more, though, because she blamed herself entirely. When she had submitted her application, she'd sealed Sarah's fate.

Several times throughout her shift, she tried to get a hold of Rose to pick her up when her shift ended. The last thing she wanted to do was go home to Amanda's apartment, but her mother didn't answer. Most likely, it was one of her bad days. Luna wouldn't force her to drive in that condition. Especially not after what had happened to Sarah.

Without another place to go, she returned to the apartment. She held her breath as she unlocked the front door, but the living room was dark. The light above the stove guided her through the apartment.

Easing her posture, she crept down the hall. Maybe she could still have a peaceful night after all. She pushed her bedroom door open and switched on her light. Chance was on her bed. His eyelids were closed, and he was stretched out on his back, arm tucked under her pillow.

Her heart rate increased, waiting for some type of trick, when she realized he was asleep.

I guess there is rest for the wicked

On an ordinary day, she would've preferred wandering the streets to dealing with him. But this hadn't been an ordinary day. She thought of Sarah's tiny, sad memorial. The life that had been taken far too soon. This *man* was responsible for it. Yet, he didn't care. He continued to cause pain day in and day out, but nothing came back to affect him.

Luna wasn't used to feeling rage, but it flooded through her raw and uncontrollable. She stormed toward him, ready to beat him until her fists were bruised and her throat was raw from screaming. Luna slapped him across the face, the echo of skin on skin loud in the quiet apartment. His eyes flew open, his long fingers wrapping around her delicate forearm. Luna growled and broke free. "What the hell are you doing in my bed?" she demanded.

"Waiting for you," he said, sitting up. He straightened the creases in his shirt and added, "Didn't intend to doze off."

"You didn't answer my question."

Chance rolled his eyes, fishing a small box from his pocket. "I would've given you this days ago," he started, "but since you were MIA for your birthday, I didn't get the chance. So, here." He shoved the box toward her like it was a peace offering.

Luna crossed her arms, refusing to meet his gaze. "I don't want it."

Chance snapped the box open and took out a silver necklace, the pendant shaped like a rose. "But it's perfect for you."

Luna's stomach twisted. She hated it. Before she could protest, Chance slid an arm around her waist, steadying her as he lifted the chain. The cool metal brushed against her skin as he looped it around her neck.

She squirmed, trying to get away, but his grip tightened. She stilled as he clasped the necklace closed, brushing back a lock of her hair to see it against her skin. "It looks good on you," he whispered, fingers smoothing out the tiny kinks in the chain.

Luna would rip it off and throw it away at the first

opportunity she got. Chance didn't seem to notice her disdain. He moved his hands from her neck and shoulders to her waist, locking her in place.

"We need to talk," he said.

"No," she refused, trying to drive her heel into his shin. "I've had a long day at work, and I want to sleep. Please, this one time, grant me a favor, and *leave*."

He took a deep inhale of her scent. "I don't think so."

With a frustrated grunt, Luna managed to slide from his lap and made a move for the door, but he grabbed her wrist. "We *need* to talk," he repeated, dragging her back to the bed and making her sit down. "Running away isn't going to change that."

Luna pressed her lips together, forcing herself to peer up at him. If he were a normal person, their situation would call for them to have a *lot* to talk about. But with him as he was, it wouldn't help either of them. "What could you possibly want to talk about?"

He crouched down to eye level and said, "What we've done." Luna tried to escape again, but he clutched her jaw, forcing her to stay put. "You can't ignore it forever."

She slapped his hand away. "How fucked in the head are you?" she asked in a whisper. "You want to break me. You *did* break me, and now you expect me to *talk* to you about it? I've known what you were since high school, but this? It's like you almost feel guilty. Or you want me to go to the police." She paused to sniffle. "Not that they'd believe me anyway. No one ever does."

The gentle expression on Chance's face vanished. "You know I don't want that."

"Why talk about it, then? This is so pointless, all of it. You've won! I don't know what else you want, why you're still hanging around."

Chance's eyes darkened, but he was almost tender as he reached up and stroked her cheek with the backs of his fingers. "I want *you*. Nothing else."

Luna shut her eyes tight, bracing herself. When she opened them again, she sprang to her feet and fled, dashing straight into Amanda's room. She was sprawled out in bed, asleep, and Luna was relieved to see such a normal sight.

Chance hurried after her, but Luna barely noticed as she tossed the blanket aside and curled up next to Amanda, clutching her close like a lifeline. "I'm staying here," she snarled, teeth bared. "Whatever you have to say, you can say it in front of her."

Chance smirked, but Luna was willing to bet money it was fake. She had beaten him for the time being, and he knew it. Counting his losses, he left the room, slamming the door behind him.

Luna let her head fall onto the pillow beside Amanda, who snored softly, utterly oblivious to the storm swirling a few feet away. Luna envied her peace.

Chapter Forty-Nine

WHEN LUNA WOKE, a sharp poke jabbed her side. Her eyes snapped open, expecting to see Chance, but it was Amanda hovering above her, brows furrowed in confusion.

"Good morning, sleepyhead," she greeted.

Luna glanced at the clock. "Is it morning already?"

Amanda nodded, then pointed between Luna and the bed. "Quick question."

Luna frowned, rubbing her temple. "I was . . . having night terrors again. Hope you don't mind."

"Not at all," Amanda said, full of warmth. "But I gotta head out to go help my sister pick up her centerpieces. If you need anything, let me know. I'll have my pager."

Luna sank back into the pillows, the heaviness of her thoughts settling around her like a fog. She lost track of how long she lay there until a sudden shift in the room made her freeze.

Sitting up, she caught sight of Chance framed in the doorway. Panic flared, and she scrambled out of bed while she still could. His piercing blue eyes locked onto her, and all she could think was, *Would her baby have his eyes or hers?*

"What do you want?" she asked, watching warily as he approached her.

His eyes were on the necklace she'd forgotten was clasped around her neck. Gently, he reached out, clutching the rose between his fingers. In a husky whisper, he asked, "Can we finish our talk now, please?"

A surge of nausea caused her to clamp a hand over her mouth, and he let go of the necklace. She hurried past him to the bathroom. She locked the door behind her, then puked up everything in her stomach. Morning sickness would get very inconvenient, very quickly.

Pounding sounded at the door. "Luna! Luna, let me in. Please."

She curled inward, arms clutching her abdomen so tightly that sharp pains stabbed through her ribs. The last thing she would do was open that door. She'd rather stay locked inside this small room until it became her tomb.

"Luna!" Chance called again, desperate and pleading.

She counted the minutes in her head. He stopped before her tremors did. After the nausea disappeared, she went through her morning rituals of brushing her teeth and hair. With a satisfying *ting*, she tore the necklace off and winged it into the trash.

That's where it belongs.

Out of excuses to stay in the bathroom, she cracked the door open, peeking warily into the hall for any sign of Chance. He was gone. Relieved, she hurried back to her room and sat on her bed. Not for the first time, she regretted ever moving out of her mother's house. For years, she'd been desperate to get out from under her father's strict rules, imagining that when she was free she would be happy. If anything, the opposite was true.

The problem is me, she thought.

Her father wasn't around anymore. All she had left was her mother. *If I went back home, would Chance hurt her too?*

When she'd chosen to stay with Sarah, his first move had been to threaten Amanda. If Luna never came back, he wouldn't spare her anymore. He wouldn't need to.

When Luna blinked, her mind conjured the image of Susan's withered corpse in the cabin, and she shivered. Was there such a thing as a place where Chance *couldn't* follow? Idly, Luna thought about the way things were during Chance's coma—the best years of her life. She missed being able to sleep in her bed without the fear of having to share it. She missed her body being her own.

I can't worry about her anymore, Luna decided. Amanda knew Chance's backstory and had chosen to stay with him. When Luna was well enough, and the opportunity presented itself, she would put herself first and run for her life.

WHEN LUNA FINALLY rolled out of bed a few hours later, the apartment buzzed with life. Amanda hummed a soft, cheerful tune in the kitchen while Chance flipped pancakes with practiced ease. Luna moved quietly, avoiding their eyes as she poured a glass of orange juice.

"Oh, Luna!" Amanda called, catching a glimpse of her friend from the corner of her eye. "You're up!"

A sharp pang of nausea twisted in Luna's stomach at the

scent of rich syrup and butter mingling in the air, but there was nothing left to throw up. She lifted the glass slowly to her lips, sipping carefully before pulling out the chair across from her roommate.

Amanda tapped her fingers lightly on the table next to her empty plate. "Would you like some breakfast?"

"No," Luna said, studying the way Amanda chewed on her bottom lip.

"You've got to eat something," Chance insisted, placing a plate of pancakes in front of her.

They were picture-perfect, like everything he did, but Luna didn't trust them. He could've put anything in the batter, and she would rather starve than risk suffering from some kind of poisoning. The longer she stared at them, the more she hated them. They were perfectly symbolic of her life, and Chance himself—innocuous on the outside, but questionable on the inside.

"No, *thank you*," Luna said, her tone sharper.

Next to the plate lay a folded newspaper, the headline barely visible. She spotted the word *Obituaries* and instinctively brought the paper closer. Amanda's face tightened, as if she'd been bracing for this moment. She quietly slid the plate of pancakes toward herself.

Close to the top of the page was a picture of Sarah.

In Loving Memory of Sarah Amelia Cross

Sarah Amelia Cross, 21, of Lima, passed away peacefully on June

23rd, 1992.

Known for her intelligence and boundless curiosity, Sarah had a natural way of making people feel seen and heard. A recent graduate of Shawnee High School, Sarah was excited to pursue her future. Her love for literature and learning was matched only by her devotion to her family and friends.

Though taken from us too soon, Sarah's spirit will live on in the stories we share, the lives she touched, and the community she helped build. She is deeply missed.

Beneath it, the date of her funeral: *July 3rd, 1992.* Tomorrow.

Chance glanced at her from his place by the sink. The creases between his eyebrows told her he had something to say. Something he *couldn't* say because of Amanda, who took a bite of her food, oblivious to the silent exchange.

"We're going to hang out with some friends later, and I think you should come," she announced.

Luna placed a hand on her stomach and glared at her roommate. "I don't think that's a good idea . . . considering."

Amanda held her palms up defensively. "I'm sorry to spring this on you—"

"You spring EVERYTHING on me," Luna interrupted.

"—at the last minute, but I think we could both use a night out. It might help you feel better. Or at the very least, forget about things for a little while."

Luna didn't have to speak to make her disinterest apparent.

Chance turned toward the sink, hiding his face.

What does he think of the idea? Luna wondered.

Amanda continued. "You can wear your pretty new dress, and we can go eat somewhere quiet and nice. It'll be fun."

Luna sighed, resigned to her fate. It wouldn't matter what she answered. It never did.

A FEW HOURS later, they dressed and climbed into Chance's truck. It took effort for Luna to keep herself from having a panic attack as Chance folded the driver's seat forward for her to climb into the back. Amanda sat in the passenger seat, oblivious. As he drove, Chance kept an eye on Luna in the rearview mirror.

Luna's dress was itchy and thick, clinging to her clammy skin in a way that frustrated and exhausted her. Sweat trickled down her temple, and she had a hard time deciding whether it was from her hormones or the fabric of her clothes. When they arrived at their destination, Luna was struck with déjà vu—the place was a lot like the one Violet had taken Chance and Luna to so long ago.

Outside the front door, a man waited for them. He was a bit taller than Luna with greasy, shoulder-length brown hair, wearing a dress shirt he didn't look comfortable in. Luna guessed that in a casual situation, he'd wear grunge clothing. Amanda introduced him as Drew, to which Chance was eerily silent.

Luna side-eyed Amanda as they went into the restaurant. She'd expected a group hangout, but now she understood exactly what Amanda was trying to do. This was a double date.

Chance must've come to the same conclusion because, as they neared the table, he blurted out, "Let's not sit next to our dates."

Amanda laughed, her fingers trailing down his arm. "Why not?"

Chance smiled, soft and sincere. "I think it's more romantic to sit across from your date, so you can look into their eyes." He leaned in and pressed a gentle kiss to Amanda's lips.

Luna wanted to puke, and for once, not because of morning sickness. Tightening the shawl around her shoulders, she glanced at Drew. He shrugged and got into the booth without a word. Luna cast a glance at Amanda but saw no protest in her shining eyes, only adoration for Chance.

Luna shook her head. *Have you no shame?*

Resigned, she eased into the booth across from Drew. Chance settled beside her, close enough that the hidden dagger in his pocket pressed sharply into her hip. A warning.

What in God's name is he planning now? Is he really thinking of trying something here, in front of all these witnesses?

"Hey, shouldn't it be girls on one side, guys on the other?" She floated the idea out loud in her best attempt at sounding friendly.

Chance visibly bristled when Amanda tilted her head in consideration. "Too late for that, girl. We're already sittin' down."

Chance smiled at Luna. "Don't worry, I don't bite."

Luna's gaze dropped to the table as Amanda jumped into small talk. She let her mind drift, silently reciting organic compounds from her last class, grounding herself somewhere far away.

Chance's fingers brushed across her knuckles. She looked down at their hands, then back at his face. His eyes were all for Amanda, as if his arm operated separately from his body.

Luna jerked away from his grip and set her hand on the table. "Don't touch me."

Chance held his hands up innocently. "Sorry. It was an accident."

Amanda shot Luna a petulant glare. She thought she was causing problems.

Of course.

Frowning, Luna shifted her focus to Drew, forcing a smile as she tried to engage him in friendly conversation. But then Chance's hand settled heavily on her thigh. She stiffened. Neither Drew nor Amanda seemed to notice.

Why? Why is he doing this? Luna wondered, then caught a split-second bitter glare Chance sent Drew's way. *He's jealous.*

She wanted to call him out for touching her again, but Amanda had nearly gone venomous. An idea popped into her head. Luna reached across the table, clasping Drew's hand. Chance's fingers dug deeper into her thigh, but Luna ignored them, batting her lashes in her best Amanda impression. Chance fidgeted in the seat beside her, losing control of his temper. How much more would it take for his rage to take over so Amanda could see who her "sweet" boyfriend really was?

Amanda dismissed herself to go to the bathroom, and Drew did the same. Luna was ready to join them, but Chance refused to move from his seat, blocking her in the booth, up against the wall.

"What do you think you're doing?" he demanded, drumming his fingers on the table as soon as Drew and Amanda were out of earshot.

"I was talking to my date," she replied, jutting out her chin.

"Your *date*? Really? We both know you don't give a shit about him. You just want to piss me off."

"I don't know what you're talking about," Luna lied sweetly.

Chance scoffed and leaned toward her. Without any trace of emotion, he said, "You will if I empty his guts all over the fucking parking lot."

"Why would you do that?"

"Because you're mine. You're—" He stopped just before Amanda and Drew sat back down at the table. The fury vanished in an instant, replaced by a bright, easy smile. A smile he and Luna both knew was fake.

She shrank back against the wall, trying to disappear into the wood and plaster, tension curling tight in her chest.

"Everything all right?" Amanda asked, her eyes flicking between Luna and Chance, trying to read the air.

"Of course," Chance said, voice breezy. Practiced. "We should get a round of drinks to celebrate."

Amanda giggled, any concern melting away as quickly as it had come. "Celebrate what?"

Chance's gaze locked onto Amanda, warm and steady. "Blossoming romance," he said smoothly. Beneath the table, his fingers slid toward Luna's leg again, cold and deliberate.

Amanda and Drew whooped in agreement.

Chance cut Luna a sideways glance. A flicker of amusement? A threat? Whatever it was twisted her stomach. *He knows.*

"N-no, that's okay. I'll just have water," Luna said.

Chance raised an eyebrow, a partially amused expression on his face. "Oh, but why not have something more relaxing?"

There was only one answer, and the way Chance watched her made her almost certain he expected her to say it.

Amanda grabbed Chance's hand, saving Luna from speaking. "Oh, give her a break. She hasn't been feeling well."

"That's too bad," Chance said, the friendly smile belying the monster in his eyes.

Luna shot Amanda a grateful glance. "Yeah, it is."

Lighthearted conversation resumed, and Luna slumped in her seat. How much longer until this was over? She considered slipping out to the bathroom and calling Rose to see if she could come get her.

Chance's hand brushed hers again, and she tensed before it gave way to annoyance. Maybe she was going about this the wrong way. Playing defense was getting her nowhere. It was time to take some shots of her own. Instead of tearing herself free again, she forced herself to keep her hand there, letting his palm slide into hers. He glanced at their entwined hands from the corner of his eye, smirking slightly.

Luna ground her teeth, letting a few minutes pass before she squeezed tight and plopped their clenched hands onto the table for Amanda and Drew to see. Her roommate's nostrils flared, her expression somewhere between anger and humiliation as Chance ripped his hand away. Amanda's bitter eyes zoned in on him, but he plucked a cigarette from his pocket and hurried toward the door.

Amanda stood up, dragging Luna from the table to the alcove by the bathroom. "What the hell is your problem?" she hissed. "I invite you out for dinner, and you act like this? So not cool."

Luna held her hands up. She wasn't going to have this argument again. "I know what you're thinking, but he keeps touching me under the table. I know you don't care, so I'm going to find a pay phone and get Mom to pick me up. Tell Drew I'm sorry for bailing."

Amanda's face softened. She glanced in the direction of the door, then back to Luna. Her nostrils flared again, but she seemed more annoyed than angry. "Wait."

Luna did.

"Honestly . . ." Amanda started with a great gust of a sigh, "I thought it was weird the way he insisted on sitting next to you. I've noticed a few other things that were weird too. I wanted to believe it was because he was sweet and could see you were in a rough place, but I'm not so sure that's what's going on anymore."

The tiniest flicker of something bright blossomed in Luna's chest. What had she seen that finally planted the seed of doubt? Was there anything Luna could do to deliver the final blow?

"He's been odd lately. Distant, quiet. Has weird marks and

wounds, and I—" She stopped as if she couldn't finish that thought. "I caught him leaving your room a few weeks ago in the middle of the night."

Luna stilled, the words knocking the air from her lungs. This whole time, could it be that Amanda *knew* what Chance was doing and had allowed it to happen? Swallowing down a surge of nausea, she asked, "You *what?*"

"He said he heard you screaming, your night terrors, but I shrugged it off, thinking he was surprised because I didn't warn him. I . . . It all seems dumb now, Luna. I'm so sorry I didn't tell you."

Luna's head filled with static, unable to decide which feeling was the most appropriate—anger, betrayal, sadness, despondency?

"I've been thinking about breaking up with him," Amanda added.

The static cleared away, leaving behind something eerily similar to hope.

If Amanda kicked Chance to the curb, there'd be no reason for him to be in the apartment anymore. There was a long way to go before things could ever be okay again, but that would be a huge step in the right direction.

A step toward getting her life back.

Chapter Fifty

THE HOPE DIDN'T last long. Not that Luna expected it to.

The ride home was awkward and tense and seemed to take forever. Luna was quick to leave Amanda and Chance alone so her roommate could do what she needed to do. But hours passed, and Luna heard no screaming or crying. Nothing happened at all. When she strained hard enough, she could hear the television playing in the living room.

The anxiety in Luna's brain taunted her, *She's not going to do it. Nothing is going to change.*

Those thoughts were accompanied by the look on Chance's face in the restaurant. What had he been about to say before Amanda returned from the bathroom? Luna would likely never know. She curled up in bed, mad that she hadn't taken the opportunity to call her mother and go home with her. This was going to be a long night. Made even longer by the fact that it was unlikely she would fall asleep anytime soon.

Tears running down her cheeks, Luna dug her backpack out of the closet and emptied all of her textbooks onto the floor.

Leaving was her best bet. She'd done everything else and failed. Her last option was to cut the cord of this life and try again. If everything went according to plan, she would stop by Sarah's funeral, then make her way to Rose's.

A floorboard creaked in the hallway, and Luna tossed a blanket over her half-filled backpack. Same as when she started staying with Sarah, she didn't plan on telling Amanda she was leaving. A head start was the best thing she could hope for. When she looked up, Chance stood in the hall, his form outlined in shadows. She went back to searching for the bare essentials. She didn't care if he watched her scavenge to collect random items so long as he didn't know what they were for.

"Luna," he greeted.

She ignored him.

"You're planning something," he said, face creased in frustration as he tried, and failed, to get her attention.

Footsteps thudded on her floor as he approached, grasping her shoulder to bring her toward him. "Will you stop running from me already? Let me in. *Accept* me. It's time, don't you think?"

His face was an inch from hers, so there was no way he missed the exact second her mask fell. "Three years," she whispered. "Every week for three years I visited you in the hospital. I moved all the way out here to keep an eye on you just to have some semblance of a life, and now, it's all gone. Everything I've worked for."

"You've centered your life around me, and you still think you hate me?"

"I don't think. I *know.*"

"In three years you could've been on the other side of the world, but you stayed by my side, waiting for me to wake up. That doesn't say *hate* to me."

Luna curled her lip at him. "My mistake was that I didn't kill you when I had the chance."

Chance smirked. "You could never kill me. You need me."

"I owe it to Max."

"Okay," he said, blue eyes sparkling with amusement. He dug his dagger from his pocket and handed it to her. "If you hate me so much, then go ahead. End it for both of us right now. I won't stop you." He lifted his shirt, tapping his chest. "My heart is right here, baby."

Luna's lip quivered, her fingers inching toward the blade. She could imagine taking it and sinking it into his neck, ending all her problems in one fluid movement. *If only things were that simple.*

"I'm not putting my fingerprints on that thing," she said, retracting her hand.

Chance smirked, slow and cold, before sliding the knife back into his pocket. "Yeah. That's what I thought. You don't want to be alone. Without me, who are you? Just a sad story with no villain to blame."

He took a step closer.

"No scapegoat. No distraction. Just you and the truth. That your life didn't fall apart because of me. It was already broken. I just made it harder."

Luna's chest felt like it was caving in. Rage flickered, but it couldn't find oxygen. Everything inside her was too hollow, too cold. She *wanted* to scream, but she had no energy to back it up.

"You want to know what I think?" He continued, eyes gleaming. "I think you *like* having me around. I think you crave the chaos. But you're scared. Scared people won't get it. That they'll look at you like you're sick." He leaned in. "News flash! Anyone who might've judged you? They're already dead."

"Malcolm!" Amanda's voice rang out, sharp and distant.

Luna's lips parted, but no sound came. Her body felt weightless, as if her soul had begun retreating just to protect itself.

He held her gaze like a vise, his smirk tightening ever so slightly. "This isn't over."

"Malcolm!" Amanda shouted again, closer this time.

Finally, he stepped back.

Luna forced a smile, brittle and venomous. "Bye-bye, Malcolm."

As soon as he disappeared down the hall, she wilted. What would he do when he realized she was gone and not coming back? Would he follow? Who else would he hurt to get to her? Was running away really her best option or would it only make things worse?

I have to try.

So far, nothing else had worked. Luna didn't know exactly what plans Chance, and those mysterious men, had for her, but she didn't want to wait to find out.

Chapter Fifty-One

AMANDA GLANCED AT Malcolm from the corner of her eye. He sat beside her, relaxed against the couch. His gaze locked on the television as if everything was fine. As if he hadn't blown up their entire relationship two hours earlier.

She stayed silent, hoping he would bring up what happened on his own. He didn't. He would barely look at her. Did he sense the tension between them? Did he care? Amanda started to think of her conversation with Luna again, and about everything she had seen in her journal.

He's an asshole for sure, she mused, wondering if Luna would let her see the pictures in her book again. Then she scolded herself. Did she really need pictures to work up the nerve to dump some jerk who was treating her wrong?

Malcolm rose without a word and started down the hall like she wasn't even there. Amanda's fists clenched at her sides, nails carving half-moons into her palms. Her legs trembled with the raw effort it took to stay still, to keep from lunging after him and dragging him back by the collar. She followed anyway, silent as a shadow. When he went into Luna's room and shut the door behind him, something in her snapped. Her vision tinted red, hot and pulsing, and the hallway suddenly felt too narrow to contain her. She debated whether to rip all her hair out or to storm in there and rip his out instead.

That was it. She stormed forward, hollering down the corridor.

"Malcolm!"

No answer.

Her pulse spiked. Her throat burned.

"MALCOLM!"

Luna's door creaked open a beat later, and he emerged. When his eyes landed on her, he froze for half a second. Just long enough for Amanda to spot the flash of panic before it disappeared behind something softer.

A smirk.

Gentle. Familiar. Like he wasn't an absolute slimeball.

"What's wrong, baby?" he asked with false sweetness as he leaned in like he could kiss it better.

She stopped him with a hand on his chest. "What's *wrong?* Are you kidding me right now? This is the most you've spoken to me in two hours."

He kept his silence.

"And it's only because you know I saw you in her room. *Again.*"

"She called me in there and I—"

Amanda held her hand up even higher. "We both know that's bullshit. I don't know what kind of game you're trying to play here, but I think you should leave."

"But, sweetheart—"

Amanda tipped her head back to stare into his eyes for a full minute, then said, "Go."

He stared back, scoffed, and stormed out of the apartment without another word. Only when the door clanged shut behind him did Amanda let her face fall.

Chapter Fifty-Two

LUNA GOT OFF the bus in Lima early the next day and made her way through her hometown. The plan was simple. She would attend Sarah's funeral, then make her way home. She didn't know how she would explain herself to Rose yet, but she would worry about that later.

At the cemetery, Luna sat alone in a chair in the back row of Sarah's funeral, mostly ignored by her relatives. Luna was used to that. Used to blending in with the background. She dissociated, replaying those last terrible moments in the car full of Sarah's terrified wails.

Luna was so used to crying that she could no longer do it. Her eyes burned with the sensation, but inside, she was dead. She didn't hear the priest giving his homily. She didn't hear anyone. When a tear landed on her hand, pulling her back from the dissociative state, she stared at the glittering globule for a full minute. It was a small reminder that she was alive. That meant she still had the opportunity to make her situation better. That was more than she could say for Max and Sarah. Dead, they were unable to change their fate.

When Sarah's casket was lowered into the grave, Luna left the ceremony, cutting through the field. The rainwater was deeper in several places, making her backtrack numerous times in an attempt to get to the road. She started to run, hoping to make it home without getting caught in the worst of the storm. Rain dripped from her hood into her eyes, blurring her surroundings. Boot catching on something, she flew to the ground. Her first instinct was to protect her stomach, curling into herself as she fell on the grass. She sat up, groaning in pain. Dazed, she glanced at what she'd tripped on. A small plaque. She recognized the name engraved on it.

"Violet Bulrey, rest in peace," she read aloud. Droplets pelted the ground around her, the perfect soundtrack.

For a long time, she stayed like that. Rain began to soak through her clothes, freezing her skin, but she didn't move. Her mind was trapped in a whirlwind.

Violet, her late best friend.

There was no reason Luna should've survived instead. She was just a broken girl stumbling through the wreckage of her life while the people who mattered most lay in the ground.

Hands trembling, she pushed herself up, fingers digging into the dirt for support. Each movement was a small victory against the ache clawing inside her. Her feet found the narrow path leading out of the cemetery. Steps slow and uneven, she walked, passing cracked sidewalks and weatherworn houses. The town blurred around her, familiar and unrecognizable at the same time.

Luna slowed her pace as she came to an intersection, contemplating what she would tell her mother. What would be the easiest way to sum up all that had happened? Was there such a thing?

She made a move to cross the street but stopped. A man stood on the other side, dressed head to toe in black. His hood was low, shadows swallowing the top half of his face. He was watching her.

The hairs on the back of Luna's neck rose, anticipating danger. She tried to ignore it. *I'm getting in my own head. He's not watching me,* she thought, but when she glanced at him again, he was moving. In her direction.

Paranoid, she started to walk faster. And so did he. She shifted direction, heading back the way she'd come to test what the man would do. He stepped into the street, crossing toward her.

There was no doubting it now. He was after her. Luna started to run, unsure what to do. This part of town was far from any of her friends or family. The closest thing to safety she had was the woods. As much as she hated them, there was familiarity there. Familiarity she prayed the man didn't have. She burst through the undergrowth, listening to him crashing behind her. A small bush caught her eye, dense enough to offer cover. She dove in, curling into herself, lungs burning. Hands shaking, she clamped one over her mouth, willing her breath to slow. If she could stay quiet, maybe he'd pass her by.

To her horror, the footsteps got *louder.* Closer. She lost her nerve and bolted from her hiding spot, terrified to see the man only a few feet behind her.

"What do you want from me?" she hollered over her shoulder.

He didn't respond. His face was drawn, eyes focused and

empty of anything remotely human. She had seen that look many times in Chance's eyes. It spoke of danger. She'd learned to avoid it.

She put her all into running. Her walks around Bowling Green had given her better endurance than the last time she'd had to do this run. She jogged so long, in fact, that she surprised herself when she busted into the clearing of Chance's cabin.

Of course.

The man was still a good distance behind her, but she had a dilemma on her hands. She'd come this far, but she couldn't run forever. She would have to rest, and soon. But would the cabin offer her shelter or would it only trap her?

Snap!

That decided it. She hurried toward the cabin and went inside, closing the door behind her. Dust and stale air made her cough as she rushed through the living room, frantic to find the best place to hide. There wasn't enough furniture in the front room, and she didn't have time to search anywhere else before the door burst open. The man entered, face red, hair wild from the run.

When he spotted her, he grinned and pulled a blade from his pocket. "Seems I've got you all alone."

"Why are you doing this?" she asked, taking one step backward.

"I have orders," he said. "It's nothing personal, okay?"

Luna grabbed a candleholder off the table and brandished it at him. The man held out his weapon and came toward her, swinging it in various directions. She dodged several slashes and tried to jump backward, stumbling over an uneven wooden plank, and fell, landing heavily on her backside.

Sneering, the man hovered over her, knife raised. Footsteps came from the door. Luna peered around her attacker's legs, fearing a second assailant. Chance wiggled his dagger back and forth as he leaned in the doorframe, the backdrop of the gloomy rain-filled sky completing the horror scene. "I knew you were plotting something. And it looks like I got here just in time," he said.

Then he grabbed the man's collar and yanked him backward, reaching around to stab him in the stomach. With a grin, he tossed him aside, leaving him bleeding on the floor.

Luna couldn't tell if he was dead or not, but she was no longer afraid of him. Her attention was on Chance and the damn Cheshire-cat grin on his face as he approached her. Luna stood her ground, too tired of the nuance to be afraid. Tired of letting him get the best of her. Tired of being at his mercy.

Just *tired.*

He grabbed her arm. "I don't know where you thought you were going, but you're not going anywhere without me." She felt cold metal as Chance pushed his knife against her windpipe, smearing blood onto her skin. She should've been scared, but she was listless.

At the very least, death would reunite her with all those he had already slain. "Kill me if you're gonna do it."

In her peripheral vision, Luna could see the unknown assailant picking himself up. He groaned once, then stood on wobbly legs and lunged at them. Chance struck out so fast that

Luna didn't have time to get out of the way as he embedded his blade in the man's chest. She gasped and took a slow step backward, cradling her arm. One long slash appeared, from her elbow halfway to her wrist.

"Get out of here!" Chance yelled at her as he faced the man.

A strange chill burned through the wound. Instinctively, Luna pressed her hand on the injury, warm blood running through the cracks of her fingers.

She obeyed Chance. She ran.

Chapter Fifty-Three

CHANCE COULDN'T DO IT.

Luna had been in his clutches, his blade to her throat. Ending his problems had been as easy as one swipe. One single swipe, and he'd be in the clear. He'd even had a witness who could vouch to Cody that he was following orders. Yet, he couldn't bring himself to do it.

When he opened his eyes, she was long gone. He didn't know where she went, but he was glad. Until he regained control over his anger, he didn't want to risk the possibility of harming her further. He was well on his way into *that* mind and it couldn't be stopped.

Amanda's rejection had had him on edge all night. He'd fallen asleep in his truck, thinking of ways to make it up to her. To get her to let him back inside the apartment. Then he'd seen Luna sneaking off early in the morning and followed her, thinking this was a better opportunity than anything he could've thought up.

When he'd spotted one of Cody's men, he had no choice but to intervene. Chance stared at the man. He was still alive, clutching at the deep gash across his chest. Red rivulets cascaded to the floor, creating a puddle beneath him. Taking his dagger, Chance plunged it straight through his heart with a sickening *pop*.

Wide eyes stared up at him. He struggled to live against the blood drowning him.

Chance let out an irritated sigh. "Would you just die already? Damn. You're taking up my whole morning."

He wrenched his knife free, a torrent of blood welling from the wound. Blood pooled onto the floor around him, staining the tips of his fake blond hair a muddy maroon. Carefully, Chance wiped the blade clean on the edge of the man's pants and stood up.

He took his last breath, his body shuddering, then lay still forever. Chance was relieved. Although he'd have to spend the rest of the day disposing of the body, he'd kept Luna and himself alive for another day. Now, he had to keep his fingers crossed that Cody wouldn't find out.

Chapter Fifty-Four

BY THE TIME Luna made it out of the forest, the rain had stopped. The trees dripped, and her boots squished in the grass. Her arm was in searing pain, and although it wasn't a deep wound, it was long. Long enough to make her lose a decent amount of blood. Horrid, ragged sounds came from her chest, her ribs aching with phantom pains from her accident. Tears mixed with the rain. She cried for her lost loved ones. Cried for herself. But mostly, she cried at the fact that there was such evil in the world.

Amid her agony, it struck her what had happened. She'd been in danger, and Chance *saved* her.

Her arm was soaked in blood as she hurried toward town, toward help, convinced Chance would be right behind her if she turned around. She pushed herself to go faster.

The more she exerted herself, the worse she started to feel. Dizziness swirled through her, sending the world tilting in an unsettling blur. She stuck her arms out, trying to keep herself balanced. The edges of her vision flickered, colors bleeding together. Her knees buckled, and the blackness reached up to claim her.

***

WHEN LUNA CAME to, she was confused. The room around her was too bright. Empty of anything. She didn't remember what had happened or how she arrived here, but her arm was in pain. She glanced down at the bandages, and it all slowly trickled back to her.

The cabin. The man. Chance.

"You're in Bowling Green Hospital," someone said. She jumped, glancing at the doctor beside her with the sudden realization of his presence. "You were brought here by ambulance from Lima. You needed twenty-five stitches."

She stared at the bandage, mystified. The wound could've been to her throat. It would've been if he hadn't hesitated, but Chance changed his mind for whatever reason. He'd *saved* her.

"She's awake," the doctor called into the hallway.

The same officer she'd spoken to at the police station entered her room. "Your name's Luna, right?" he asked, moving a stool over to her bedside. Luna forced herself to peer at him, trying to remember his name. His face was weathered, marked by years of worry, with lines etched softly around his eyes and mouth. Deep-set eyes, the color of faded denim, held a quiet kindness as he observed her. "We met before. I'm Officer Steerling. A concerned citizen called in an unconscious woman in the road. Can you tell me what happened?"

Luna sat back, tracing the lines in the ceiling with her eyes. The wound on her arm was an *accident*. Chance hadn't been trying to hurt her. *This time.* That hadn't always been the case.

So what if he helped me? He's a murderer, she reminded herself.

He'd killed Max. *Bragged* about it. He'd killed Violet, and Susan. And she was pretty sure her father too.

"Does this have to do with your last trip to the station?" he prompted when she didn't answer the first question.

Luna opened her mouth and three years' worth of trauma spilled out.

Chapter Fifty-Five

CHANCE CONNECTED THE sirens to Luna's departure. He hadn't been able to dispose of the body. Hell, the best he'd been able to do was light a fire and hope the cabin went up in flames. He barely had time to escape the clearing before it was surrounded by cops.

That little bitch. He seethed. *After everything I've done for her.*

He wanted to find Luna and hurt her in every way possible for betraying him. Hurrying out of the woods, he ditched his truck and hot-wired the first car he came across. It was ugly, and the fact that he *had* to drive it filled him with the slightest bit more loathing. Back in Bowling Green, he ditched the car not far from Luna's apartment complex, running the rest of the way. He burst through the door, ready for a fight. When Amanda greeted him, he stilled. There was no sign of anger or fear on her face, only bewilderment.

She doesn't know what's happened, he realized. *Luna hasn't been here.*

The sirens were getting louder, and his intuition warned that they were coming for him.

"What the hell are you doing here?" Amanda demanded.

"I'm sorry, okay? I forgot my . . . wallet. Gonna grab it and go," he assured her, flying past.

"Uh, sure." She watched him warily.

"Thank you," he said and hurried out of the living room.

She was still reeling in stunned silence when a knock echoed through the apartment.

Chance sprinted down the hall and out the bathroom window just as Amanda opened the door to the cops.

Chapter Fifty-Six

WHEN LUNA WAS released from police custody later that day, it was with a rock in her stomach. Chance could be *anywhere*, and it brought her little comfort to think of the police scouting Lima and Bowling Green for signs of him. If he was as crafty as he used to be, he'd leave no clues for them to follow. She tried to force herself to relax as Officer Steerling drove her to her mother's, but her hands shook when she opened the car door and thanked him for the ride.

As Luna stared at the front of her childhood home, she took a deep breath to calm her tattered nerves and went inside. She followed the clanking of dishes from the kitchen.

"Mom. Can we talk?" she asked.

Rose turned to face her, surprised. "I didn't hear you come in," she said, wiping her hands on the nearest dish towel. When she noted Luna's expression, some of her brightness dimmed. "What's the matter?" she asked, eyes on the bandages wrapped around Luna's wound. "What happened to your arm?"

"I fell at work and needed stitches," she lied, not wanting to go into details until she was in a better place, mentally, to talk about it. "I wanted to see how you were doing."

Her mother sighed, exhaustion heavy in her voice. "It's hard, Luna. It feels like time is going by so slowly, but I'm sure you feel the same and don't need me reminding you."

"It has been hard," Luna agreed. "Ever since Dad died, it feels like something is missing."

Her mom's eyes softened. "We're all trying to figure it out. Some days I feel like I'm just holding on by a thread."

"Is it . . ." Luna started, then paused, unsure how to drop her question. "Would it be okay . . . if I moved back home? At least for a little while?"

Her mother's expression shifted, a mix of concern and surprise. "Where is this coming from?"

"I just . . . I need to be somewhere familiar."

"If you're sure," Rose said. "What about Amanda?"

Luna's stomach clenched. With any luck, the police would catch Chance before he could hurt anyone else, and Amanda would be just fine. "She's gonna stay in the apartment, I guess. I haven't actually talked to her about this. We're not getting along as well as we used to."

Rose placed her hands on her hips. "And what of school? Are you going to make an hour drive there and back every day in the fall?"

Heat rushed to Luna's cheeks. "No. I'm . . . I'm not going back."

Rose's brow furrowed. "What?"

"It's . . ." Luna peeked up at her before shame had her studying the floor again. The words were there, on the tip of her tongue, but there was something about actually saying them out loud.

Rose placed her hand on her daughter's shoulder. "What

is it?"

Luna met her eyes. *Here goes nothing.* "I'm pregnant, Mom."

Rose went still as a statue. She reached behind her, grabbing the back of a chair to steady herself. "Did I . . . hear you right?"

Luna bobbed her head once, curtly, unable to decipher the expression on her mother's face.

Slowly, she steadied herself and gathered her daughter into her arms. "That's such wonderful news!"

Luna broke from the embrace, stunned. This was the opposite reaction she'd expected. For Luna's entire life, Rose had driven home the point of living your own life first, of not starting a family until she was ready for it. Luna had expected anger, dismay, aloofness, but this? "Wait . . . you're not disappointed in me?"

"Honestly, Luna, there was a time I might have been, but after your father passed, I've done some reevaluating of my life. Family should come first." She paused and swiped a thumb across her chin. "No matter what."

"Does that mean I can move back home?"

"Of course it does. You can have your old room back if you'd like, but I should give it a proper cleaning first. There's quite a bit of dust in there."

"You don't have to trouble yourself," Luna said. With everything going on, dust was the least of her concerns.

Chapter Fifty-Seven

"I'M GONNA GET dinner started," Rose said. "Are you—" The phone rang, cutting off whatever she was about to ask. She scooped it up and held it to her ear. "Hello? Amanda? Yeah . . . she's right here. Luna, it's for you."

Luna drew her eyebrows together and hesitantly took the phone. "Amanda?"

"Luna! Where are you?" She sounded frantic, but not afraid.

"Are you safe?" Luna asked.

"Yeah, I'm fine, but—"

Luna hung up with a *click*. If Amanda was okay, then that meant Chance was still on the run, that the cops were doing a good job of scaring him away, and with any luck, he would *stay* away.

Rose gave her an odd look as she set the phone back on the base. "Is everything okay?"

"Yeah. I should get back and get started on packing," Luna said, gesturing to the phone. "I think Amanda's starting to worry."

"Be careful, Luna. And call me as soon as you get there."

"I will." Luna offered a small, tired smile.

Rose went back to her food, and Luna slipped out into the

cool evening air. She started her walk to the bus stop, her mind void of thoughts as she rode to the apartment. On the way through Bowling Green, she stopped at a convenience store to gather some boxes.

Amanda was ready to ambush her right when she walked through the door. "Where have you been?" she demanded, pulling Luna into a hug. When they broke apart, she lightly slapped her on the arm. "There were cops here for Chance. I was worried when you cut our phone call short, and . . . Oh my God!" She gently touched her bandaged arm. "What happened?"

"Chance hurt me again. When they catch him, the police are going to lock him away for a long, long time. I hope you kissed your precious boyfriend goodbye."

"I dumped him last night," Amanda said.

Luna stopped, the words knocking the wind out of her sails. "You what?"

"I broke up with him," she reiterated. "Told him to leave. He came back through here earlier and then, maybe a minute later, the cops showed up."

"They told you everything?"

Amanda rolled her bottom lip between her teeth. "He's wanted for questioning in connection to some murder."

"At least you know now that I was telling the truth," Luna said and stepped into the hall.

Amanda grasped Luna's undamaged arm. "I-I'm so sorry . . . for everything." She moved to hug her again, but stopped, staring at the cardboard tucked under her arm. "Why do you have boxes?"

"I'm moving."

"I didn't think you were serious!" Amanda exclaimed, trying to tear them from Luna's hands. "You can't go! What about Mal— Chance?"

"Stop it, Mandy. I've had enough, okay? Mom said I could come home, and that's what I'm going to do. It's too dangerous to stay here when he knows every detail about this place. You said he came back once. Well, you best believe he'll be back again, and I'm not gonna wait for that to happen. If you're smart, you'll stay with one of your sisters for a while until they catch him."

In a small voice, Amanda asked, "Do you think he's going to come after me for kicking him out?"

Luna shrugged, refusing to look at her. It was hard not to blame her, not to think about the fact that if Amanda had taken her warnings seriously from the beginning, they might be in a different situation right now. A better one, most likely.

Chapter Fifty-Eight

I T WAS ODD how life had a way of coming full circle. The hovels Chance had escaped from were the only places he had left to go now that the cops were hot on his trail. The winos and drug addicts had as much to lose as he did by talking to the police, so in a way, they were the best sort of protection he could muster.

But he was tired. So very, very tired.

After killing Cody's recruit, he feared going to sleep. What would he do the next time he saw him? But sleep was inevitable. Chance closed his eyes for a second, but it was a second too long. When he came to, he was in DreamWorld. He panicked until he recognized the beach. Reese's dream cycle.

As soon as they made eye contact, Reese's expression softened with sympathy. "I saw the news, man. Tough break."

"Yeah," Chance said, running a hand through his hair. "I'm fucked. Royally."

Reese was silent, and Chance scoffed, plopping down onto the sand to stare out at the ocean. He didn't know what he expected Reese to say, but the silence further irritated him.

"There's always something that can be done," Reese said at last.

"Like what?"

"Do you still have the Rosebone?"

"Yeah. Why?"

"Then we have a plan," Reese said, smiling up at the sky. "As long as you don't mind dying, of course."

Chapter Fifty-Nine

O N THE NEXT day, the Fourth of July, Luna wasn't in a festive mood. Impending doom clung to her mind as she worked on moving her stuff back to Rose's. Amanda wasn't handling the situation as well as Luna thought she would. She'd made plans for the two of them for the holiday, to which Luna grudgingly agreed after Amanda pestered Rose for an hour. It would be a sort of goodbye. Plus, it didn't hurt that Luna could keep an eye on her and make sure her friend was protected, in case Chance tried to use the holiday confusion to make a move.

He had been mysteriously absent the last twenty-four hours. Had he left to save himself or had he finally been captured by the people he'd been so desperate to escape from? Luna didn't know. His face had been plastered all over the news, but police hadn't found him. The longer the search went on, the more unsure Luna became. If Chance was still out there, hunting her, it would only be worse when he finally caught her. He's an animal. Everyone knows to never corner one that's injured, even if it is just his pride.

"Hey, I'm ready to do the fireworks now," Amanda called cheerfully to Luna, peeking in what used to be her room.

"Okay," Luna said as she filled the last box of her belongings. Amanda's eyes hinted at sadness, at words unspoken, but she hid all of that with a smile as she left the room. Luna made sure she was gone before she grabbed her notebook. She added the details of Sarah's death to it, making sure to write it on the same page as Susan's.

"Luna!" Amanda called from the front room.

With a huff, Luna grabbed the box and trudged outside. The apartment complex was oddly empty, but she guessed most of their neighbors had gone to visit family out of town. The fireworks already in the sky seemed to be a long way off.

Luna dumped the box in the trunk of Amanda's car and went back to the porch. She kept her back to the building, the brick under her hands grounding her to reality.

Amanda carried the first firework out to the center of the grass strip. She struck a match, lit the fuse, and stepped back. When it exploded with a sharp, piercing *bang*, red light spilled across the lawn like a sudden wound tearing through the night.

Luna flinched, shrinking into herself. The sound a brutal echo of Chance's gunshot—the same merciless noise that had silenced Violet forever. The red a reminder of the blood that flowed.

The pressure of pretending she was fine was suddenly too much. Luna's face crumpled, and she ran as fast as her legs would allow, giving Amanda no time to stop her.

Everything would always remind her of the past she had somehow survived. The past that, despite all her trying, she couldn't escape.

Chapter Sixty

FROM HIS HIDING place at the back of the lot, Chance watched Luna's figure grow smaller and smaller. Her cries pierced the quiet, and the urge to chase after her gnawed at him. Clenching his hands into tight fists, his nails dug into his palms, the sharp sting grounding him and reminding him why he was here. What he needed to do. His gaze shifted to Amanda as she trudged over to the porch.

No reason to drag things out any longer, he thought.

He was Bowling Green's most wanted man. Not only that, he was at the top of the hit list for Cody's men. He needed to split town, but he couldn't do that until all his business had been taken care of.

Chance emerged from the foliage, heading toward his "ex-girlfriend" on the porch. He exaggerated the sound of his footsteps, waiting for her to see him. When she did, she jumped to her feet and bared her teeth.

"Judging by your expression, I take it you know all about the real me," he said, swinging his dagger back and forth like a pendulum.

"You're a murderer," Amanda hissed.

"And the last horse crosses the finish line!" Chance laughed.

"Everything Luna said . . . it was true. She stiffened, face going pale. "She told me it was Max's, but . . . the baby is yours, isn't it? That's why I caught you in her room. You sick, twisted . . ."

Chance didn't hear the rest of her rant as he stilled, the words about Luna's pregnancy an unexpected blow.

She told her it was Max's? Betrayal stabbed into his chest. Why hadn't he considered that possibility?

"So, what . . . *now* you care about Luna?" Chance snapped, stalking toward Amanda to hide his hurt. "What about all the times she begged you to listen to her, *pleaded* with you, and you ignored her? And yes. I know how hard she tried."

Amanda fidgeted, studying the malice in his face. A flash of panic sparked in her eyes, then Amanda dashed for the door, Chance right on her heels.

"Don't flee, little rabbit!" he taunted.

He waited until they were both in the apartment to grab her long blonde hair, wrenching her head back. The gesture exposed the white skin on her throat.

"I should've listened to Luna," Amanda sobbed, twin trails of watery mascara running down her cheeks.

"Yes, you should've. But I guess I'm too captivating for that," Chance said, keeping the blade against her throat. "All I had to do was smile and use cute words, and girls like you turn to butter. So predictable."

"You never cared about me."

"At least you realize that now," Chance said with zero remorse.

Amanda's crying grew louder, the sound grating against

the inside of his head, but he wasn't ready to kill her yet. He moved her through the apartment to Luna's room. A hard shove knocked her to the floor, then he dragged his blade across her throat. Crimson flooded over her pale skin, and she collapsed onto the carpet. Chance dipped his fingers in her blood, stepping over her outstretched hand to scrawl a message on Luna's bedspread.

Chapter Sixty-One

LUNA SPED MOST of the way to Lima. Fireworks illuminated the sky, then stopped all at once when rain erupted as if Mother Nature had grown tired of the festivities. Water streamed from her eyes, making it hard to see.

Back home, she carried the last of her boxes inside while Rose quietly tidied up the room. When Luna set the final box down on her dresser, she sank into the chair in front of her vanity.

"How much more stuff do you have?" Rose asked, glancing at the scattered boxes. "I don't remember you moving this much out of the house."

"That's everything," Luna said, rifling through the contents of the box beside her. Horrified, she didn't see her notebook and dug deeper, but it wasn't there. After adding Sarah's details, Amanda had distracted her, and she'd forgotten to pack it. "But . . . I need to give Amanda back her car."

"Do you want me to follow you so I can bring you back home? It's getting late."

Luna shook her head. "The buses run for a few more hours. I'll be fine."

"Okay, I'll see you when you get back."

"See you," Luna said, hurrying outside. Of all the things to leave behind, she couldn't believe she'd left her *notebook*—

arguably, the most important item of all her belongings. She was desperate for the day to be over with, but her trip back to the apartment was harder than when she'd left. The closer she got to Bowling Green, the heavier the downpour. At the complex, sheets of water made it impossible to tell if Amanda was still outside.

Jogging to the door, Luna welcomed the dry warmth of the apartment as she stepped inside. Out of habit, she flipped the light switch but nothing happened. The apartment remained dark, the furniture reduced to silhouettes in the gloom.

The rain must've knocked the power out.

"Amanda?" Luna called, feeling her way through the darkness.

Luna waited a long, tense moment for a response that didn't come.

"Something's wrong," she whispered to herself.

A tiny light glowed down the hallway from her old room. It flickered and danced in the darkness. Candlelight. Luna shivered, not liking the foreboding that ran down her spine.

"Amanda, this isn't funny!" she called out, clinging to the idea that it was her friend playing a mean trick on her. Which was better than the alternative.

No response came. Luna lifted her hands to the sides of her head, her breath quick and uneven with fear. From the doorway, her eyes locked onto the candle. It sat in a familiar golden holder. She took a step back, ready to bolt, when her gaze landed on a shape beside the bed.

"Amanda!" she exclaimed, dropping to her knees.

She scooped up her limp body, seeing the massive wound

across her throat. Luna cuddled her to her chest. She was smaller in death. Amanda hadn't deserved this cruelty. Her only crime was being Luna's friend. She'd been in the wrong place at the wrong time.

"I'm sorry," she whispered, and with bleary eyes, set her down. As she sat back, she spotted the words that had been smeared on her bedding in blood: *TIME'S UP.*

Luna screamed and shot to her feet, ready to run, when a figure disconnected from the shadows in the corner of the room. A hand closed around her throat, choking off her cry for help. Luna tried to throw herself backward, out of his grip, and her heel knocked the candle over. The force tightened. She was lifted off the ground, then slammed against the wall. Choking, she raised her knee and jabbed it hard into Chance's manhood.

With a groan, he released her. She fell to the floor, gasping for air as she darted down the pitch-black hallway, fast and blind. Blood pounded in her ears, and she prayed she wouldn't stumble over her feet, that she wouldn't bring about her own downfall. She rounded the corner into the kitchen, searching for a weapon.

"Luna!"

She gave up her search and ducked beneath the table, contemplating her next move. She wanted to make a run for the front door, to try and flag down someone for help, but that would be foolish. He'd see her open it, and she knew from experience how quick a runner he was. He would catch her.

"It's over, darling!" Chance called over the echo of his footsteps.

Luna held a hand over her mouth, desperate to stifle

herself.

"I'm not angry, kitten. Honest. Show me that pretty face of yours, and we can put this all to rest."

Chance's footsteps drew closer, and she feared he already knew her hiding place. That like the predator he was, he could sense her, even in the dark. Her heartbeat was so loud she was sure he could hear it. The smell of burning material hit her nose, and she remembered the candle she'd knocked over, further amplifying her fear.

"Come out, come out, wherever you are!"

Luna bolted across the dark apartment, hoping the shadows would cover her well enough until she could either find a new hiding place or a proper weapon. Her foot caught on the edge of the table leg, sending her to the floor. Chance chuckled with glee and rushed toward the sound. She rolled away as quickly as she could, but Chance wrapped an arm around her waist, bringing her close. His blade found its way to her bare throat.

"Finally decided to come out and play, did you?" he taunted in her ear.

Luna clenched her teeth and slammed her head backward. A roar of pain erupted from Chance, letting her know she'd hit her mark. His grip slackened enough for her to break free. He stuck his foot out and Luna tripped, slamming into the nearby wall with a groan. Chance lunged at her, his hand once again on her throat. He ignored the blood leaking from his nose and stared down at her with haughty eyes.

"No!" Luna tried to gasp, watching orange flames flicker and engulf the doorframe of her room, spreading into the hall.

A flash of silver glinted in the firelight, his dagger at the ready to draw blood. He put force behind the metal as he held it to her throat, and she stilled. Chance rested his forehead against hers. "I'm sorry it had to come to this."

Tears brimmed in Luna's eyes. After everything she'd survived, she would die here, like this. And for what?

"Why?" she whispered, defeated. "Why couldn't you just let me go?"

"All you had to do was love me," he said, a quivering mix of sadness and anger. "Was that so hard for you to do? Everyone I've ever met has let me in, except you. You kept me out when I made it clear what I felt. I—" He stopped, turning enough for the light to catch his face. His sapphire eyes shimmered, glistening at the edges.

He wasn't completely dead on the inside.

"I'm sorry," she forced herself to say, praying it would be enough to elicit a response.

Chance released her, waiting for her to catch her breath to press the tip of the blade into her throat hard enough to draw a drop of blood. "What did you say?" he demanded.

"I-I said I'm sorry."

Chance said nothing as the room behind him was engulfed in flames. Luna could suddenly smell the gasoline and understood Chance's plan. He'd wanted her to knock over the candle.

He wanted to kill them both.

"Chance, we have to get out before the fire stops us," Luna whispered, desperation clawing at her insides.

"We'll die here," he said, "together." Chance's eyes glazed

over and that scared her more than the blade at her throat. "What do you think it's like . . . to die?" he asked so softly that Luna barely heard him.

She was too petrified to reply. For all her schooling, she'd never been taught how to handle a psychopath of his caliber.

"I've seen people's eyes when the light leaves them. It's terrifying. People say death is peace, but it seems like such a struggle."

"Please don't put me through that," Luna pleaded, throat dry from inhaling smoke.

"It'll be quick," he said, eerily soothingly. "And when the fire eats us up, we won't feel a thing."

"Chance, please. You don't have to do this," Luna sobbed, wet streaks running down her face to soak her neck and collarbone.

"What else am I supposed to do?"

"You can start over! No one knows your past but me and you."

"And all the damn cops in Ohio," he sneered. "Not to mention Cody's men."

"B-but DreamWorld can help hide you, right? You can get out of here and have a fresh start somewhere else. We don't have to die," Luna whispered, balling her hands into fists at her sides. "You can start over."

"You hate me. That's why you went to the police," he argued, and this time his eyes opened to stare down at her. "If I let you go, I'll regret it for the rest of my life."

"If you let me live, I promise I won't say a word," Luna

vowed, her stomach twisting in disgust. That promise went against everything she believed in, against everything she knew to be right, but if it meant saving her baby, it would be worth it in the end. "We can go our separate ways and pretend none of this ever happened."

"It doesn't matter what you do now. It can't take back what you've already done. When Cody catches me, he'll kill me. If I'm doomed to die anyway, then it's gonna be on my terms."

Luna breathed in. She had exhausted all the other cards in her hand, but she had one left. The ace of her entire deck, and it was time to play it. "Chance, I-I'm pregnant," she said, closing her eyes. It was too dark to see much of his face, but what she could make out was too much.

Chance's dagger dropped off her. He reached out, grabbing her arm to help her to her feet, and she stared into his eyes, terrified for whatever would come next. This was the first and only time she admitted it to him. She had no way of knowing he already knew.

"I know," he said softly, his fingers digging into the skin on her wrist, a complete contrast to his voice. "I tried to talk to you about it, to decide what *we* were going to do, but you wouldn't hear it."

"I didn't want you to know," she said against the tightness in her throat.

"Why? Because it's not mine? Amanda said you told her it was Max's."

Desperation yawned inside her. The lie came back like poison, choking her. *What if he believes that?* "It was a *lie*. I didn't want her to know . . . what you did to me. She asked if it was Max's, and I went along with it. It was easier that way."

"And how do I know you're not just saying that now?" he asked, cocking an eyebrow.

A hot flush of shame crept up her neck as she dropped her gaze. "You're the only one I've ever been with."

A beat of silence, then Chance grabbed her chin, forcing her to look at him. "So, you are pregnant with *my* baby?" he asked, tone unreadable.

"Yes, Chance," she whispered. "Yes." Her hands gripped the tops of his arms, the fire crackling louder behind them, heat licking closer. "Please . . . let me go. Let our baby live. Please."

Eyes narrowed, he searched her face as if he was trying to decide whether or not she was telling the truth.

Please believe me. Please let this be enough.

His expression shifted. She couldn't tell if it was relief, resignation, or something darker as he said, "Let's get out of here."

Chapter Sixty-Two

LUNA'S HOPE LIT up something behind her eyes. Something Chance thought he'd stamped out of her a long time ago. They burst from the burning apartment an instant before the doorway caved in, and landed together on the grass, coughing. Chance's eyes streamed with water as he gulped down the fresh air. The rain had stopped, though the grass beneath them was soaking wet. From somewhere not too far, sirens wailed.

Luna was still on the ground trying to regain herself as Chance stood up. He grasped her arm gently and pulled her to her feet. She stared in quiet horror at the blood on his hands, and until then, he'd forgotten it was there. He said nothing as he held her in place, reaching toward her stomach. Luna's eyes were wide as she watched him. He made sure no emotion showed on his face, but that was certainly far from the truth. It was early in her pregnancy, but Chance couldn't resist. He pressed his palm on her firm stomach.

"I'll never have a fresh start," he said, retracting his hand. "But if we're going to stay alive, we can't stay here. There's targets on both of our heads now, so I'm taking you with me."

"No," she tried to protest.

"Thing is, it's not up to you. This is *our* baby," Chance said, running his hand over her stomach. Irritation flared in the back of his head, but he was trying to stay calm. If he was aggravated, it would only be harder to think. If there was ever a situation that required his full attention, this was it. "And I'm going to fulfill my obligations to take care of you both."

The sirens were louder. People would come. Not all of them friendly.

"Not to mention the fact that it's in your best interest to disappear." Luna's face scrunched, ready to argue. "This is your home. They're gonna search and only find one body, which means you'll be their first suspect."

Her face softened as she stared down at the ground. Quietly, she asked, "What happens now?"

He sighed. "It's gonna be a tense few days. If the police catch us, we're done for. We'll figure out what to do next once we find a place to settle down."

Luna was silent, staring down at the grass. He could imagine the thoughts in her head right now. She was debating what to do: listen to him or turn him in. She thought the cops could help her. She didn't understand that they were as much of a threat to her as he was.

"The police aren't good guys," he added, hoping it would make her decision making easier.

She looked up, eyebrows wrinkled in confusion.

He elaborated. "Maybe some of them, but a lot of them are in as deep as me."

Understanding flashed through her eyes. She didn't argue as he began to lead her away from the burning apartment. A neighbor crossed the grass toward them, hollering something.

Chance didn't want to wait to find out what. He started to run, dragging Luna with him.

Thankfully, the man didn't follow as they rushed through the gap in the gate to the sidewalk beyond. He stopped to gauge their location. There was a gas station across the street, and thankfully, he still had his wallet.

"Come on," he said.

Luna hesitated again.

"We don't have time for this." Irritated, he grabbed her wrist, yanking her along with him.

They slipped into the building, the tiny *ding-ding* announcing their arrival. Chance kept his face angled to the floor, hoping it would be hard to make out, in case there were any cameras around.

The cashier was a thin teenager with acne dotting his face. He leaned on the counter, bored or annoyed, maybe both. *Good*, Chance thought. He likely wouldn't be too vigilant.

"You really think you'll be able to get out of here without anyone recognizing you? Your picture is everywhere," Luna murmured as they slid down the first aisle.

"I'll be in disguise," he said, picking up a box of hair dye from the shelf. "And so will you."

"Okay," she said, sounding as if she didn't have much faith in the idea.

He grabbed a hat and ripped the tag off, putting it on his head. Luna scanned the aisle warily as he followed it up by cramming the box of dye into his pocket. "Grab that dress right there."

Luna obeyed and handed it to him.

He shook his head. "Stick it under your shirt."

"But—" she started to argue.

"Do you want to go pay for it covered in blood?"

Her shoulders slumped. She murmured, "No," and stuffed the dress under her shirt to look like a pregnancy bump.

It's like I'm looking into the future, he thought. Out loud, he didn't comment on it. He peered around the edge of the aisle, gauging the distance to the door.

"All right, ready?" he asked.

Her eyes widened, startled.

"Go!"

He ran down the aisle and out of the store, waiting to hear angry shouts, but they didn't come. Either the cashier didn't notice or didn't care. Luna came out behind him, and Chance hurried her around the building to the bathroom. He held the door open, ushering her inside, then immediately followed. It was a single cubicle with a sink, toilet, and trash can.

Perfect, he thought, then turned the lock.

"Change your clothes," he told Luna before he went over to the sink and washed the blood off his hands. There was none on his clothes, at least. A smear colored the side of his neck and a crust lined under his nose, but all in all, he looked better than he originally thought.

He expected Luna to argue, but as he patted himself down with paper towels, she dropped the last of her bloody clothing onto the floor. The dress was baggy as it fell into place, going past her knees and hanging around her elbows, but it was simple in a way that wouldn't draw attention to them.

Chance piled the discarded clothes together, wrapping them in paper towels and toilet paper before tucking them in the trash can beneath wadded-up tissues.

"Ready?" he asked.

She nodded sheepishly.

He unlocked the door and peeked at the parking lot. There was one car at the nearest gas pump, but no one was outside. Slightly relieved, he said, "Let's go," and led the way down the street.

Bowling Green always had decent traffic, but in his paranoia, there seemed to be people *everywhere*. They needed to get over two streets. How many people would see them in that amount of time?

"There's a pay-by-the-hour hotel a couple blocks over," Chance said, glancing over his shoulder at his accomplice/prisoner. "We'll stop there for a minute. It'll give us a chance to rest."

Luna stayed silent. Chance tried to keep his irritation to himself as they ducked across the road and wove through the streets, slowing down once they hit the parking lot of the hotel. Chance stopped her by the door, handing her a twenty-dollar bill.

"Check us in," he told her.

She stared at him, another war in her mind.

"No funny business," he added.

She pushed open the door, announcing their presence with the tiny *ding* of a bell. The lobby showed the amount of care the owners had for the place. Faded wallpaper peeled at the corners, revealing cracked plaster underneath. A threadbare carpet, stained in mottled shades of brown and gray, muffled their footsteps as they crossed to the front desk. The man who sat there was older, with a scruffy beard and wearing a small, brimmed hat. He was reading a magazine but pushed it aside as Luna approached.

Nervously, she said, "Hi, um . . . I'd like to rent a-a room, please."

"How long you want it?" he asked and picked up a cigar from his ashtray, clamping it between his yellow teeth.

Luna cast a glance at Chance. He wished she would stop doing that. How much more obvious could she make things? "Two hours?"

"A'ight," he said and set the cigar down. "Twenty bucks."

Chance nearly sagged with relief as Luna handed him the bill. He suspected this man of doing his own shady things. Why else would he own a place like this? Most likely, if he did see the red flags, he was going to look the other way. Smiling, he stuck the money in his pocket and grabbed a key off the set of hooks behind him.

"You kids enjoy," he said, tossing it to Luna.

She was silent as they left the desk, heading toward a sketchy set of stairs at the back of the room. Chance snagged the key from her but made sure she led the way up the stairs. The hallway reeked of old sweat and cigarette smoke, but something about it comforted him. Finally, they came to their room. He didn't let out a full breath until they made it inside and the door closed behind them.

Chapter Sixty-Three

THE WALK UP the stairs to their room felt like walking to her own execution. Luna's footsteps were measured and cautious, as if the slightest misstep might shatter whatever fragile mercy kept her alive. When the door finally closed with a soft *click*, the weight in her chest dropped like a stone. A cold, sickening dread settled deep in her gut, twisting tighter. This wasn't like the last time he'd taken her. She'd gone with him willingly, hadn't she? She'd said no, but she hadn't fought. She'd let him bring her here.

He coerced me, she thought, feeling his looming presence behind her. Did it count as kidnapping if she had a reason to go with him? *This is crazy. Why didn't I run? Why didn't I ask the guy at the desk for help?*

The police aren't good guys. Maybe some of them, but a lot of them are in as deep as me, Chance had said.

She had a theory that the police were helping him back in Lima. Considering how sloppy his crimes were, that had to be the reason why he kept getting away with things. If that was true, and Cody had men there, too, then Chance was right. No one and nowhere was safe.

What if it's all a lie to get me to go with him?

Sarah's death was a reminder that there was some truth to his words: there were other threats besides him.

Fear curled in her stomach, her mind a whirlwind of conflicting doubts. How was she going to get out of this?

Chance walked around her, taking off his hat to sling it on the bed as he pulled the crumpled box of stolen dye out of his pocket. Luna hovered by the door; the desire to open it and run down the hall bounced around inside her head alongside everything else.

She must've made a face because he said, "I want to remind you how vulnerable a position you're in right now. I'm being nice because you've been somewhat cooperative. It can stay like this. We can work together and make things go smoothly, or you can fight me, get hurt, and have it happen anyway. Like last time."

Luna closed her eyes, trying to process all that had happened. Trying not to think about the cabin and how that experience had gone.

"I'm going to try to get this done quickly so we can get the hell out of here," he said. When she didn't move, he pointed at the bed and said, "Sit there, where I can see you."

Luna's lip trembled. Another dying spark of who she used to be rumbled up, and she opened her mouth, ready to argue. Then she remembered Amanda's lifeless eyes and felt the spark fizzle out. Her body sagged, emotionally and physically spent, and she sat in the exact spot he pointed to.

He eyed her but said nothing else as he gathered his things and went into the bathroom, leaving the door open. She didn't watch him moving around inside. Dissociating, she stared at the ugly red walls, thinking how much she hated the color.

How did I get here? she wondered. *I did everything right.*

She replayed it over and over in her mind, each time the words growing more distant, as if they belonged to someone else. Everything she had been taught, everything she believed would keep her out of harm's way as a woman, she had done. Drinks never left her sight. She kept her distance from anyone who set off a warning bell deep inside her. She kept her head down, minding her own business, always polite, always careful.

And yet, here she was.

The only thing she'd ever truly done wrong was say no to one man. That truth settled over her like a cold fog, numbing and relentless. Time blurred, dragging her away from herself. Somewhere in the middle of it, Chance finished with his shower. When he emerged, he was dressed, with hair so dark brown it was almost black.

"What do you think?" he asked, running his fingers through it. "Suits me, right?"

Luna said nothing.

Chance sighed. "Are you okay?"

She didn't answer.

"It's time to go," he said and reached for her hand. "Nothing stupid, all right? I don't want to hurt you, but it's always an option."

As if Luna could forget.

"As soon as we step out of this room, your best bet is to stay quiet," he warned.

He paused, eyes scanning the hallway through the cracked door, weighing the risks before making a move. As soon as he opened it to its full extent, she could understand his concern. People were everywhere, coming and going from the other rooms and hanging out in the stairwell. If she was quick enough, any of them could be her savior. Chance's grip on her arm tightened as if he could hear her thoughts.

"Don't," he warned in a low growl. "Just don't."

A second later, something hard pressed against her back. His dagger at the ready to do damage. She moved with him as he quickened his pace, leaving no room for her to break free.

When they crept into the parking lot, Luna asked, "What are we doing now?"

"Getting a new set of wheels," he replied, scanning the nearby row of cars.

"I thought you were trying to keep a low profile. Carjacking doesn't really fit with that."

He glanced at her, eyes dark and sharp. "I am, that's why I need a new car. My truck is hot."

Maybe the car could distract him long enough for her to wave someone down and escape. But Chance was careful. He scanned the nearly empty lot, finally settling on a car parked toward the back. The owner had left it unlocked. He nudged her inside, belting her into the passenger seat before he slid into the driver's seat and hot-wired the ignition to life.

Eyes shining, he said, "Sounds like a good sign."

She said nothing. If she had spoken, her words would be laced with anything but happiness.

He sped out of the parking lot, and Luna's chest tightened. Each passing block felt like a countdown to something worse. He was really taking her away, and there was nothing she could do.

"Not much farther now until we say goodbye to Bowling Green," he said, voice dripping with mockery. He was enjoying her turmoil. Enjoying the fact that he had won.

Then he hit a red light. Beside them, a police cruiser rolled into the lane next to them.

This is it, she thought. *My chance.*

She braced herself to slam her fist against the window, to scream until someone heard. Then a cold, sharp pressure pressed against her body. Steel biting through fabric. The blade was aimed at her stomach and the baby inside.

"I know you remember what this feels like," he said, low and venomous. "Don't make me remind you."

The light turned green. The police car drove away.

Chance withdrew the blade, the cruel smile returning as he merged into the flow of traffic. Luna's hope slipped away, leaving only cold helplessness behind.

***

THE DRIVE WENT on for hours and hours. In the midst of her silent crying, Luna fell asleep. When she opened her eyes again, it was dark outside. Her body sagged in the seat, neck stiff and aching from the unforgiving angle.

"You awake, kitten?" Chance asked, deceptively gentle.

Luna winced, but the charade of sleep felt useless now. She shifted upright, blinking against the dim light, trying to focus on the window beside her. The car was still, parked in a patch of shadow so deep it swallowed every hint of the world beyond.

"Where are we?" she asked.

Chance's eyes gleamed in the darkness as he pointed toward a faint glow in the distance. A lone house. "Scouting out a place to sleep for the night. I've been watching this place for a while. Looks like the guy lives alone."

A cold knot twisted in Luna's stomach. "Can't we find somewhere abandoned? Somewhere no one lives?"

"No," he said. "This is the only place I've seen in miles. Besides, I'm sure you need to use the restroom by now, and you'd probably like to sleep in a real bed, right? I promised I'd take care of you, and I'm going to do exactly that."

"An innocent person shouldn't have to die for that," Luna murmured.

Chance ignored her as he continued. "You're going to knock on the door and say you're hurt. When he opens it to let you inside, I'm gonna rush him."

"He's not going to fall for that," she said. "I'm *not* hurt, and all it would take for him to see that would be a glance through his peephole."

Chance bobbed his head and summoned his dagger. Luna flinched, assuming it would come toward her, when he lowered it to his palm instead. He cut a line across his pale skin, watching the blood ooze out. Carefully, he smeared the warm sticky substance along the side of her neck and onto her collarbone. Luna gritted her teeth, trying hard not to gag at the feeling or the smell of it.

Chance drew another exaggerated line under her chin.

"That should be convincing enough."

"I don't want to do this," she said, peering up at him through her eyelashes.

Chance's gaze was cold, unyielding. "It's a dog-eat-dog world. Sometimes you've gotta do things you don't want to in the name of survival. Haven't you learned that by now?"

He wouldn't cave. She was going to have to go through with this. Luna pushed open the door and stepped out onto a gravel path, following it into the darkness. She glanced over her shoulder, but Chance was already out of the car, lost to the nearby woods.

Maybe if I'm quick enough, I can get inside before Chance does, and I can have the guy call 911, Luna thought as she walked toward the front of the house. *Or better yet, maybe he won't answer.*

Her hand hovered inches from the worn wood of the door. She stopped, eyes darting behind her, searching the blackened tree line. Chance could be anywhere. Gathering every shred of courage, she knocked.

From the other side, a rough, suspicious voice barked, "Who is it?"

"Please! I need help!" Luna called out weak and raspy enough to leave little doubt.

There was no immediate response. She could imagine the man peering at her through the peephole, trying to decide if it was a trick. Then, with a slow *creak*, the door swung open. An older man stood in the dim light, hunched and worn, dressed in a loose T-shirt and faded striped pants. His eyes widened in shock as he took in Luna's trembling form.

"Oh my Lord, child, what's happened to you?" He reached out as if to steady her.

Chance pushed past her, dagger raised. "That's none of your concern."

The man screamed and tried to run, but Chance grabbed the back of his shirt, knife pressed against his throat. "Who else lives here?" he growled in the man's ear.

"Please! Take whatever you want but don't kill me!" he begged, breaking down into a sobbing mess.

"Answer the question," Chance demanded. The blade dug in enough to draw the smallest drop of blood.

The man yelped and said, "I live alone!"

Chance started to walk him forward. "Now that wasn't so hard, was it?"

"Chance, please don't do this," Luna said when she finally found her voice.

He didn't listen. He walked the man into the bathroom and made him step into the tub. Luna followed, hysterical. Chance showed no remorse as he dragged the blade across the homeowner's throat. Squirts of blood splashed over Luna's skin, morphing with Chance's drying streaks. Chance dropped the man's body. His hands, arms, and clothes were soaked in blood as he stepped out of the tub. Sighing, he closed the shower curtain, hiding the dying man from sight. Guttural groans came from the other side. And an attempt at the word "Help."

Chance pulled his shirt over his head and went to work unfastening his belt. His pants fell to the floor, and he stepped out of them, approaching her. "You should get out of that dress before the blood dries. It'll be uncomfortable when it does."

Luna shook so hard she couldn't think. The man had been visibly concerned for her when he opened the door, and he died for it. Luna was so tired of people dying for her. Chance sighed, grabbed the bottom of her dress, and yanked it over her head. She shivered in the cold bathroom, recognizing the gleam in his eyes. He caught her lips with his and brought her close.

Luna didn't fight, just let him scoop her into his arms and carry her through the house. She had to put effort into not seeing the pictures on the walls. Smiling images of the man she had watched die. Chance found the bedroom and threw the comforter aside, setting her down on the bed. When he crawled over her, her mind was on the fear in the old-timer's eyes, his final moments of terror.

Chance started to kiss her neck and collarbone. "I know today has been rough," he whispered. "But it'll be worth it in the end. I promise."

Luna said nothing, lost in her trauma as Chance pushed himself inside of her. His grunts and groans filled the room until he came. Sighing in satisfaction, he rolled off her, gathering her into his arms as he whispered, "I love you."

The first real tear leaked from her eye, but she hid it by burying her face in the pillow. Chance's fingers ghosted gently over the side of her face as he wiped her hair away, trying to get her to look at him. He planted a gentle kiss on her lips and reached for something on the table beside the bed. Cold metal wrapped around her wrist. Handcuffs. She expected him to loop the other end to the bed frame, but he clasped it on his own wrist instead.

"I can't have you running away during the night." He tossed the key across the room to where it clattered on the floor, lost to the shadows. "From now on, consider us glued at the hip. Wherever you go, I go."

Chapter Sixty-Four

HOURS PASSED, AND Luna, unsurprisingly, had a difficult time falling asleep. Every time she closed her eyes, she heard the old man's screams, smelled his blood, and she wanted to scrub her brain clean of all of it. *It's my fault*, she thought. *I let him die.*

Amanda's death, the burning apartment, being kidnapped, leaving Bowling Green . . . all of that had been *one* day. Less than twenty-four hours of being on the run with Chance, and it was the longest day of her life. She regretted the choice. Regretted not running when she had the chance. Whatever Cody's men had planned for her might be more merciful than a life like this.

What have I done?

If she somehow made it out of this, she would never be the same again. Of course Chance's violent tendencies were nothing new, but this was the first time she'd been a witness to the crime in action. And she would never forget it.

Luna pulled her wrist, the cold metal sinking into her skin. Beside her, Chance didn't move, deep in his slumber. How did he do it? How did he manage such peace after all the violence he caused? She yanked the handcuffs again, trying to fold her thumb in and slide her hand out. There was a bit of wiggle room, not a lot, but enough to keep her going.

She pulled harder, forcing the biggest part of her hand against the metal until she could feel her skin break open. Blood started to drip, but she wasn't about to give up. Pain shot up her arm, but she didn't stop. The blood helped her slip her hand further, serving as a twisted lubricant.

She gasped when the pain became too much and quickly covered her mouth, terrified of waking Chance. He continued to sleep. Her wrist throbbed with pain, but she couldn't get free. She stared at the ceiling. What would happen to her tomorrow? Where would he take her? What would he make her do?

I need to get out now, she thought, staring in the direction he'd thrown the key.

Luna took a long, deep breath and closed her eyes. Falling asleep was probably the hardest thing she ever had to do. Fear and anxiety rioted in her blood, so it took effort to calm down enough to sleep. When she opened her eyes again, she was still in the room, but it was hazy, blurry at the edges.

The DreamWorld version of it. She sat up, relieved when she could ease herself off the bed. Beside her, Chance didn't move. He wasn't active on this side. She assumed he was still in the process of reviving his magic. Whatever the case, it was a break, and she'd take it. Hurrying to the corner of the room, she dropped to her hands and knees to pat the dark surface, bumping into the key with a soft *ting*.

She scooped it up in both hands and closed them tight, holding them against her chest. With her ability, she could bring things through to reality. Chance had taught her that, except when she'd done it last time, it hadn't been on purpose.

She'd been afraid, desperate to get herself to wake up, and in the process, it had happened.

I can do this, she thought.

Luna swallowed and squeezed the key tighter.

"Wake up," she told herself.

The room stayed in place.

She tried again. "Wake up!"

Her eyes flew open. She was once again in bed beside Chance. At first, she didn't dare breathe for fear she might've hollered out loud and woken him. Peering at him from the corner of her eye, she eased. He was still asleep.

Luna opened her hand. The key sat in her palm, small and impossibly powerful. She didn't move at first, afraid that if she blinked, it would vanish. She grabbed it with a sharp exhale, the sound more like a sob. Her fingers shook as she guided the key into the slot, turning it with a faint *click*.

The cuff loosened. She was free. Shaking, she inched the open cuff toward the bed frame and wrapped it around the steel bar before closing it. Cradling her injured wrist to her chest, she slid off the bed, knees weak, adrenaline pumping like ice through her veins. Her eyes darted to the door. A dozen options screamed in her mind, all tangled in panic, but she didn't have time to weigh them. She had seconds to figure it out.

Her feet barely touched the floor as she darted into the hallway, ears straining for any sign that Chance had woken. It was silent. She didn't know where he had put the keys to his stolen car, and she wasn't going to go back into the room to look. By the front door, a ring of keys hung on a rusty hook. Her hand shot out and grabbed them, the metal cool against her skin. As her fingers closed around them, something shifted in her chest, sharp and sudden.

These weren't just keys.

They were a remnant of the man who had died. A stranger who had been in the wrong place at the wrong time and whose only crime had been concern for another person's well-being. His death had been brutal. Senseless. He'd never see the sunlight again, and here she was, holding the keys to his life.

I'm sorry, she thought as she ran outside. If she survived this ordeal, she would take the time to properly mourn him.

Night air sliced against her bare skin as she sprinted across the yard. Branches clawed at her as she reached the vehicle hidden in the trees, fingers trembling as she yanked open the door. She flung herself inside, heart crashing against her ribs.

A car phone sat nestled in the middle console.

Luna's eyes welled with sudden, desperate hope. She turned the key, and the engine roared to life with a violent thrum that shattered the quiet like a gunshot. Every nerve screamed at her. Call. Drive. Run. Hide. She shook violently, her mind splitting in two—one part begging her to call for help, while the other urged her to drive, to vanish into the woods before it was too late.

Then came the roar.

It erupted from the house, unmistakable in its fury. Her stomach dropped. A second later, the front door exploded open and Chance barreled out. His shadow stretched across the yard like a monster from a nightmare.

She was caught.

Slamming the locks down, she lunged for the phone, fingers fumbling over the buttons as she pressed *9 . . . 1 . . . 1.*

It started to ring.

A blur of motion, then Chance appeared beside the passenger side door, his face twisted with rage. His eyes found hers through the glass. She barely had time to brace before his fists crashed against the window with a bone-jarring *thud, thud, thud.* He screamed her name, raw and hoarse, the punches growing harder, more desperate, like he could break through the glass with sheer will alone.

She pressed the phone tighter to her ear, breath coming in shallow gasps.

"You bitch, don't you leave me!" he screamed, the thuds enunciated with tiny tinks from the chain of the broken handcuff still fastened to his wrist.

"911. What is the nature of your emergency?"

"Please help," Luna whispered. "I don't know where I am. I've been kidnapped."

There was a beat of silence long enough to feel the weight of the world on her shoulders.

"Do you know who took you?" the dispatcher asked, calm and steady.

Luna met Chance's eyes. Voice cracking, she said, "Yes."

"Where is he right now? Are you safe?"

"He's right here," she said. "I'm in a car with the doors locked, but . . . I don't know how long they'll hold. I think he's going to break the window."

"Okay, listen to me. Help is on the way. Stay calm. Can

you start the vehicle?"

"It's already running."

"You need to move if you feel you're in immediate danger. Can you drive?"

Luna's hands trembled on the gearshift. Chance slammed his fist against the window again, then a flicker went across his face. The realization that he no longer had control over the situation.

He stepped back, eyes burning into hers. Then he bolted for the stolen vehicle nearby. Headlights flared, tires crunched over gravel, and he vanished into the night.

Luna sat motionless, chest heaving. The woman on the phone continued speaking in her ear, but all she could hear was her pounding pulse and the sudden, terrifying quiet Chance left behind.

Epilogue

LUNA TRUDGED ACROSS the cemetery, struggling to keep hold of her armful of bouquets. Carefully, she sank to her knees by the nearest grave. With a *plop,* the entire lot of flowers fell to the grass beside her.

It had been such a long week. She'd been in and out of the police station so many times that she knew the layout of the building. She didn't know where Chance had gone when he'd disappeared into the night, and the police didn't either. They assumed she was holding back information, which of course, she was, but his location wasn't part of it.

Luna tried not to think about that as she ran her hand over the plaque beside her. Out loud, she read the name engraved on it, "Max Cazmea."

She sorted through the flowers, trying to ignore the blossom of pain in her chest. Would it ever get easier with time or was that saying a lie? Sniffling, she decided on white roses, the prettiest of all her bundles, and put them in the open spot in the plaque. She did the same for Violet.

Sweeping away a layer of dirt, she stopped. A small, folded piece of paper had been hidden there. With shaking fingers, she picked it up. The rose pendant from the necklace Chance had given her tumbled out, and she started to shake as she read the note.

Luna,

I suggest you read the paper. I think it'll cheer you up, if nothing else.

Chance

Had he turned himself in? She set the final bouquets in place for Susan, Sarah, and Amanda. With a long, pained glance at each of the tombstones, she stood and ran to the nearest store. Tucking a newspaper under her arm, she hurried to the counter and threw some money at the clerk, not waiting for change.

She meant to find a private place to react to whatever the newspaper had to offer, but after only a few steps from the store, curiosity made her open it. The front-page story caught her attention.

Local Man Dies After Fall During Police Standoff

Luckily, there was a bench behind her because Luna's legs gave out. Breathing through her mouth to keep from fainting completely, she continued to read:

BOWLING GREEN — A recent manhunt ended tragically today when 21 year old Chance Welfrey, also known to some as Malcolm Sanders, died after falling from the roof of a six-story building downtown.

According to police reports, Welfrey climbed to the rooftop following a standoff with law enforcement late yesterday afternoon. The situation escalated, prompting a large emergency response including crisis negotiators and tactical units.

Officers attempted to negotiate with him for several tense hours, but efforts to de-escalate the situation were unsuccessful.

At around 5:30 p.m., Welfrey fell from the rooftop. Emergency medical personnel arrived promptly, but he was pronounced dead at the scene. Authorities are still investigating the exact circumstances surrounding the incident.

Welfrey had been the subject of a widespread search in connection to the murder of a thirty-year-old man Friday morning. Local police described him as dangerous and had urged residents to remain cautious during the manhunt.

"This is a tragic end to a very difficult situation," said Police Chief Harold Jensen at a press conference. "Our thoughts are with the families affected by these events. We are continuing to investigate and will provide updates as more information becomes available."

Authorities are asking anyone with additional information related to Welfrey, or any recent incidents, to come forward.

Survive at Midnight (Rituals of the Night Series Book Three)

Death doesn't always bring peace.

In the wake of Chance Welfrey's death, Luna Ketz is doing her best to rebuild her life, but the ghosts of her family and friends refuse to let her go. Moving on feels impossible, especially with her due date looming. As the days slip by, Chance's buried secrets begin to surface, dragging Luna back into the darkness of his past.

Her dreams become a battlefield where the dead don't whisper. They demand her attention, pulling her deeper into a nightmare she can't escape. The only way out is to trust the one person who has already destroyed her. Chance.

But trusting him could cost her everything—her future, her sanity, and even her soul. As the lines between reality and trauma blur, Luna realizes the true horror isn't the secrets Chance left behind, it's losing herself to the darkness.

About the Author

Raised in Michigan but moved to Texas, Kayla has experienced the best and worst of both. She has interests in the dark and macabre and enjoys '80s music and movies. A little neurotic and a huge lover of Halloween, creepy stories and cats are totally her jam.